Dedication

To Jerry, Ske (Dean), Gene, Henry, Tom, Jeff and the rest of the Tuesday lunch bunch

Acknowledgements

Natalie Lund played tour guide on our research trip to Kentucky "bourbon country". The tours and sightseeing provided me with so much research material I "geeked out" when writing the first draft and had to trim about a hundred pages of bourbon making chemistry from this final version of the book.

As always, Deanna Wilson reads the rough first fragments of my draft and saves me endless hours of proofreading and typo corrections while keeping the police and horse stuff right. Julie Hovey endures my hours of research and keyboard work, then hauls boxes of books for my library and bookstore events. Frannie Brozo, Clem MacIlravie, and Mike Westfall comment on early proofs to make sure the details are correct. Natalie Lund, Anne Flagge, and Deanna Wilson do the final proofreading.

Despite their best efforts, I still manage to insert a typo here and there.

Thanks to Jude, JD, and Susan at BWL Publishing for your support, editing, and marketing efforts.

"I have never in my life seen a Kentuckian who didn't have a gun, a pack of cards, and a jug of whiskey."
– Andrew Jackson

"Bourbon reflects the soul of America, complex and full of character."
– Thomas Jefferson

A Bourbon to Die For
Doug Fletcher mystery #17
Dean L. Hovey

Print ISBNs
Amazon print 9780228635758
Ingram Spark 9780228635765
Barnes & Noble 9780228635772
BWL Print 9780228635789

BWL Publishing Inc.

Books we love to write ...
Authors around the world.

http://bwlpublishing.ca

This book is a work of fiction, a product of the author's imagination. Any resemblance to actual events, people, or locations is coincidental and unintended. Some actual locations are used fictionally.

Table of Contents

Prologue

The shadows from the setting sun cast a camouflage pattern of light and dark on the trail as Alistair McInnis walked the wooded portion of Abraham Lincoln Birthplace National Historic Site. With his head down and his hands in his pockets, McInnis was deep in thought when a person emerged ahead of him. Frowning, he asked, "What are you doing here?"

The visitor marched down the trail until they were face to face. Clenching his jaw and keeping his hands in his pockets, McInnis shook his head in resignation. "Just leave. I have nothing more to say."

"You're right. There *is* nothing left to be said."

McInnis turned, waiting for the visitor to leave. He ignored the rustling sounds which preceded the blow to his head. Reeling, he fell to his knees while trying to process what was happening. The second blow knocked him unconscious. He fell face down into the creek.

The most primal of human instincts kicked in when he inhaled water. His head jerked up, and he sputtered, trying to draw a breath of air while his arms and legs failed him. The visitor's knee pressed on McInnis' back, holding his face in the water. Unable to hold his breath any longer, McInnis exhaled, and air bubbled up around his face. Then he inhaled, filling his lungs with water.

The visitor's adrenaline surged as McInnis struggled to draw a breath. The rush faded as McInnis became inert. "I guess you'll never get to enjoy your *perfect* bourbon."

Chapter 1

I was drafting my Medora kidnapping report when my phone rang. Happy to be interrupted, I answered without looking at the caller ID. "Fletcher."

"Have you unpacked yet?"

Recognizing my boss, Jack Pardee's voice, I replied, "Jill is washing the last load of laundry while I'm slogging through my report."

"There's been a death at Abraham Lincoln Birthplace National Historic Site and the State Department has requested our assistance."

Thinking I'd misheard what had been said, I asked, "The State Department?"

"The deceased is a prominent British citizen. The US State Department and the British Consul General have been talking about how to best handle the investigation."

My mind reeled, thinking about the bureaucracy involved when two major countries discuss investigating the death of a foreign citizen. "And they think using the US Park Service Investigative Services Branch is a better solution than requesting assistance from the FBI?"

Jack chuckled. "No, the Secretary of the Interior, our boss of all bosses, wants his people to lead the investigation. He stepped forward while the FBI was still discussing who should have jurisdiction."

"Please tell me the Secretary didn't ask for me by name."

"No. He asked me to send my best investigator."

"Best, as in the most skilled or the most diplomatic investigator?"

"By sending you and Jill, I cover both of those needs. Repack your bags."

"Lincoln's birthplace?" I asked as I picked up a pen and flipped to a blank page in my notebook. "Where in Illinois is that?"

Jack chuckled. "Get out your history book. Lincoln spent his adulthood in Illinois. He was born in Kentucky. His birthplace is near Elizabethtown, about halfway between Louisville and Nashville."

I pulled up the park's website as Jack spoke. "Is there anything special about the deceased?"

"He's the son of a prominent Scottish distiller who's become a local Kentucky icon of sorts. Nearby Bardstown is the center of the bourbon-making universe. The deceased had been the head taster or blender or something at a startup distillery. The Secretary said the victim left his family's distillery to create a bourbon start-up. I guess this new operation was within months of releasing their 'much anticipated' new brand."

Having overheard me talking on the phone, Jill stuck her head into my office. "What's up?" she mouthed.

I motioned for her to join us. "Jill just walked in. Please repeat what you just told me."

Jack gave a quick recap of the request as Jill nodded. After the overview, she asked, "Was this dead guy well-liked in the community, or did they see him as an interfering outsider?"

"We didn't get into that level of detail. The one unspoken thing I surmised was that the victim was important. The British Consul General doesn't call the US Secretary of State when a poor peon dies."

"Do we know the cause of death?" I asked.

"The Secretary said it appeared the victim drowned."

Jill grinned and leaned close to the speaker. "This sounds like something out of a British mystery. Did he die in a vat of bourbon?"

"His body was found inside the park. So probably not."

"If you have the victim's name, we can check the local news reports," I suggested.

I heard Jack's computer keys clicking. "It's an unusual name. Here it is. The victim was Alistair McInnis."

Jill entered the victim's name into her phone while Jack reminded me to submit my expense voucher for the Medora trip before we departed for Kentucky.

Staring at her phone, Jill said, "I found a story in the *Lexington Herald*. The article says more about Mr. McInnis than it does about his death. He was from Scotch whisky royalty. His family has operated a distillery on the island of Islay since the 1600s. Alistair was the youngest of eight children. He told the reporter his prospects for operating his own distillery were better in Kentucky than sharing the family business with his siblings on Islay."

"Is there any information about his death?"

"It says he drowned. His body was found in the creek that runs through the Abraham Lincoln Birthplace National Historic Site." Jill paused with her head cocked. "This seems strange. I'm looking at a newspaper picture of investigators at the scene. The stream looks like it's barely more than a couple of feet wide and maybe inches deep."

"Maybe he wasn't sober," I suggested.

"Maybe he was killed," Jill countered.

"You two will get those details in Kentucky. Give me a call after you've spoken with the local police."

I ended the call and referred to my notes. "Jack said the park is halfway between Louisville and Nashville. Find out which city has the best connections from Texas."

Jill shook her head. "Having driven in rural Kentucky, I know that many of their *highways* are two-lanes wide with stone fences inches from the edge of the pavement. It appears there is a *real* highway between Nashville and Elizabethtown. I vote for Nashville."

I shrugged as I pulled up the expense voucher database. "Make the reservations while I work on my expense voucher." I paused, then added, "Unless you'd rather fill out my voucher."

"My voucher is done, as is my trip report," Jill said as she smiled and walked out of the office.

As she walked away, I said, "Your trip report is done? Good, I'll cut and paste."

* * *

After submitting my expense voucher and trip report, I called the historic site. The eager young female voice with a mild southern accent seemed genuinely pleasant. "Hi, I'm Doug Fletcher, a Park Service investigator. I'd like to speak with the superintendent."

"He's off site right now. Is there something I could help you with?"

"I'm flying from Texas to Kentucky tomorrow. Is there a motel or hotel near the park you would recommend?"

The woman chuckled. "Most Park Service visitors stay in E-town, where there are several chain motels. Personally, I'd recommend a B & B in Hodgenville. You'll get a better taste of local culture than you'll get from a stuffy ole chain motel."

"Is there a B & B close to the park?"

"Um, sure. Aunt Mary's Inn is in Hodgenville, about ten minutes from the park. Do you want their number?"

"Sure, give me Aunt Mary's number."

A second later, the ranger was back. After repeating a phone number, she added, "Be sure and tell Bitsy you're a ranger. You'll get a special discount."

"Bitsy? I won't talk to Aunt Mary?" I asked, joking.

"Oh, no. Aunt Mary died right after the war. Her daughters and granddaughters have always run the place since then."

"The war?" I asked.

"Pardon me?"

"Which war did Aunt Mary die after?"

"Where are you located, Mr. Fletcher?"

"I'm flying in from Texas. Why do you ask?"

"Down here, there's only one war that gets mentioned. The people of southern Kentucky were split between the Union and the Confederacy. The graveyards are a mix of round-top Union grave markers and pointed-top Confederate markers."

"Thanks for the history lesson. Maybe you'll be able to fill me in on the man who drowned in the creek, too."

"Well, Mr. Fletcher, it was downright odd. I mean, that man was face down in the creek, which is only about six inches deep this time of year. If he'd just pushed himself up, he wouldn't have drowned."

"Do you think someone held him down, or did he maybe get drunk and fall into the creek?"

"Well, sir, LaRue County is dry."

"Dry, as in, the creek isn't running?"

"Dry, as in, they don't sell alcohol here."

"They don't sell alcohol there? I thought you were in the heart of bourbon country?"

"Oh, you're not from here. Kentucky has wet counties, dry counties, and moist counties. Dry counties don't allow liquor sales. Wet counties have liquor stores and bars."

"What's a moist county?"

"Well, sir, Moist means it's between wet and dry."

Assuming my leg was being pulled, I said, "I kind of thought that's what moist generally meant. What does it mean for liquor sales?"

"I guess some dry counties considered how much tax revenue they were losing when people drove to the wet counties to drink and buy booze. Some are allowing restaurants to serve alcohol. It's kind of a sliding scale depending on the size of the restaurant and the county."

"Where do you go to drink?"

"Me? I'm Baptist. I don't drink at all."

"I assume we'll be at the park sometime tomorrow afternoon. Will you be on duty?"

"I should be. My name is Patience Weller. If I'm not at the information desk, ask for me."

"We'll see you then!"

I found Jill in the bedroom with two open suitcases on the bed. "I moved some underwear directly from the clean clothes basket into your suitcase. You'll have to choose the rest of your wardrobe yourself."

Removing golf shirts from hangers, I replied, "We've barely had time to wash clothes in between assignments."

"Yeah," Jill sighed. "I don't have time to keep up with the weeds popping up in the flowers."

I folded the shirts and laid them in the suitcase. "We don't have to do this."

That comment froze Jill. "What do you mean? Are you going to call Jack and refuse this assignment?"

I walked around the end of the bed and pulled Jill into my arms. "We can retire. We don't have to do this."

Burying her face into my neck, she drew a deep breath. "I don't think I'm ready to retire. I mean, what would I do?"

"Weed the garden. Read."

Jill leaned back and looked at me before shaking her head. "We can't retire here. We'll have to move to South Dakota."

"Because of the horses?"

Jill frowned. "Not the horses. Our parents are going to need us."

"You've convinced me. Retirement is a bad idea. Forget I ever mentioned it."

Chapter 2

Our flights left us plenty of time to read the background information downloaded onto Jill's phone and laptop. The front-page newspaper article about the McInnis death was the most informative. After reading it, I turned to Jill and asked, "What do you think about the veracity of the information in this article?"

"I'd say it's slightly more trustworthy than the internet and slightly less useful than a police report."

"Your gold standard is a police report?"

Reclaiming her laptop, Jill clicked on icons until she found the report filed by the law enforcement ranger who'd been dispatched from Mammoth Cave National Park to assist immediately after the body was discovered. "Read this. The author sounds rational, reasonable, and reliable."

Taking the computer, I started reading as I said, "Are you hinting this is unlike my reports?"

"Your reports are perfect. All you ever do is cut and paste my reports into a form with your name on top."

I slid the computer back to Jill. "You're right, Calvin sounds professional. He states facts and doesn't speculate. On the other hand, he didn't know anything except where the body was found."

Smiling, Jill replied, "There you go! You didn't want speculation. Calvin said what he knew and quit."

"I spoke with Patience from the visitor center yesterday. She agreed with you about the creek not being a drowning threat. She also threw cold water on the theory that the victim was drunk and passed out in the creek. The entire county around the park is dry, without liquor sales."

Still smiling, Jill asked, "When you were drinking, wouldn't you have driven to a bar or liquor store in the next county?"

"True, there's probably no law against transporting liquor between counties. It only restricts sales," I agreed.

"I filled in at Mammoth Cave National Park when one of the rangers was out on maternity leave. As I recall, the superintendent told the rangers living on site they couldn't drink outside of the residences. No cop was going into the house to tell you to dump out your beer, but they would stop if a bunch of rowdy people were drinking on a porch or while pitching horseshoes."

"Really? They'd ticket people for drinking on the porch?"

"Yes." Jill paused, then asked, "You've booked us into a bed and breakfast?"

"Aunt Mary's Inn, which is a few minutes from the park. Patience recommended it over the corporate motels in Elizabethtown, which is farther away."

"Staying at a B & B always seems like I'm intruding in someone's house. I mean, the one in Hawaii was okay, but it's still easier to slip in and out of a 'sterile' corporate motel than interacting with our host and the other guests who sometimes linger in the living room and get to know each other over breakfast."

"You just don't want me chatting up the next-door neighbor women," I said, referring to Hawaii where a neighbor who worked in a strip joint asked us to help her out of a difficult personal situation.

"Have you noticed how we seem to attract strays? The waitress in Florida. The stripper in Hawaii."

"You have your own strays, like Uncle Chet."

Frowning, Jill looked at me. "Chet isn't a stray. He's been like a family member for as long as I can remember."

"Ahh, so it's your family who attracts strays. I don't recall having an affinity for helping assorted needy people before I married you."

The seatbelt sign came on, and the pilot announced our descent into Nashville, effectively ending the discussion. Jill packed up her laptop and slipped it under the seat. As we stepped out of the jetway, I looked for a sign directing us to the baggage claim. I felt Jill's hand on my arm, then looked in the direction she was staring. A law enforcement ranger, who looked like he'd just retired from the Marines, nodded to me. He stood at parade rest, just out of the flow of people.

"Inspector Fletcher?" he asked as we approached.

I put out my hand to him. "Doug and Jill will be better."

"Yes, sir. Doug and Jill. I'm Calvin Woodrow."

"Nice to meet you, Calvin," I said as we stepped away from the moving masses of people.

"We're unaccustomed to being met at the airport," Jill said. "This is a pleasant surprise."

A forced smile flashed on Calvin's face, then disappeared. "I thought it would be best if we had some time alone before we got to the park."

"Uh oh," Jill replied. "That sounds ominous."

"Ma'am, I was an NCO. Sometimes it's better for us working folks to discuss reality before we meet with the officers."

"What makes you think we're not officers?" I asked as we started walking with the flow of people toward the baggage claim.

"I've read up on you two. In my experience, officers decide what should be done, then tell the NCOs to figure out how to make their vision happen. Your history has been filled with getting things done and not telling other people what to do."

"Sergeant?" I asked.

"E-6."

I nodded, understanding he'd been a staff sergeant. "I was a corporal when I left. Please excuse Jill, she's a reformed park superintendent."

"Reformed?" Jill asked.

"You quit giving orders and started doing the work."

"Ahh. I'm reformed. Yes."

Calvin frowned. "You two must've worked together for a while."

"Worse," Jill replied, "we're married."

The confusion on Calvin's face was humorous.

"Yes, we're married partners," I explained. "It makes for interesting dinner conversation."

"I bet it does," Calvin replied. "My wife doesn't want to hear anything about what happens at work."

Our conversation ended at the baggage claim when I moved to the carousel. Calvin and Jill moved away from the crowd to be nearer to the wall, where he scanned the crowd as they spoke. He was a head taller than Jill and probably weighed 250 pounds. Watching them, I felt reassured. Calvin was the kind of person I'd want watching our backs if we were ever in a standoff.

I rolled our bags to them and Calvin led us to the park service vehicle he'd parked in the driveway with the light bar flashing. An airport police officer stood next to the vehicle, perplexed by the obvious police vehicle with no one around. He had his citation pad out but hadn't written a parking ticket.

Calvin walked up to the cop and extended his hand. "Thanks for watching my vehicle."

The flustered cop nodded, then watched Calvin load our luggage into the back of the pickup. The suitcases, which weighed close to forty pounds each, looked like bags of marshmallows when Calvin handled them. Jill opened the rear door, leaving me riding up front with him.

"What can you tell us about the murder?" I asked.

"Well, that McInnis guy was found face down in the stream. The visitor who found the body pulled him out and was doing chest compressions when the EMTs arrived. Based on the condition of the body, the EMTs determined the guy was way past the chest compression stage and well into the decomposition stage."

"Was he found in a well-traveled area of the park?"

Calvin shook his head. "There are two units in the park. Most people visit the birthplace in the southern unit. That's where the memorial and visitor center are. There's a northern unit, the site of Lincoln's boyhood home. The victim was found in an out of the way part of the south unit."

"Are the south and north units connected?"

"They're about ten miles apart. The birthplace unit is a couple of miles south of Hodgenville. It's got a visitor center and a memorial building housing a replica of Lincoln's cabin. The park is crisscrossed with hiking trails. The guy who found the body was walking a trail along the creek."

"How remote is the area where the body was found?"

"The body was discovered less than a mile from the visitor center."

"But in an area that doesn't get much foot traffic?"

"Nearly all the visitors go to the memorial and visitor center. The trails in the south unit aren't what serious hikers want."

"Did the autopsy estimate the time of death?"

Calvin glanced at me, then back at the road. "I don't mean to be morbid, but McInnis had been dead for a couple of days. His face was..." After a pause, Calvin added, "he'd been face down in the water for a while. There was no question in my mind that he'd departed this world a few days before. The medical examiner estimated two days, based on the passing of rigor mortis and the body's decomposition."

Jill coughed in the backseat. "And the person who found him was doing chest compressions?"

"Yes, ma'am. He was a well-intended Good Samaritan. I assume he'd never seen a dead body outside of a funeral home."

"What was the cause of death?" I asked.

"There was water in his lungs. He drowned."

"The stream didn't appear to be a raging torrent."

Calvin chuckled. "It's hardly flowing. He must've worked hard to drown there." He glanced at Jill; apparently afraid she would be offended by his description of the body. "I mean, if he'd done a pushup, his face would've been out of the water."

"How was he identified?" I asked.

"He was carrying a wallet full of credit cards and cash. His face sort of resembled the picture on his driver's license. The ME made a positive ID from dental records."

From the backseat, Jill asked, "Had he been reported missing?"

"Yes, ma'am. His wife reported his disappearance to the Elizabethtown police. She initially thought he'd spent the night at the distillery. She called his office the next morning and was surprised to hear he wasn't there."

"Is she the prime suspect?" I asked.

"I guess she's broken up over the death." Calvin paused, then added, "The distillery had something big coming up and he'd been working night and day to prepare."

"Something big?" I asked.

"He's the main guy at a new distillery. They've been operating for like seven years and were preparing to release their first bottles of bourbon. It was a really big deal."

"So, not a suicide?" Jill asked.

"Apparently not. I mean, he was *the man* at this new distillery. It's been all over the local news. His family made Scotch, and he'd brought all his knowledge to this new bourbon operation. He told the newspaper his new release was about to turn the bourbon industry upside down."

"It sounds like he might've been making his competitors nervous," I suggested.

"Not really. I mean, the distilleries here are mostly owned by big conglomerates now. In the old days, he might've been a threat to the local family-owned bourbon makers. Today, the headquarters of the big companies are far away. I don't think any of them felt threatened by this little start-up operation. Hell, he's only got two rickhouses." Calvin glanced in the mirror. "Sorry about my language ma'am."

Jill smiled and waved off his apology. "Calvin, I've heard a lot stronger language than you're using."

"Just the same, I don't like to swear in front of ladies."

I glanced at Jill, grinning and weighing her response. "Thank you, Calvin. I work with a bunch of cops. It's not often anyone addresses me as ma'am, watches his language, or calls me a lady."

"That's not the way I was brought up, ma'am. Men don't swear around ladies."

"Only around other men and only when they're drinking?" Jill asked.

A grin tickled the corner of Calvin's mouth, then disappeared. "Mostly when dealing with livestock, ma'am. Horses, cows, and pigs can drive a man to profanity."

Laughing, Jill said, "I understand that. I've sworn at a couple of horses and steers myself."

"You grew up on a farm?"

"I grew up on a South Dakota ranch. I'm handy with a rope and can ride, too."

I watched Calvin's expression change from concerned to amused. "The McInnis distillery co-owner is a thoroughbred breeder from Lexington. I guess their logo is one of his champion studs."

"I read your brief, concise report."

Calvin glanced at me to see if I was being serious or joking with him. "There wasn't much to say."

"I like a report that gives me the facts without offering suspicions and suppositions. On the other hand, I'd like your observations, too."

"All I know is that McInnis drowned, and his body was found inside the park. It appeared he died there."

"Do you think he died where he was found?" I asked.

"That path isn't well traveled by visitors, but it's not at all remote. I thought it unlikely someone hadn't noticed him lying there for more than two days."

"How far was the body from the nearest parking lot?" I asked.

"The parking lot isn't terribly large, but the body was found closest to the most remote part of the lot. This time of year, there aren't many people who choose to park in the corner farthest from the visitor center. It's kind of an overflow parking area, and there aren't a lot of visitors for another month."

"Are there security cameras?" Jill asked from the back.

"The only cameras are in the visitor center and inside the monument. McInnis never walked through either of those buildings."

"I looked at the park's website. Isn't there an Inn opposite the visitor center?" I asked. "Have you interviewed the guests and staff?"

"The Inn and guest cottages closed during Covid and never re-opened. Greta, the woman whose family built and ran the Inn, still lives in a house there. That far corner of the parking lot is hard to see from her residence." Calvin's lips twitched into a smile that disappeared as fast as it arose. "Greta lives alone. She told me she sometimes peeks between the blinds if she hears something going on. She's called the visitor center to have a ranger deal with people who are rowdy or poke around the cabins. She's not one to step into a situation."

"Did she peek between the blinds the day McInnis was murdered?"

"She was actually in the visitor center, working at the reception desk when the body was discovered. She didn't see anything that morning, or the previous evenings."

As we turned off I-65 at the Sonora exit, Calvin pointed to a billboard with the picture of a young woman who appeared dressed for the prom. Below the picture were the words *Missing* and *Reward*. "That's Cybill Cantwell. She'd been missing for three months before she was found in Florida. You'll be working with Kristina Blake, the detective who found her. Kristina has become a local hero who's been interviewed by every television network and the newspapers."

"That's quite an accomplishment," I said as we exited the highway outside of Elizabethtown. "I think only about a quarter of missing girls are ever located."

"Yeah, like I said, Kristina is a local celebrity. You'll like her. She's a good investigator." Calvin slowed as we passed through Elizabethtown. Just outside of town, I saw the sign for Hodgenville.

"Kristina and I are pleased you're here. This investigation is…*target-rich*."

"Define target-rich," Jill requested.

"There are at least a dozen people with motives to kill McInnis."

"Besides his wife, who is on your list of possible suspects?" I asked.

"There's always the spouse, although she seems broken up over his death. Then, there are all the local distillers, suppliers, and the horse people."

Jill leaned forward. "You said all the distilleries are owned by big conglomerates."

"They're *owned* by conglomerates, but the employees are local. The local folks are always worried about their jobs. McInnis claimed that he was about to reinvent bourbon using science and technology. Most of the locals consider bourbon making to be an art. If he really reinvented the process, some people could lose their good-paying jobs."

"What about the horse people?" Jill asked.

"They're aloof and above the riffraff. They're the likely buyers of the new high-end McInnis bourbon. If McInnis really is making the best there ever was, bottles of really expensive booze will become passé. There's talk about a few of the locals scooping up all of the McInnis bourbon to maintain the value of their collections. Add to that the potential loss of farm income."

"What lost farm income?" I asked.

"McInnis developed his own strains of corn, barley, and rye. He's paying big bucks to a few farmers who are protecting the integrity of his genetics. If other distilleries go out of business or cut production, corn and barley prices are going to tumble."

"It sounds like a few farmers are going to do well if he's successful," I replied.

"At the expense of their neighbors."

Calvin turned into Abraham Lincoln Birthplace National Historic Site and drove to the parking lot adjacent to the visitor center. An unremarkable black vehicle was parked near the visitor center in a spot reserved for law enforcement.

"Certainly, his distillery will carry on after his death," Jill suggested.

Calvin shrugged as we walked toward the visitor center. "McInnis was bigger than life. Conversations stopped when McInnis walked into a room. He'd become local royalty. I'm not sure there's a brand without McInnis at the helm. His death makes life more secure for quite a few people."

"This is just wonderful," Jill said, her voice dripping with sarcasm.

"Like I said, ma'am, it's a target-rich environment."

Chapter 3

Inside the visitor center, we found a trim woman talking to an overweight man wearing Park Service gray and green. The man stepped forward and offered his hand. "I'm Bud Parker, the superintendent." As we shook hands, he nodded toward the woman with a badge and holster clipped to her belt. "Kristina Blake is the LaRue County investigator assigned to the case."

Without smiling, the woman extended her hand to Jill, as I shook Bud's hand. "You must be Jill Fletcher."

"It's nice to meet you, Kristina. Are you the lead investigator?"

"I'm the lead and *only* investigator."

"We heard you're good," I said as I shook her hand.

Kristina glanced at Calvin and Bud before answering, "The sheriff assigned this case to me and said it was my baby—another chance to shine. In reality, Calvin and I think the case is a stinking pile of manure that no one wants to touch. I spoke with an FBI special agent who said, 'he'd leave the case 'in my capable hands.'"

I nodded my understanding. "We've been assigned to a few of those."

"What makes this untouchable?" Jill asked.

The superintendent looked around at the visitors who were close enough to hear what was being said. He nodded toward an open door in the far corner. "Let's continue this discussion in the office."

Closing the door behind us, Calvin said, "I told Doug and Jill about the political aspects of the case."

Kristina set out five paper cups and poured coffee from a carafe sitting on a credenza as if she'd been spending a lot of time in the room. "I've already had a call from the British Consulate in Chicago asking if they needed to 'send someone down to *facilitate* the interview with Tamsin McInnis,'" Kristina continued as she handed out the coffee cups. "I told them they were welcome to send Mrs. McInnis anyone they wanted, including a lawyer. They tried to go off the record and asked if she was our prime suspect."

"How did you respond?" Jill asked.

"I told them there wouldn't be any off-the-record statements. I said Mrs. McInnis is as much of a suspect as anyone else in LaRue County right now."

"Are the Brits sending someone from the consulate?" I asked.

"They are 'considering a local *solicitor*' who might sit in with Mrs. McInnis if we question her. I had the impression they hoped I would tell them Mrs. McInnis wasn't a suspect, and she wouldn't need a *solicitor*."

"Have you spoken with Mrs. McInnis at all?" I asked.

"I made the death notification with her Episcopal minister. Mrs. McInnis explained her whereabouts at the estimated time of the victim's death. Like many innocent people, she'd been home alone with no one to provide an alibi. For what it's worth, she seemed genuinely upset over the death of her husband."

"I take it she didn't request a lawyer, nor did she ask you to contact the consulate?" I asked.

"She called the consulate to discuss the paperwork required to repatriate her husband's remains, which is how they became involved. She called me back and asked about making funeral plans. I said it would be a few days before her husband's body would be released." Kristina paused, then said, "In case you're wondering, Tamsin McInnis isn't going anywhere while this investigation is ongoing. I have her passport."

"Who else is on your suspect list?"

"Mr. McInnis has a financial backer, Robert Joseph Carlisle III. I'm trying to determine what happens to the partnership now that Alistair McInnis is dead. They incorporated *Running Acres Distilling* before they poured the distillery's foundation. Their business registration with the state says Robert Carlisle owns fifty-one percent of the stock. The remaining portion is owned jointly by Mr. and Mrs. McInnis."

"So, Carlisle stood to lose a lot if the business sinks because McInnis died," I summarized.

Kristina sipped her coffee and nodded. "Depending on who you talk to, Carlisle either wins big by losing a stubborn partner, or he loses big because he's lost the big-named Scot who claimed he knew how to make the best bourbon anyone has ever tasted."

"Have you spoken to Mr. Carlisle?" I asked.

Kristina looked at her watch. "I'm meeting him in half an hour at his lawyer's Elizabethtown office. You're welcome to join me."

"At his lawyer's office?" Jill asked with a smile. "Carlisle must have a guilty conscience."

"Mr. Carlisle is a shrewd businessman who didn't fall off the turnip truck yesterday. His lawyer contacted the sheriff and suggested that we meet with Carlisle at his office."

"Is the sheriff joining you?"

Kristina snorted. "He's a busy man who delegates well. I was asked to deliver his apology."

"Elizabethtown is about fifteen minutes away, right?" I asked.

"Fifteen minutes in rush hour," Kristina replied.

Calvin chuckled. "There really isn't a rush hour in Elizabethtown, unless you get stuck behind a combine or tractor."

"Have you been to the distillery, Kristina?" Jill asked.

Kristina nodded. "I got as far as the tasting room. I was told I needed a search warrant to go any farther or to look inside Mr. McInnis' office."

"Did you learn anything?"

Kristina leaned back and thought before answering, "I've toured nearly every Kentucky distillery over the years. Some are rustic and some are fancy. Running Acres Distillery is in a category of its own. Most of the distillery tasting rooms are 'homey' to make a normal person feel comfortable. Running Acres Distillery's guest room looked like it was ready for the King's visit."

"Did you learn anything related to the case from them?" I asked.

"They're convinced Running Acres Distillery has created a whole new bourbon category. A luxury bourbon that'll put the others to shame."

"Did they tell you how they planned to do that?" I asked.

"Not really. Charlotte, the manager, spoke about using 'chemistry instead of artistry.' Whatever that means."

Jill looked at me. "It sounds like we may have to buy a couple of bottles for my dad and Uncle Chet."

Kristina shook her head. "Not unless you have a lot more disposable income than I do. They're auctioning off their first release. They expect it will fetch thousands of dollars a bottle."

"A bottle?" I asked.

Kristina nodded. "For each bottle."

I scrambled to do the math in my head. "If they're selling one-liter bottles, that's over one hundred dollars a shot!"

"The bottles are 750 ml," Kristina replied. "It's more like two hundred dollars a shot."

Jill grinned and asked, "Don't you think Dad and Uncle Chet are worth that?"

"I doubt their palates could discern the difference between this new booze and a shot of Gentleman Jack."

"I don't know that anyone but a professional taster could tell the difference between any high-end bourbons," Kristina said. "Snob appeal will sell this product."

Calvin cocked his head. "I took a marketing class. One of their case studies was Smirnoff vodka. The company was having a hard time getting into the market, which was flooded with cheap vodka. Some marketing geniuses convinced the company management to put a silver label on the product and double the price. Once they did that, Smirnoff couldn't make enough vodka to cover the demand. On top of that, they quadrupled their profit on each bottle. Snob appeal is a real thing."

Kristina glanced at her watch. "I've got to leave now for my meeting with Carlisle and his attorney. Calvin, Doug, and Jill, would you like to join me?"

"Sure," I replied, "if you can deliver us to our inn afterward. We didn't rent a vehicle."

Kristina tossed her paper coffee cup into the wastebasket and gestured to the door. "I'll drop you wherever you want to go."

Calvin opened the door for us. "I'm passing the baton to the Texan experts."

Kristina put on a stage impression of being disappointed. "I thought we were partners."

"Are you kidding me? After calling me the cave cop for a week, you're disappointed when I have to go back to my *real* job?"

Kristina bumped fists with Calvin as she passed. "You're okay for a park ranger."

"Bring your kids to the cave sometime. I'll give them a behind-the-scenes Mammoth Cave tour."

I shook hands with Calvin as we split up outside of the visitor center. "You don't have an ongoing role in this investigation?"

"My role ended when I summarized my report and delivered you to the visitor center. You've got the ball." He paused, then added, "stop by if you have time for a tour of the big hole."

After transferring our bags to the trunk of her vehicle, Kristina drove out of the park and turned toward Elizabethtown. "Calvin said you two are from Texas?"

"We work out of Padre Island National Seashore."

"How did you end up here?"

"We are assigned Park Service investigations all over the country. We just wrapped up an investigation in North Dakota. The boss called and told us to pack our bags and fly to Kentucky."

Kristina glanced at me. "So, you two aren't run-of-the-mill law enforcement rangers?"

"We're part of the Park Service Investigative Services Branch. We're dispatched to assist local law enforcement officers with their investigations."

"You're here to take over the investigation?"

I shook my head. "This is your baby. We're here as a resource to help you."

"'We're from Washington, and we're here to help,' is not a welcome phrase. I've dealt with the FBI, DEA, DOJ, and Homeland Security. Once they arrive, I've usually been relegated to copying files and fetching coffee."

"You're an experienced investigator with local knowledge we don't have. Our role is advisory. We'll help however we can and try not to step on your toes."

"And you'll call a news conference to announce the arrest of the murderer."

"With any luck, Jill and I will be back in Texas before there's a news conference."

Kristina glanced at me. "Are you serious?"

"We have no need to stand in front of a camera. But our bosses would appreciate it if you mentioned the assistance of the Park Service at your news conference."

Kristina glanced in the mirror at Jill. "Do you agree with that?"

"Doug and I didn't even pack uniforms to wear at a news conference. You're the local hero."

"I'm not sure I'm much of a local hero."

"You found a missing teen," I said. "That's huge."

Kristina sighed. "Yeah, I found a broken teen who'd been pimped out two or three times a night for six months. She's in a detox facility trying to kick a heroin addiction. Her family is trying to wrap their head around the whole thing. If she can stay clean, she's going to need years of counseling."

"But she's alive," Jill said quietly. "And you got her out of the hell hole she was in. She's got a chance."

"Yeah, I guess I've given her a chance."

* * *

The law offices of Cooper, Cooper, and Taylor were located on the second floor of a rehabilitated building facing the historic courthouse in the center of Elizabethtown's square. Rather than waiting for what appeared to be an antique elevator, Kristina walked up the stairs two steps at a time. Jill followed, and I took the steps more slowly. When I reached the second floor, Jill and Kristina were already inside the law office anteroom, speaking to a receptionist. I overheard, "...they're waiting for you in the conference room at the end of the hallway."

Two dapper men, drinking from sweating glasses of what I assumed was iced tea, were seated at the far end of a table arranged to seat six. A younger third man was gathering papers he'd been discussing with the others. Both of the older men smiled and stood as we entered. The young man closed his laptop and slipped it into a backpack.

A hefty man wearing a golf shirt with a horse logo circled the table. "Kristina Blake, it's truly a pleasure to make your acquaintance. You deserve a medal for saving that child." He introduced himself as Robert Carlisle.

"The sheriff sends his regrets for being previously engaged," Kristina said. "He asked me to update him after the meeting. He offers his assurance that our department is doing everything we can to solve the McInnis murder."

The second older man leaned close to the guy who was packing up and whispered, "Looks good, Reggie. Go with that plan."

The young man nodded to us as he passed. The man he'd spoken with approached me and said, "I'm Kyle Cooper. You must be one of the rangers assigned to Kristina's case." He was about the same age as Carlisle but looked healthier. He wore a dress shirt and looked like he could put on a suit coat and tie and be standing in a courtroom within minutes.

"Doug Fletcher. I'm actually a US Park Service investigator, as is my partner, Jill."

Cooper raised his eyebrows, as if impressed by my title. It was done in a way that made me feel it was a move he practiced to manipulate people.

Cooper introduced himself to Jill, then thanked Kristina for her great detective work on Cybill's case. Kristina accepted his praise gracefully.

Carlisle approached me. "It's a pleasure to meet you. I apologize for the delay while we finished our meeting with my financial advisor."

"No problem," I replied. "Thanks for meeting with us."

Cooper gestured for us to take seats. Our hosts waited until the ladies were seated before taking their chairs. "Would any of you like a glass of tea?" Cooper asked, lifting a sweating cut glass pitcher from a serving tray that held an ice bucket and several tumblers.

Kristina declined. Jill and I both accepted. After one sip, I remembered that Southern iced tea tasted like equal parts tea and sugar. I tried not to grimace.

Cooper read my reaction and quickly said, "If you'd prefer, I have a bottle of bourbon in the cabinet."

"Thank you, no," I replied, setting the glass carefully on a stone coaster printed with the firm's logo.

Cooper leaned forward and smiled at each of us. "Let's put our cards on the table. Mr. Carlisle has graciously offered to answer your questions about the death of his partner. His cooperation is voluntary, and his interests are aligned with yours; he wants to solve the murder. He will cooperate fully, to the extent that he can. However, if your questions become accusatory or confrontational, this meeting will be over, and my client will decline any further questions. Is that acceptable?"

Resigned to the terms of the interview, Kristina nodded.

I raised one finger and smiled at Cooper, then Carlisle. "I apologize, but my partner and I have only been on this case for a few hours. Because of our...unfamiliarity with the case and the people involved, we may ask more probing questions in an effort to get up to speed."

Carlisle looked concerned. He turned to Cooper, who was smiling. Cooper said, "This is not a deposition. Mr. Carlisle isn't under oath, although we do understand the penalties for lying to federal investigators. We will afford you latitude in your questioning. However, if you exceed the scope of collecting background information, I will advise my client not to answer your questions and advise *you* that the interview is over."

Jill, who was unaccustomed to dealing with lawyers or courtroom situations, turned to me with a look that asked, *what the hell did you two just say?*

"If hypothetical answers and generalities will bring us closer to understanding what happened to Mr. McInnis, we'll be happy to agree to your terms for this interview," I replied to Cooper.

I glanced at Kristina, who was smirking. I got the impression she found my response amusing. I nodded to her and said, "Detective Blake, we're your guests here. Why don't you ask the questions? Jill and I may ask for clarification."

Kristina nodded, smiled, then asked, "Mr. Carlisle, did you kill Alistair McInnis?"

Carlisle was unprepared for that direct question and looked at Cooper. The lawyer nodded to his client, then smiled at Kristina. "As I said, we're laying our cards on the table. Let me state unequivocally that my client was in no way involved in the death of his partner. What's your next question?"

"Mr. Carlisle, have you been in or near the Abraham Lincoln National Historic Site in the past week?"

Carlisle looked at his lawyer, who gestured for him to answer, giving the appearance that he'd been coached on what to say. "I haven't been anywhere except my farm, Elizabethtown, and in Lexington for the past week. I'm not even sure where the Abraham Lincoln thingy is."

"What happens to Mr. McInnis' ownership stake in the distillery?"

Carlisle seemed surprised by the question. "I assume it'll pass to his wife, Tamsin."

I jumped in before Kristina could ask another question. "Do you have insurance on the business and partnership?"

"I have life insurance, if that's what you're asking."

"Does the distillery have life insurance on the owners?" When he didn't reply immediately, I added, "The value of the distillery must be impacted by McInnis' death. He's your main guy. Is the distillery even a viable venture without him?"

Carlisle and Cooper stared at each other for a second before Cooper leaned over and whispered something to his client. Carlisle nodded and composed himself. "Mac, as I called Alistair, has been training the Running Acres Distillery team for years. We have a succession plan with people who are ready to step up."

"But none of them are Alistair McInnis. How much of the Running Acres Distillery's value is determined by the McInnis name and reputation?"

Carlisle snorted. "It's impossible to know! With our first bottling coming out, we've been banking on the tasting results. Sure, Mac led the team in crafting our bourbon, but his whole focus was on putting science to the art of bourbon making. We've done that! Our people understand what Mac's been doing. Besides, we have rickhouses full of seven years of aging bourbon. When people taste this first release, we'll have them hooked. Our biggest challenge is financing our expansion, and that has everything to do with marketing the brand and little to do with Mac's involvement."

I nodded as Carlisle spoke, then asked, "Are you now the bourbon maker?"

Carlisle smiled. "I've never been a bourbon maker. I'm a financier. I know what Mac's been doing, but I don't get all the talk about chemicals and the biology of barley. That's all been Mac's baby. Well, Mac and his team. Sophia Thackery is Mac's chemist. I have every faith that Mac taught Sophia everything he knew."

"Isn't that risky?" Jill asked. "Sophia could move to one of your competitors tomorrow."

Cooper cleared his throat and said, "All of the Running Acres Distillery's employees are bound by non-compete agreements."

Carlisle nodded. "Sophia is our analytical chemist. She's been key to understanding the materials, processing, and storage that give our bourbon its unique character."

"Ah," I said, "so McInnis was expendable."

Carlisle's face turned red as he prepared to respond. Anticipating an outburst, Cooper put his hand on his client's arm. "I think our interview is over. If you have any other questions, please submit them to me in writing." Cooper stood with his hand on Carlisle's shoulder.

Kristina was quiet until we got into her vehicle. We sat idling, waiting for the air conditioner to start blowing cool air. "That's it, isn't it? McInnis did such a good job of coaching that he was no longer needed."

"Who wins?" Jill asked from the back seat.

"I suppose that depends on if the buyers are as excited about their first taste of this bourbon as Carlisle hopes they'll be," I stated. "If they spit it out and call it turpentine, I suppose everyone loses. If it's a big hit, Carlisle stands to make handsome profits for decades."

Kristina nodded. "So will Tamsin McInnis."

"It depends," I replied. "We're assuming she inherits Mac's portion of the business. If there's a buyout clause in the bylaws, she may get a check for some predetermined amount and then be pushed aside. Or, if the business has life insurance on Mac, we'll have to see who the beneficiary is."

We drove a few miles, then turned onto a side street in Hodgenville. Kristina parked in front of the stateliest house in the neighborhood. The entire block looked like it had been built in the 1800s. Each house was two-story and had a porch with rocking chairs and wooden steps. A small, hand-painted sign stood alongside a concrete sidewalk read, *Aunt Mary's Inn.*

"I'll arrange meetings with Tamsin McInnis and the distillery manager for tomorrow. Will you two be ready to leave by nine o'clock?"

"We're early birds," Jill said as she unbuckled her seatbelt and opened her door. "By nine, we will be showered, dressed, fed, and caught up on email."

"Caught up on email if Aunt Mary has Wi-Fi," I added.

"Remember that you crossed into the Eastern time zone just south of Hodgenville." After helping us unload our suitcases, Kristina stepped back. "You two are okay...for feds."

"If we're needed, we've got your back. We're not going to hide behind cover while you're shot at."

Kristina laughed. "Let's hope it doesn't come to that. I've never fired my weapon anywhere but on the range. I'd like to maintain that record until I retire." She paused, then cocked her head. "You make it sound like you might've been involved in some shooting situations."

"I've put down a couple of rabid animals," I replied.

Smiling and nodding, Kristina patted her holster. "That, I could see happening." Fingering her keyring, Kristina wished us a nice supper and good evening. "I've got a middle school girls soccer game to attend if you guys are bored." She paused, then added, "Personally, I've never been that bored."

Chuckling, I said, "I think we need to adjust to the time change. But thanks for the kind offer."

"Are you sure? At the last game, there was a discussion about the side effects of Ozempic and Zepbound."

"You don't look like you have a weight problem," I observed.

"Not eating regular meals is a side benefit of this job. It's hard to gain weight eating a granola bar for breakfast, drinking coffee all day, then eating two bites of whatever my husband whipped up for supper as I rush out of the house to sit at my kid's ball game or PTA meeting."

"Good night," I said as she climbed into the car.

Chapter 4

We carried our suitcases up the steps, stopping at the front door. A hand-written sign read, *The door is locked after 9:00. Ring the bell if you're late.* I held the door for Jill, and we stepped into a time warp. The living room we entered felt like an 1800s museum. The hand carved sideboard and the brocade covered furniture all looked like genuine antiques. There wasn't a television or any sign of electronic devices. A grandfather clock ticked in the corner. The sideboard was filled with classics by Robert Louis Stevenson, Walt Whitman, Emily Dickinson, Arthur Conan Doyle, Edgar Alan Poe, and Mark Twain.

The creaking stairs preceded the appearance of a slender Black woman whose smile exuded warmth. "Checking out my library?"

"You've got quite a collection. I read most of these when I was a child," I said as I ran my finger across the titles on the books' spines.

"I'm Bitsy," she said, extending her hand to Jill. "I assume you two are the Fletchers?"

"Jill and Doug. You have a museum."

Bitsy laughed and gestured toward a row of small, framed paintings mounted on the wall leading up the stairs. "I'm the caretaker of this place, which was founded by my great-grandmother, then minded by my grandmother and mother. None of us was named Mary after our great-grandma."

"It's lovely," I said. "But I'm afraid to sit on the furniture."

"Don't be. These are all reproductions of antiques. Everything in the house is meant for use." Bitsy nodded toward an open door. "Let me give you a tour of the first floor."

Setting our suitcases aside, we walked into a dining room with eight chairs set around an oak table. One wall featured a built-in sideboard displaying plates, glasses, and serving dishes. "Dinner is a set menu served here at six o'clock. Breakfast is available from seven to nine."

From the dining room, we walked through another time warp into a twenty-first-century commercial kitchen with stainless steel countertops and modern appliances. The aroma of baking cookies filled the air.

"Wow!" Jill exclaimed as she turned and looked around. A young woman with her hair in cornrows, wearing a white apron, glanced at us, then quickly looked away before donning a pair of potholder mitts. She removed a tray of cookies from the oven and set the baking sheet on the table.

"If you'd like to freshen up," Bitsy said, "I'll take you to your room. The cookies should be cool enough to sample by the time you come back downstairs."

We followed Bitsy upstairs to a hallway lined with wooden doors. "Each bedroom has its own bathroom." She opened the first door on the left, then led us into a luxurious bedroom with a canopy queen-sized bed. "This is your room. If you need anything, my room is at the end of the hallway. Knock anytime, day or night."

"I doubt we'll have to disturb you," I replied.

Bitsy's smile turned from professional to homey. "I've had a few law enforcement people stay here over the years. They're polite guests who respect me and my staff. I've never had one of them break anything or raise a ruckus. On the other hand, I know that your days are sometimes long and unpredictable. If you miss a meal, there's always bread in the breadbox, cold cuts in the refrigerator, and fruit in a bowl on the counter. Help yourselves to anything."

Jill checked out the bathroom while I set our suitcases on stands next to the bed. "Your cook looked a bit nervous when she saw us," I said.

Bitsy smiled. "That child has had a few scrapes with the law. I'm sure she was surprised to see your badges and guns. Don't worry about Mindy. I'm guiding her back on the right path. She works hard and is putting her past behind her, although some of those scars run deep."

"That's kind of you to help her."

Bitsy shook her head. "It's what good Christians do, Doug. We help those in need."

"Having spent my life dealing with criminals, many of whom are repeat offenders, I have a hard time turning the other cheek."

Bitsy continued to smile. "I choose to give sinners another chance. On the other hand, I do keep an eye on things. It's always prudent not to leave cash laying around." Stepping to the door, Bitsy said, "You two freshen up, then come downstairs. I have tea and lemonade in the refrigerator. I can make coffee if that's your beverage of choice."

After Bitsy closed the door, Jill emerged from the bathroom.

"Did you hear that our cook is a criminal?" I asked.

Jill shrugged and opened her suitcase. "She's the criminal we know about. How many motel employees are crooks that haven't been introduced to us?"

I sighed and opened my suitcase. "I suppose that's true. Washing dishes in a restaurant or vacuuming vehicles at a car wash seem to be entry-level jobs for paroled felons."

"There you go! The devil you know versus the devil in disguise."

"We've got half an hour before supper. Do you want to take a shower?"

In a theatrical move, Jill sniffed her armpit. "Aside from being worn out from traveling, I think I'm good. How about you?"

"The cookies sound tempting, but I'd hate to ruin my dinner."

Picking up a laminated card from the dresser, Jill read, "The Wi-Fi is *Maryshouse* with the password *roomone*." Jill looked surprised. "There is technology here! I'm going to check email," she said as she removed her laptop from a carry-on bag.

"I'll have a glass of lemonade and cookies while you play with your computer."

Bitsy was sitting at the dinner table opening the mail. "Ready for tea or lemonade?"

"I'll take a glass of lemonade and a cookie."

I followed Bitsy into the kitchen, where the enticing cookie aroma mingled with roasting ham and subtle hints of sweet potatoes. Bitsy filled a glass with lemonade from a pitcher. Mindy looked nervous and scrubbed the cookie sheet intensely, making sure not to make eye contact with me. I followed Bitsy back to the dining room, where she set a coaster on the table for my lemonade, then set down a plate with three fresh cookies.

She took a seat across from me while I took a bite of a cookie, washing it down with lemonade.

"Where y'all from, Mr. Fletcher?"

"First of all, please call me Doug. We live in Texas, but we travel all over the country."

"Doug, that's not a Texas twang in your voice. Unless I'm mistaken, it reminds me of that movie 'Fargo.' I remember that hooker's line, 'Go Bears!' when she was talking about her home team."

"I'm originally from Minnesota. The White Bear 'Bears' were a high school rival."

"Western Kentucky is a long way from Minnesota or Texas. What brings you here?"

"We're assisting with the investigation of the guy who died at Lincoln's Birthplace."

Bitsy nodded while reflecting on the news about the murder. "Too bad it wasn't one of the local Bubbas who was killed. There's always some conflict. There are generations of people here who will hold grudges over stupid stuff the present generation can't even remember."

"Like the Hatfields and McCoys?"

"Yes, something like that. It's not that they're trying to kill each other. It's just that it doesn't take much provocation to touch a nerve that results in a punch being thrown. Some of it dates back to the 'recent unpleasantness.'"

Intrigued, I stopped with a bite of cookie halfway to my mouth. "The recent unpleasantness? Was there a recent dispute I should know about?"

Bitsy chuckled. "You're a Yankee. You might not recognize the Southern term for the Civil War. By the way, the war isn't over—the fighting has abated, for now."

"You're kidding. Lee surrendered one hundred and sixty years ago."

"Lee surrendered the Army of Virginia. There's the whole rest of the Confederacy who stopped fighting without laying down their swords."

"I doubt that Alistair McInnis' death has anything to do with 'the recent unpleasantness.' He was Scottish."

"You've got a good point, Doug. That said, you haven't eliminated any suspects with that conclusion."

"The usual motives are love, money, or drugs."

Smiling, Bitsy said, "The wife did it?"

"A person known to the victim is the killer in about ninety-five percent of murders."

"Who asked you to assist with the investigation?"

"My understanding is that the request came from the US State Department because the victim was a well-known foreign citizen."

"I'm surprised the sheriff didn't dump the case in your lap and run like the last striped-fanny ape."

"Why would the sheriff want to dump the case?" I asked, already aware that he'd handed it to Kristina like a hot potato.

"Mr. McInnis was...universally distrusted by anyone outside of the distillery."

"Distrusted, not hated?"

"I don't think anyone displayed outright hatred toward him. At this point, there are rumors and suspicions. Next week, there would've been someone whose ox got gored."

"What's going to change next week?" I asked, knowing about the premiere of the new bourbon, but wanting the local perspective.

"They were going to pour the first glasses of the new McInnis/Carlisle bourbon."

"And that was going to ignite some hatred?"

"Someone was going to be unhappy. If his booze is as good as Carlisle is bragging, every local bourbon maker and their suppliers will be on edge and their product at risk. If it isn't as good as they say, all of the distillery employees and McInnis' suppliers are going to take a hit. They've all bet big on McInnis, and if the bourbon isn't a gold medal winner, they'll all have invested seven years while McInnis and Carlisle blew smoke up their skirts."

"How was McInnis blowing smoke?"

"Every supplier, from the barley and corn growers to the bottle suppliers, and distillery workers have traded their profits and time for a future share of the distillery. They're all going to be owners, and McInnis has sold them on his grand plan to make the world's best bourbon. If the samples don't taste like pure liquid gold and have to be sold as 'bottom row booze' instead of 'fancy locked away in the rich man's liquor collection ultra-premium bourbon,' they'll all take a financial hit, and the distillery will probably fold."

"Wow. And the whole town knows that?"

"Honey, the whole state knows that. You've got rich people lined up with their checkbooks open, waiting to buy a bottle of the best bourbon in the world. On the other side, you've got twenty or thirty distillers hoping that McInnis has created something that's only good for stripping paint."

"What do you think, Bitsy?"

Pushing herself away from the table, Bitsy stood and replied, "I think you're out of lemonade."

* * *

I shared Bitsy's observations after our ham and yam dinner. Dessert was derby pie, which turned out to be a wonderful pecan pie with bits of chocolate. Jill filled up on ham and yams, leaving only enough room for one bite of pie, which meant I was obligated to finish both of our pies or risk offending our hostess. I bore that burden without complaint.

Jill was lying in bed, staring at the ceiling, when I came out of the bathroom. "What's wrong?" I asked as I slid under the covers.

58

"Everything about this case is a mess. There's a legion of potential winners and losers. Think about the outcome. Why kill him now? I mean, the tasting will happen whether he's alive or dead. It's not like it will change."

I switched off the light and snuggled against Jill's side. "Someone knows how the tasting will go. I'm betting an insider, who sampled the new booze, saw an opportunity to improve his financial stake by eliminating McInnis."

"I think there's more going on with Carlisle. Who arranges for their first police interview in their lawyer's office? That makes me extremely suspicious."

"I think Carlisle is a shrewd businessman who didn't want to have a statement taken the wrong way."

"His lawyer jumped in too quickly. Carlise barely got a word out."

I chuckled, adding, "That's what smart lawyers do. They step in before their client answers potentially embarrassing or incriminating questions."

"Carlisle stands to be the biggest winner or loser. I think he's our prime suspect."

"Hey, Sherlock, aren't you the one who said we collect the evidence and let it lead us to a conclusion?" As I spoke, I slid my hand on Jill's stomach.

She didn't resist, but asked, "How can you even think about being romantic after eating that huge dinner followed by two pieces of pie? You must be ready to explode!"

I edged closer and kissed her ear. "I think pecans are an aphrodisiac."

"If you throw up on me..."

Chapter 5

Kristina arrived just as we finished our breakfast. Bitsy met her in the living room and clasped both of her hands. "Miss Kristina, it is an honor to have you in my house."

Kristina offered a demure smile and nodded. "Thank you. How is Mindy doing?"

"Mindy's just fine. I think she appreciates your support and trust."

"May I slip into the kitchen and greet her?"

Bitsy released Kristina's hands and gestured toward the kitchen door. "I think she'd be happy to see you."

Kristina nodded to us, then walked into the kitchen where we heard murmured voices. Bitsy topped off our coffee cups.

"I take it you know Kristina," I commented.

"Miss Kristina is a good soul. After Mindy's arrest, Kristina approached me and asked if I'd be willing to take on a charity case for kitchen help. She explained that Mindy needed guidance more than she needed a stay in juvenile detention, so I agreed to work with her. The judge was touched by Kristina's suggestion at Mindy's sentencing. He asked me if I was in agreement, and I said, 'yes.'"

Kristina was smiling when she walked out of the kitchen. Bitsy pulled out a chair, then poured her a cup of coffee. After Bitsy left, Jill commented on Kristina's outreach in the community.

After sipping her coffee, she said, "Some kids are trouble, and there's not much you can do to help them turn the corner. Others, like Mindy, don't have any guidance from home and end up making a mistake. I like to help them find a kinder pathway back to society. Recidivism among teens leaving juvenile detention is abysmal. Mindy needed a guiding hand and someone to make sure she went to school every day, not a stay in a detention facility."

"What's your plan for today?" I asked.

"Tamsin McInnis agreed to meet with us. She'll be at an art class in Danville at nine o'clock."

"Where's Danville?" I asked.

"It's about an hour east of here. Her class meets in the Glass National Art Museum. It's attached to the Art Center of the Bluegrass."

Jill appeared impressed. "That sounds interesting."

"I haven't been there, but people who've toured it say it's really something. It's showcasing the work of Stephen Rolfe Powell."

"I'm not familiar with his work."

"I'm not into art beyond being able to pronounce Renoir," Kristina joked. "But I've heard this Powell guy is the Dale Chihuly of Kentucky."

"Ah," Jill replied. "I've seen pictures of Chihuly glass sculptures. They're incredible."

"The museum has thousands of Powell's pieces."

Jill looked at me as I finished my coffee. "Maybe we should check it out after this investigation wraps up."

"I'd choose the National Corvette Museum in Bowling Green or Mammoth Cave National Park over a museum full of glass sculptures. Besides, you know me. I'm *Ivanbeto*. I might break stuff."

Walking to Kristina's plain brown Dodge Charger, she asked, "What's an *Ivanbeto*?"

Jill explained, "Our Navajo friend, Jamie, calls Doug *Ivanbeto,* which means bull buffalo. Doug's earned the nickname because he has a tendency to charge through investigations without noticing the havoc he leaves behind."

Kristina snorted. "Oh, great, I'm working on a sensitive investigation involving a foreign celebrity, and I've been teamed up with a bull buffalo federal agent."

"I'm not so much a buffalo as a focused investigator who doesn't like bureaucrats or red tape." Changing the buffalo conversation, I said, "I had a nice conversation with Bitsy last night. She had some interesting insights into McInnis' situation."

"Which situation is that?" Kristina asked.

"Bitsy says someone's ox will be gored by the McInnis bourbon tasting."

"I'm listening..."

"If the product is as good as its marketing says it is, the other distillers and their suppliers will be hurt. If it turns out to be 'paint stripper,' as Bitsy called it, all of the McInnis distillery workers and suppliers will be hurt. Either way, there will be winners and losers."

"That's what I told you. I'd throw Carlisle into the mix as a potential *big* winner or loser. Aside from McInnis' reputation, Carlisle is the person who's going to take the financial hit. If it's a bust, McInnis could always pack his bags and fly back to Scotland. Carlisle will have egg on his face, in a region where people have long memories."

Nodding, I said, "Bitsy mentioned family grudges going back to the 'recent unpleasantness.'"

Jill leaned forward. "No one mentioned a 'recent unpleasantness.'"

Kristina glanced at Jill in the rearview mirror. "The recent unpleasantness is what the Southerners call the Civil War."

"That's not a *recent* unpleasantness," Jill replied, "The Civil War ended one hundred and sixty years ago!"

"Is that your view of it, Kristina?" I asked.

"My family moved here from Lexington. We lived so close to Ohio my coworkers call me a damn Yankee."

"Speaking of being a damn Yankee, Bitsy picked up my 'Fargo' accent. I always thought my accent was neutral."

Kristina glanced at me like I'd said something inappropriate. "You don't think you have an accent? Really?"

"I don't hear it," I replied.

"Jill's accent is mostly neutral. Doug, you drag out your vowels. Minnesoooota. You betcha."

Sighing, I asked, "What else can you tell us about McInnis or his wife?"

"McInnis was great at selling himself and his ideas. The investors put a lot of trust into him, considering he's Scottish and unschooled in bourbon."

"I assume his Scotch education translates to bourbon."

"I don't have an opinion on brown liquor," Kristina replied. "I never got into the 'Kentucky hug' experience."

"Kentucky hug?"

"All the bourbon drinkers talk about it. The hug is the warm glow you get when the alcohol gets into your bloodstream."

"How did McInnis get connected with Carlisle?" Jill asked.

"There's a big online article about this if you Google McInnis and Carlisle. According to the internet, in addition to the distillery, the McInnis family breeds British racing horses. The story is that Carlisle shipped a thoroughbred to Britain for a race where the Carlisles and the McInnises had adjoining owners' boxes. Liquor was being served, and there was a lot of comparison and friendly banter about the obvious superiority of Scotch over Kentucky bourbon, along with the discussion of horse breeding. At some point, Tamsin McInnis and Glinda Carlisle got bored with the *boy talk* and wandered away. The wives hit it off and made arrangements for the couples to meet the next day. More liquor was served, and Alistair explained his frustrations with his stodgy family members who were unwilling to 'take their whisky to the next level' based on the chemistry Alistair had learned while earning a Master of Science at Heriot-Watt University. Carlisle, who has no shortage of cash after syndicating the breeding rights to his prize-winning stud, suggested that they team up to make the world's best bourbon. A month later, McInnis was in Kentucky and ground was broken on a new distillery and a rickhouse."

"You've mentioned rickhouses," Jill said. "What is a rickhouse?"

"Basically, it's a barn filled with rows of racks where bourbon barrels are stored while they're aging. Legend has it that the warm Kentucky days and cool nights cause the liquor to move in and out of the charred oak barrel staves, extracting essential bourbon flavors as it goes back and forth. I'm told that the barrels nearer the outside walls see the greatest temperature extremes, so they get the deepest color and flavor. The master tasters sample liquor from the individual barrels, then blend them to get the most appealing and consistent flavor."

"Wait! You said the McInnis bourbon has been aging for seven years."

Kristina nodded. "Two years is the minimum aging required for the liquor to be labeled as bourbon. Most of the distilleries sell two-year-old liquor under their inexpensive labels. A lot of the 2-year-old is the low-end bourbon that's served in bars. The higher-end booze ages longer, generally at least three years. The theory being that additional aging mellows the liquor and adds depth to the flavor. The tradeoff is 'the angel's share,' the percentage of alcohol that's lost to evaporation from the barrels for every year of aging."

"Was McInnis' decision to sell after seven years an economic determination?" I asked.

"A number of the master distillers call seven years 'the sweet spot' of aging. The bourbon snobs claim that even older booze is smoother. Others argue that the additional years in the barrel add unappealing flavors."

"So, McInnis and Carlisle chose the sweet spot and decided to bottle their booze now," Jill summarized.

"According to the internet, which of course is always complete and correct, McInnis had always intended to age his bourbon for seven years."

"No one has leaked a bottle to the press?" I asked.

Kristina groaned. "Bad choice of words, Doug. No booze has leaked to anyone who's admitted it. According to McInnis, only he, Carlisle, and his head taster have sampled the barrels. The *big reveal* was to take place next week."

When we'd covered all of our questions about the case, Jill asked, "Who won the soccer game?"

The question caught Kristina off guard. "Um, my daughter's team won by a goal."

"Did you pick up any suggestions for weight loss medications?"

Snorting, Kristina replied, "Last night's topic was tweezing vs. waxing."

Lost, I asked, "Which body part were they discussing?" When both women stared at me, I asked, "What did I say?"

Kristina looked at Jill, not knowing me well enough to answer the question. "Women tweeze facial hair. Mostly eyebrows." Glancing at Kristina, Jill asked, "What was the consensus?"

"Going to a spa for a wax is expensive and indulgent."

"So, tweezing is the way to go?" I asked.

Kristina glanced at Jill again before answering, "Just because something is indulgent and expensive, doesn't mean it's not what we prefer. Like having your nails done is indulgent but it's a great way to unwind."

"I'll never understand that whole female grooming thing."

"You've got that right. How long were you married to Sherry, your first wife?"

"Hey, that doesn't count. She quit shaving her legs and armpits. I doubt tweezing was an issue. Can we change the topic? What sports activity do your kids have tonight?"

"My son has chess club right after school and my daughter has soccer practice, so my husband picks them up. I think we'll actually get to eat dinner as a family. Jill, you mentioned Doug's first wife. Were both of you married before? Any kids?"

"I was married to my job, so Doug is my first, and only husband. No kids for either of us."

"What are your dinner discussions like? Do you talk about work all of the time?"

"When we're on assignment, we talk about work a lot. At home, I play golf and garden. We socialize with friends and ride our bikes on the beach."

"I can't imagine working with my husband. We'd kill each other."

I nodded. "There are days like that."

"Doug likes to feel in charge. I let him live with that illusion."

"Yeah, my husband is clueless, too. He asks the kids where the kitchen utensils are kept. He's so focused on his programming that he can't remember where we keep the can opener. He once told me Einstein didn't memorize anything he could look up. I told him he'd better start an alphabetical list of everything in the house so he could find the can opener. On the other hand, he can find the ice cream scoop with the lights off in the middle of the night."

I chuckled. "The man has priorities."

* * *

Our *getting to know each other* conversation ended when we reached Danville. The Glass National Art Museum was in an old stately building on Danville's Main Street. FEDERAL BUILDING was cut into stone above the ART sign over the entrance. A stylish woman looked up from a book she was reading when we walked in. She removed her readers as she smiled and chirped, "Welcome to the Glass Art Museum." She was about to offer us brochures when Kristina showed her badge and said, "We're here to see Tamsin McInnis. Can you direct us to the glass studio?"

The woman froze, staring at Kristina. "You're the detective who found that missing girl!"

"Right now, I need to find Tamsin McInnis. Can you direct us to her location?"

"Tamsin is teaching a class. I think they'll be done in about an hour."

Kristina smiled and nodded politely, "Tamsin is expecting us now."

"Oh. Sure. The studio is in the rear of the building. You'll see a sign on the back of the main exhibit hall." Gliding from the chair, the woman opened a brochure to a map of the museum. With her fingertip, she indicated the studio entrance.

"Thank you kindly, ma'am," Kristina said, accepting the map.

As we walked away from the desk, Jill whispered, "You're quite a celebrity."

"It's a pain in the ass."

The walk through the displays was breathtaking. Our footsteps echoed inside the large exhibit area. The variety of glass pieces was incredible, from delicate glass flowers, to bowls, to six-foot vases, and abstract animals with feet and tails.

We located the studio door buried deep inside the museum. A blast of hot air struck us in the face as we stepped into the studio. A group of people were gathered around an oven near the rear of the space. The workshop was filled with tables, with glass pieces in various states of completion. Scattered about were metal tongs and other tools that looked like they'd come from a torture chamber.

A red-haired woman wearing dark safety glasses twisted a long pipe that extended into the oven while four women and a young man watched. Her words were lost in the sounds of the furnace and air handling system, but the group was intently listening to whatever she was saying.

She glanced at us and warned, "Don't touch anything!" After the admonition, she refocused on the pipe she was twirling.

A moment later, she pulled a glowing molten glob of glass from the oven and walked to a nearby work area where she spun the pipe expertly while using a pair of metal tongs to shape the molten glass. After working the glass for a few moments, she used a paddle to flatten it. "Lisa, the yellow, now!"

One of the students returned to the oven and removed another pipe with glowing glass on the end. She delivered it to the redhead, who touched the yellow to several spots on the original lump, then cut off the yellow bits with tongs. After repeating that several times, while offering a running account of her actions and plans, she signaled for the yellow to be removed. With carefully skilled actions, she spun the main glass blob while using tongs to shape it and form the yellow globs into what emerged as an animal's legs, snout, and tail.

After several minutes of manipulation, turning, and shaping, a small pig took form. The redhead handed the pipe to one of her students and said, "Finish it off in the kiln, Maddie. Then put it in the annealing oven."

The female students followed Maddie to the oven while the redhead took a deep breath and looked at us. She said something to the young man, who was the only person not in jeans and t-shirt. Together they approached us.

Kristina nodded to the redhead. "Hello, Mrs. McInnis."

Nodding, McInnis replied with a Scottish brogue, "Good day, Deputy Blake. I hadn't realized we had anything more to discuss after you told me about Alistair's death." She nodded to the young man. "This is Derek Sandborn, from the British Consulate. He's here to make sure you don't beat me with lead pipes and lock me in the black hole of Calcutta," her Scottish brogue became more pronounced as she spoke.

Kristina ignored the consular official and addressed Tamsin, "Again, I offer my sincere condolences on the loss of your husband. Secondly, I would like to ask a few questions to help with our investigation."

Derek stepped forward and inserted himself between Tamsin and Kristina. In a very British accent he stated, "My official role here is to protect Mrs. McInnis' rights. Of course, we'd like to have your investigation of her husband's death resolved quickly and to that end, Mrs. McInnis will help as best she can."

Kristina's smile was practiced courtesy, lacking happiness or mirth. "I assure you, Mr. Sandborn, that I'm pursuing the death of Alistair McInnis with urgency." Gesturing toward Jill and me, she added, "Because of that urgency, these federal officers have been assigned to assist with the investigation. This is Jill Fletcher, and her partner, Doug."

Sandborn smiled, then glanced at Tamsin, acting as if he was impressed that feds were assigned. "Remember, you are not under arrest. You're answering their questions as a courtesy, to assist with the investigation. Under US law, you are entitled to representation by a solicitor...attorney, which I can arrange. You are also not required to say anything that would incriminate yourself."

Looking annoyed, Tamsin waved off Sandborn's warning. "What do you want to know?"

Kristina looked around. "Is there somewhere more private where we could talk?"

"There's a café attached to the museum. I don't think they're open yet, so it should be empty."

One of the older students broke away from the rest and walked over as we were about to leave. "Tamsin, would you like me to come along for support?"

Tamsin McInnis smiled at the dark-haired woman who wore a bit too much makeup, and whose jeans and shirt looked like they'd been tailored for her. Looking at us, Tamsin asked, "Would it be okay for Glinda Carlisle to join us?"

Kristina shook her head, "I'm sorry. No. We need to interview you alone."

Glinda, whose clothes and makeup nearly hid the fact that she was ten years older than her companion, touched Tamsin's arm. "I'll wait for you in the exhibit hall. We'll have lunch."

Tamsin McInnis led us out of the glass blowing studio, through the museum, and past a sign announcing that the café was closed. Acting as if she owned the museum, she walked to a coffee urn and drew a cup of hot water, then selected a tea bag from the display. "Help yourselves to tea or coffee. Heaven knows that the museum owes us that much considering how much time and money I've donated to them."

I looked at Jill, who seemed disgusted by the announcement of McInnis' generosity, and apparent entitlement because of their gifts. "Would you like coffee?"

"I'm good for now," she replied.

The five of us sat around a table. Sandborn took a seat alongside Tamsin, as if physically protecting her.

Kristina took out a notepad and pen. "Mrs. McInnis, have you recalled anything more about the evening your husband died?"

Gently bobbing her tea bag in the steaming water, Tamsin replied, "There was nothing special. As I said the last time we spoke, Alistair was working late at the distillery. He called to tell me he'd be later than usual and that I should go to bed."

"Did you have any contact with him after that?"

Tamsin removed her tea bag and made a ceremony of squeezing it out with a spoon. Setting the tea bag on a saucer, she replied, "No. He wasn't at home when I woke up at about seven. His side of the bed hadn't been slept in. I assumed he worked through the night and slept in his office...again."

"And you were alone all night?" Kristina asked without looking up from her notepad.

Tamsin bristled, "Yes, I was alone. There's no one to provide me with an alibi."

"At what point did you become concerned about your husband?"

McInnis crossed her legs and leaned back with her hands wrapped around the cup. "I must've called his cell phone at some point that morning. We were supposed to attend a fundraiser, and I wanted to make sure he hadn't forgotten about it. When he didn't respond to my voicemail or text messages, I called the distillery and asked Charlotte to relay the message to him. She told me he hadn't been there that morning."

"Remind me, who is Charlotte?"

"She's Alistair's gate keeper." Seeing our confusion over that description, Tamsin said, "Charlotte's title is administrative assistant. Most of her job is fending off the press and others who want to speak with

Alistair, or who are hoping to get inside information about the upcoming release. You'd be surprised how many people think they're entitled to a taste of the new bourbon ahead of anyone else. Even the..."

Sandborn put his hand on Tamsin's arm. "I think they've got the picture." He looked at Kristina and asked, "What else would you like to know?"

"Was that when you realized your husband was missing?"

"Yes, he was missing. I didn't think he was dead. I assumed he'd spent the night...elsewhere."

"Elsewhere? When we spoke earlier you said you thought he'd slept in his office." Kristina tapped her pen on the notebook. I assumed she was hoping the silence would make Tamsin uneasy and she'd air dirty laundry. "If you know, or suspect you know, where your husband was in the hours before his death, it would help us fill in the timeline of his last hours."

I nodded. "It might also provide us with a motive and a possible suspect."

Tamsin glanced at Sandborn who shrugged. Then she sighed, as if about to drop a bombshell. "Alistair has been *mentoring* a young chemist. They'd been spending a lot of off hours together."

"That person's name is?"

"Sophia."

"Do you know her last name?"

"Thackery. Sophia Thackery."

"Do you know if your husband was with Ms. Thackery the night of his murder?"

Tamsin shook her head.

"Where does Ms. Thackery live?"

"I have no idea where the *whore* lives." Tamsin stared at Kristina. "Your next question is?"

Sandborn put his hand on Tamsin's arm. She jerked it away.

"Has anyone threatened your husband?"

"Not overtly. No."

"Please explain that."

"I'm certain the other small distilleries feel threatened by our new release. I suppose some of them would like to see us fail. Not that killing Alistair would end anything." Tamsin paused, then asked, "You know about the break-in at the rickhouse, right?"

That caught my attention. "There was a break-in where you age the bourbon?"

"Someone broke in. They took off when the alarm sounded."

Kristina made a note and said, "That rickhouse must be in Boyle County, so we didn't investigate it. I'll give them a call." After jotting a note she asked, "Is there anyone else who might have a motive to kill your husband?"

Tamsin looked Kristina in the eye. "You mean, besides me?"

Sandborn put up his hand to stop the discussion.

"It's okay, Derek. I didn't kill Alistair. Heaven knows he irritated me. What wife hasn't been irritated with her husband. Murder is a long jump from irritation, and I wasn't there." Tamsin's eyes teared up for the first time, and she set the tea down before digging a tissue out of her pocket and wiping away her tears.

Sandborn went to the counter and retrieved another tissue for Tamsin. After a moment, he looked at Kristina. "Are we done?"

Kristina nodded and folded her notebook. "Thank you for your time."

Tamsin stood and folded the tissue. "Please excuse me while I fix my makeup."

Glinda Carlisle was waiting outside the café door. Tamsin whispered to her as she passed.

Kristina seized the moment to ask Glinda a question. "Did your husband get along with Alistair, Mrs. Carlisle?"

Caught by surprise, Carlisle showed her shock. "My husband?"

Kristina nodded. "Yes. How was the relationship between Alistair and Robert?"

Rattled, Glinda babbled, "Their relationship was professional. They got along just fine. My husband is the money man and Alistair was the bourbon making expert. Yes, I think they got along famously. You know, Yin and Yang."

Tamsin joined us, her makeup mostly repaired. "Do you agree with that statement, Mrs. McInnis?"

Tamsin glanced at Glinda, then said, "They had their moments. You know how it goes. Robert wanted to see a return on his money. Alistair knew it was going to take seven or more years before there would be income from the distillery."

"Seven *or more* years?" I asked. "This was the seven-year mark. Didn't Alistair think this release of bourbon was going to be...magical now?"

"I'm sure this year's bourbon is going to be good. They spent the whole year after the first barrels went into the rickhouse fine tuning the process. Alistair thought next year's bourbon would be even better."

"So, it was really next year's release that was going to be the game changer?" I asked.

Glinda looked like she'd never been party to any previous distillery discussions. "What's going on?"

"Alistair and Sophia blended some six-year-old and seven-year-old barrels," Tamsin explained. "Alistair said they were incredible."

Glinda stiffened. "But all the labels I designed say seven-year-old bourbon. There can't be a blend of years unless..." She stopped and asked, "Did Robert know about this?"

Tamsin shrugged.

Glinda dug into her back pocket and pulled out a cell phone. Jill gently reached out and stopped her from punching in a number. "I think it would be better if your husband spoke with Sophia about what's happening at the distillery."

Glinda pulled her phone away and glared at us. Stomping away, she punched a number in. Her footsteps echoed until we heard her say, "Call the damn distillery. Tamsin just told me Alistair and Sophia have been blending different years." A second later she shrieked. "You knew!"

Tamsin looked at Kristina and said, "I think Glinda's a bit browned off."

Sandborn chuckled as Kristina asked, "Browned off?"

"You Americans don't know, 'browned off?'"

Kristina shook her head.

"I suppose it translates to…irritated…annoyed…unhappy."

Sandborn shook his head. "I'd say things at the distillery will be sixes and sevens for a bit."

Tamsin nodded.

Seeing our confusion, Sandborn clarified, "In disarray is probably the best translation."

As we walked out, Kristina sidled up to Jill and said, "Until the browned-off comment, I thought we all spoke the same language."

Tamsin and Sandborn stopped on the steps outside the gallery. Kristina gestured for us to stop inside the door so they could speak privately. "Let her consult with the embassy guy. Maybe he'll split and we'll be able to catch her alone for a moment."

Footsteps behind us preceded Glinda's arrival. Despite heavy makeup, I could tell her face was flushed. She continued to clutch her phone as if she was trying to strangle it. She stopped short of us when we turned to look at her. Steeling herself, Glinda stepped up to us. "I now understand the change in plans."

"Does it have anything to do with McInnis' death?" Kristina asked.

"No. It's been in play for a couple of weeks. Robert says they've ordered new labels that don't have an age statement. I wasn't part of that decision."

"Is that common?" I asked.

"Most blended bourbons don't contain an age statement. Those appealing to the snob market have long aging claims; eight, ten, twelve, fifteen years. Robert and Mac decided to create snob appeal by creating a superior spirit and giving it a snappy name and label."

"What snappy name did they choose?" Jill asked.

"It's part of the big reveal at the tasting party."

Tamsin and Sandborn continued their subdued conversation on the steps. Sandborn did most of the talking while Tamsin nodded.

"What's with the Brits?" Glinda asked.

"We don't know. We're giving them space."

"Did you see the sculpture we were crafting?" Glinda asked.

"It was starting to look like a pig," Jill offered.

"Tamsin is a glass blower with a Master of Fine Arts degree. When she arrived here, she got a visitor visa, which precludes her from holding a job. I hooked her up with the museum and they jumped at the chance to have a volunteer instructor with her credentials." Glinda paused, then added, "The considerable donation Robert and I made to the museum may have influenced them as well. You don't need to tell Tamsin that, although I think she suspects it."

"Do you have any personal knowledge of McInnis' death?" Kristina asked.

Glinda appeared offended by the question. "We live halfway between here and Lexington. Aside from trips to the museum, fundraisers, luncheons at the country club, horse races, and shopping in Louisville, (pronounced *lou-vull*) I don't get around much."

"You don't go to the distillery?"

"I have no need to go to the distillery. I don't like bourbon, and I don't like industrial places."

"Isn't a Kentuckian not liking bourbon sacrilegious?" I asked.

"I can smile and choke down a swallow of a mint julep at the Derby, but I walk away when the boys start drinking bourbon straight up.”

“I think they call that ‘neat,’” I suggested.

“Trust me, there’s nothing neat about it. The boys get louder, and the jokes get bawdier.”

“What do the ladies do?” Jill asked.

“We stand off in the corner talking about the garden club, tennis, and pretending we’ve never heard the foul language the boys are using.”

Our discussion with Glinda ended when Tamsin walked back into the museum. “Oh, uh, hello. I didn’t realize anyone other than Glinda was waiting for me.”

“We were just getting a view of the Kentucky lifestyle from Glinda,” Jill said.

Glinda pushed past us and put her arm around Tamsin’s shoulders. “What do you say about us going to the country club and drowning our sorrows with a couple of bloody marys?”

“I probably shouldn’t be drinking right now. I might do or say something stupid.”

“It’s the country club, dear. Everyone says and does stupid things. What happens at the club, stays at the club.”

Tamsin looked reluctant. “I don’t know...”

“Maybe Abigail can give us a double tennis lesson.”

“I don’t have my racquet.”

“No problem, I’ve got a spare in my locker.”

We watched Glinda guide Tamsin away from the museum. "I'd like to be a mouse in the corner after Tamsin has a couple of bloody marys," Kristina said as we walked to her squad car. She paused without unlocking the doors. "Let's eat lunch. There's a great barbecue spot a couple of blocks from here. The distillery is expecting us at one."

Chapter 6

Stuffed with smoky barbecue and Pepsi, we drove to the distillery outside of Hodgenville. We passed a huge barn painted dark brown. "That's a rickhouse," Kristina explained. "They're brown to absorb the sun's heat, which drives the alcohol into the oak barrel staves."

The structure was immense, housing thousands of barrels. "Storing that much alcohol in a single location seems risky."

Chuckling, Kristina said, "A couple of years ago, one of the Bardstown rickhouses was hit by lightning. It burned like a torch, with the fire quickly consuming the wooden slats that support the barrels. As the racks collapsed, barrels fell and broke open, feeding the fire. By the time the fire departments arrived, there was flaming 140 proof bourbon flowing into the river."

"I suppose there were people lined up with scoops collecting the free bourbon," I joked.

"I don't think much of that happened. The bourbon was on fire as it flowed to the river. What did happen was a huge fish kill. I guess fish don't thrive in water that has a high percentage of bourbon."

"I bet they died happy."

Kristina parked in front of an utilitarian-looking structure that reminded me of a Minnesota pole barn. The parking lot was half full with an assortment of pickups and older American cars. The only hint to the building's ownership was a stylized horse logo. Below the horse was the *Running Acres Distilling* sign. The structure's roof was dotted with steaming stacks, and a semi was parked alongside the building with a trailer full of corn waiting to be unloaded. "Welcome to the distillery," Kristina said, smiling.

The entryway was as utilitarian as the building exterior, mostly decorated with rough-sawn logs and corrugated metal barn roofing. An empty reception desk sat at one end of the room in front of an open door.

"Hello!" Kristina said as we stood in front of the desk.

A woman's bleached blonde head popped around the doorframe. "May I help you?" A second later, recognition swept the woman's face, and she stepped out of the office. "Sorry, I'd forgotten the police were coming. I've been busier than a one-legged man in a butt kicking contest." She fumbled with her phone to close whatever she'd been doing, then jammed it into a pants pocket.

Jill giggled.

"What, you've never heard that one before?" the woman asked.

"That's a new one," Jill replied. "I bet you're Charlotte."

Charlotte swept a stray lock of hair behind her ear and replied, "Well, you had a fifty-fifty chance at guessing my name. There are only two women in this place and I'm half of them."

"We heard Sophia works in the lab."

The blonde shook her head as if in wonder. "You guys must be detectives to figure that out. Who do you want to talk to?"

Kristina took out her notebook. "Can we start with you?"

"Me? I'm just the administrative assistant."

"We heard you were the person who knows everything."

Charlotte's smile said she was pleased we knew she was in charge, although she tried to act demure. "Well, that's not entirely true. I don't know squat about the distilling operation. But, as far as the rest of things are concerned, I've got a handle on what's going on." She gestured to a sliding door on the opposite side of the rustic entryway. "Let's talk in the tasting room."

Charlotte opened the door and flipped the light switch. Moving between the rooms was like going into a different dimension. The tasting room was as opulent as the entryway was homey. The walls were paneled with dark wood. Each panel had a coat of arms or a picture of a horse on it. Oak tables were arrayed around the room, each set with four or six chairs. The wood was complemented by plush red carpeting. A long bar ran along the entire wall opposite the entrance. Behind the bar was a mirror etched with the Running Acres logo. Shelves alongside the mirror were filled with Glencairn glasses, each etched with the same corporate logo. I felt like I'd walked into a Scottish lord's personal pub. The only things missing were the bottles usually lining the shelves in front of the bar's mirror.

"This is incredible," Jill said, slowly turning to take in the entirety.

"This is where we've been entertaining potential corporate customers. Once the bourbon is released, we'll use this as our tasting room. The coats of arms and tartans are from the McInnis and Carlisle clans," Charlotte explained. "The pictured racehorses are from McInnis' Scottish stable and Carlisle's Lexington farm."

Taking a seat at the nearest table, Kristina took out a pen and her notebook. "When did you notice Alistair McInnis was missing?"

"You've got to understand, when we weren't entertaining potential customers, Mac didn't spend a lot of time down here. Most of the time, he was either working upstairs with the chemists and distillers or he was on his office phone schmoozing suppliers, distributors, and industry influencers. The only time I ever saw him here was when he arrived or left. Even then, if I was busy in the office, I might not see him."

"When did you last see him?"

"I suppose it was the afternoon he was killed. He ran through here like the devil was on his heels. He didn't say hi, bye, or anything, just ran up the stairs."

I looked around the ceiling, trying to spot a camera. Not seeing any, I asked, "Do you have security cameras, or some way to monitor when people come and go?"

"There are only a dozen workers, and we all keep track of ourselves. I mean, people tell me when they're taking vacation or if they're sick. Aside from that, everyone just comes in, works their hours, then goes home when their job is done. We're all salaried, so it's not like we're on a time clock."

"How do you make sure a non-employee won't get in?" Kristina asked.

"I monitor the front door and lock up when I leave."

"You must have confidential recipes, supplier information, test data, financial, and personnel records in the offices," I said.

"Yep, and they're all locked up when the last person goes home for the day."

"So, you have no idea what time McInnis left the night he was killed, or if there was anyone with him?"

"Nope. No idea at all. He had his own keys. So do the rest of the employees." Seeing our confusion, Charlotte explained, "We're family here. It's just like at home. The first person home unlocks the door. The last one to leave locks it up again."

"Is there anyone who didn't like Mr. McInnis?"

"What was there to dislike? He wasn't anyone's buddy. He expected us all to pull our weight and do what needed to be done. As long as we did that, he was a great boss."

"Has anyone been fired? Were there disgruntled employees?" Kristina asked.

"Not in the past few years. I mean, when we started up there were a couple young guys who thought they could game the system by coming in late and going home before their work was done. They were fired."

"Did McInnis fire them?"

Charlotte thought for a moment. "I'm not sure. We're a close-knit team. I think the slackers got the message that the rest of us weren't going to carry their load. I'm not sure if Mac fired them, or if they just decided this place wasn't right for them."

"Can we look at McInnis' office?"

Charlotte frowned. "Aren't you going to ask for my alibi?"

"Did you kill him?" I asked.

"Nope. I was home watching television the night Mac was killed."

"Then, let's see his office."

Just past the top of the stairs, Charlotte opened a door and turned on the lights in a small, utilitarian office. "This is Alistair's office," she said, stepping aside so we could walk in. "It's the penthouse executive suite."

The office was anything but a suite. It reminded me of a car salesman's office with two chairs facing a small desk. The few pictures on the walls were of horses or British racing cars, brands and models I recognized, but couldn't name. A picture of Alistair, his wife, and two adult children sat on the corner of his desktop, which was otherwise empty. One wall of the office was taken by a sofa; another featured a window overlooking the parking lot. Rumpled pillows on one end of the sofa made me reflect on Tamsin's comments about Alistair's late nights...and possible affair.

"Mr. McInnis was tidy," Kristina observed.

"Yes, he didn't like to leave papers on his desk. I think he was paranoid about someone walking in and seeing his secrets." Charlotte looked at the desktop and frowned. She reached over and adjusted the angle of the family photo, so it made a perfect triangle with the desk's corner.

"Secrets?" I asked.

Charlotte chuckled and gestured for us to leave. "You know, the typical distillery secrets like suppliers, mash bills of different batches, tasting notes."

The next office's lights were on. Unlike McInnis' office, the room was a laboratory. The lone desk was littered with paper. There were forms with handwritten notations spread across a lab bench. Two machines hummed on a counter, one displaying a countdown to some event. Charlotte let us look but blocked our entry. "Please excuse the mess. It appears Sophia has abandoned her rat's nest and is down on the floor."

After walking us back down the stairs, Charlotte led us into an open warehouse area where the walls were lined with racks containing boxes, barrels, and pallets of various items. The entire space was filled with the aroma of bourbon, which gave me a flashback to my drinking days. It was the most organized and clean manufacturing site I'd ever visited. Charlotte handed each of us a yellow hard hat from a rack on the wall. After arranging her own hard hat carefully to not mess up her perfect hair, she led us to a row of bourbon barrels lined up down the center of the open space. Each barrel was held in place by pairs of wooden wedges. A young woman, with a kinky black ponytail sticking out from under a white hard hat, stood at the end of the row holding a long copper tube in one hand and a glass beaker in the other. The woman scowled when she saw us and stopped in the middle of whatever she was doing. "Char, no visitors are allowed back here."

Ignoring the rebuke, Charlotte gestured to us. "Sophia, these are the people investigating Alistair's murder. Kristina Blake is from the sheriff's department. Doug and Jill Fletcher are with the US National Park Service. Sophia is our chemist."

Showing impatience, Sophia gave us a practiced, albeit fake, smile probably reserved for customers and potential investors.

I nodded toward the two-foot-long copper tube with a pointed tip she was carrying and said, "That looks like something you'd drive into a vampire's heart."

Sophia lifted the device. "It's called a whiskey thief. We use it to sample the barrels." She gestured toward the row of barrels, each with a wooden plug resting alongside an open hole on its top.

"I'm sorry to interrupt," Kristina said, "but we'd like to ask you a few questions about the night of Mr. McInnis' death."

The question seemed to rattle Sophia. She held a beaker under the tip of the whiskey thief, then lifted her thumb. A stream of brown liquid ran into the beaker. "Can you wait five minutes? I really need to taste this sample and make notes."

Without waiting for a reply, Sophia turned away and walked to a workbench where a line of beakers containing bourbon were lined up. Charlotte, obviously skilled at redirecting people, gestured toward the racks behind us. "These are representative barrels that Sophia and Alistair have chosen from the rickhouse. The marking on the end shows the barrel number, which distillation batch is in the barrel, the percent alcohol, when the barrel was filled, and the rickhouse location where it was aged." She turned and gestured toward the row of barrels resting on the floor. "Sophia is sampling these barrels which represent different distillation batches. She's making notes about their flavor components and mouth feel. The aging process pulls flavor elements from the charred barrels. With age, the liquor shifts from the sharpness of clear moonshine to mellower brown bourbon with hints of toasted oak, caramel, and vanilla."

"You add vanilla and caramel to the whiskey?" Jill asked.

Charlotte appeared shocked. "We don't add anything to the barrels except the distilled liquor. The alcohol extracts the vanilla and caramel flavors from the charred wood as it ages. Each year in the barrel, the bourbon picks up more flavors from the oak. Over time, the vanilla and caramel become more pronounced, and the bourbon becomes smoother. Once past seven years of aging, the process slows, and we trade off the loss of 'the angel's share' evaporation against the additional mellowing and extraction of flavors like graham cracker, orange, and candied cherry. Really old bourbon, like over fifteen years, picks up subtle dark chocolate, cinnamon, and wet leather flavors."

I focused on Sophia who'd taken the beaker to the workbench. After hanging the whiskey thief on a hook, she swirled the bourbon in the beaker and inhaled the scent. After a moment of consideration, she sipped the liquor, then set the beaker aside and made notes. She then repeated smell and taste tests on the row of samples, making additional notes on three of them. A forklift entered the area and placed a pallet in an open warehouse slot, then disappeared through a set of open doors. Intrigued, I walked down the warehouse, looking at the barrels and pallets loaded with boxes.

"Doug!" Charlotte called to me. "We don't allow visitors in that area. There's too much forklift traffic."

I walked back to the group as Sophia walked down the row of barrels she'd sampled, returning the plugs to the open bungs. I was struck by the contrast between Charlotte and Sophia. Charlotte was the prim and proper face of the company, greeting visitors. Sophia wore a t-shirt and jeans, no makeup, and hair was tied in a rough ponytail secured by a rubber band; the nerdy scientist was more concerned about her samples than her appearance.

Once the plugs were pounded into place, Sophia looked up at us and smiled. "Sorry. The bourbon changes as it airs. I needed to evaluate the sample and make my notes immediately. What can I do for you?"

Kristina raised her voice over the hum of fans and the commotion coming from the other side of the double door where the corn was being unloaded from the trailer and asked, "Is there somewhere we could talk?"

Sophia gestured down a narrow aisle between the racks. "We can chase the guys out of the break room."

Charlotte appeared less than pleased with the suggested location. Her phone vibrated as we approached the door. After checking the screen she said, "I need to leave you with Sophia while I deal with this call."

Sophia led us into the break room, which consisted of two long cafeteria tables, each surrounded by ten chairs. As predicted, Sophia asked two men if we could interrupt their break. Nodding and smiling at us, they picked up their litter and left.

Showing amazing poise for someone who appeared to be in her early twenties, Sophia shook hands with each of us. "I'm Sophia Thackery." When the introductions were complete, she gestured toward the counter. "There's sweet tea on tap, coffee in the urn, and Coke in the refrigerator. Help yourselves."

We declined beverages, then gathered around the end of one table. "Sophia, we're investigating Alistair McInnis' death and trying to build a timeline of events during the day and evening before he died."

"How can I help?"

Kristina took out her notebook and leafed through the pages. "It seems Mr. McInnis spent the day of his death here, in the distillery. Is that correct?"

"I wasn't with him the entire day, but I bumped into him off and on. Near the end of the day, we set out the barrels you saw on the warehouse floor."

"What time was that?"

"I wasn't looking at the clock. It was some time after the workers had cleared out. I suppose around three o'clock."

"How long did you spend with him that day?"

"Again, I wasn't paying attention to the clock." Sophia paused, then leaned forward. "You've got to understand where we're at. With the customer tasting a week away, we're scrambling to prepare."

"Explain that."

"Al and I are...were working all kinds of crazy hours, day and night, to sample and test barrels. Al was getting everything set for the bottling and tasting event. I was sampling the barrels and running them all through the GC and mass spec."

"You referred to Alistair as Al?" I asked.

Grinning, Sophia replied, "It's an American thing. Brits don't use nicknames. The guys started calling him Al, instead of Alistair. He was amused by our need to give him a nickname, so he went along with it, at least inside the building. He asked me to address him by his full name when we met with outsiders."

Getting back to the interview, Kristina asked, "How late were you and Mr. McInnis, Al, sampling?"

"I suppose we spent an hour here. It's kind of hard to say. When we sample barrels, time becomes irrelevant. I mean, we pull the samples with the whiskey thief, sniff each beaker, then we discuss our impression of the aromatic notes we smell. It's...tedious. Tedious isn't the right word. There's nothing tedious about it. It's a..."

"A labor of love," I suggested.

"I guess that describes it. I mean, this is our lives. Everything depends on the subtle flavors of the bourbon. Everything."

"Do you know how late you and Al tasted the samples?"

"Not exactly. I mean, it was like two o'clock when I started running the samples through the GC. I was running back and forth from the floor to the lab."

"What's a GC?" Kristina asked.

"The gas chromatograph. I inject the samples into the GC. It prints a graph showing peaks representing the chemical components in the bourbon. Each chemical compound goes through the GC column at a different rate. The time it takes for each peak to emerge tells me which chemicals are in the sample. The height of the peak tells me the amount of that chemical in the sample."

"It's not just the taste?" I asked.

"It is, but it's not. I mean, the flavor and mellowness are the reasons people pay extra for a particular bourbon. The more subtle flavors are characteristic of long aging. As is the mellowness."

"So, why run the GC if it's all about the flavors?"

Sophia smiled. "Because I can tell you what makes up the 'good' and 'bad' flavors. I can identify the subtle pleasant compounds and the nasty tasting bad actors. Through experimentation with the grain genetics, barrel toasting, fermentation, yeast strain, and distillation process, Al adjusted the ratios of the subtle flavors."

"What was Mr. McInnis doing while you were running the GC?"

"He went into his office when I took the samples to the lab. He stuck his head in to look at the peaks about halfway through the tests."

"Can you tell me what time that was?"

Sophia shook her head. "I'm not..." A thought obviously struck Sophia, and she paused. "The GC has a time notation on each sample. I can tell you exactly when each of them started and ended. I think Al checked on the GC progress about three o'clock. If we go to the lab, I can give you an exact time because he made notes on the graphs of the samples I'd run before he left."

"Before we do that, do you know when Mr. McInnis left the building?"

"Not exactly. His office was dark, and the door was closed when I finished the last GC sample. I got home after six thirty."

Without losing her rhythm, Kristina asked, "Were you and Mr. McInnis having an affair?"

Sophia lost her composure and stared, her mouth agape.

"Were you having an affair with Alistair McInnis?"

Recoiling and shaking her head, Sophia said, "God, no! Why would you even ask that? Did someone start that rumor?"

"We need to know the nature of your relationship with Mr. McInnis."

"Al and I were...colleagues. That's not right. He was my professor of bourbon. We spent all kinds of time together, but the only thing we had in common was bourbon. He was busy making bourbon, teaching, and marketing. I did chemistry. He was only mentoring me. We were NOT hooking up!"

Kristina waited for Sophia to add to her comments. When it was obvious nothing more was forthcoming, she folded her notebook. "Let's look at the GC timestamps."

In the lab, Sophia went to a file cabinet and removed a file folder while we stood at the end of a lab bench, which was covered with machines, sample containers, and notes. Joining us, she spread strips of paper on the counter that resembled EKG readings. She pointed to a small, printed timestamp at the start of each strip. "Here's the first sample, which started at 13:43. You can see where Al circled peaks and made notes. Here's a later sample. That's the last one Al marked up. The timestamp says it started at 15:02."

"Each sample takes half an hour?"

"Roughly," Sophia replied. "The column retention time is about twenty minutes. I like to let the GC rest for a couple of minutes before injecting the next sample."

Kristina pointed to the fifth strip. "This one is stamped 16:51."

"Yes, and you'll note the handwriting is different. I made the notes on this one."

"You started the last sample at 17:50 and it took half an hour?"

"I guess so. They all take a little less than half an hour. It must've ended about 6:20 PM. I made notes, shut down the equipment, then went home."

"Can anyone confirm your whereabouts after you left the distillery?"

Sophia appeared to freeze for an instant before gathering the GC printouts and answering, "My...roommate."

"What's your roommate's name?"

"Theodora Smith. She goes by Teddy. She was watching television when I got home."

"Teddy was definitely home when you arrived?"

Sophia nodded but looked extremely uneasy. "She and our daughter. We ate supper together, then watched TV."

Kristina closed her notebook and nodded to Sophia. "Thank you."

Sophia led us downstairs and to the entrance. I stayed back as Jill and Kristina exited. "Why did one of your sample barrels have Scotch marked out and other handwritten information on the end?"

Sophia hesitated. I'd done hundreds, maybe thousands, of interviews and her look was the classic warning seen when I was about to hear a lie. "Scotch?"

"Scotch."

"Oh, that! Al had a barrel of Scotch shipped from his family's distillery. We use that as a control when I run GC tests."

"I don't think so. Someone crossed out the Scotch logo with a marker and wrote bourbon barrel identification next to it."

Aware that she'd been caught in a lie, Sophia glanced past me to where Jill and Kristina were waiting just outside the door. "Your partners seem impatient."

"They're accustomed to waiting for me. What's the deal with the Scotch?"

"I'm afraid that's trade secret information I can't divulge."

"You're blending Scotch into your bourbon?"

Shock replaced Sophia's guilty look. "God, no! That would be...illegal. Blending in Scotch would mean we couldn't market the product as bourbon." I waited quietly while Sophia stared at me. Finally, she blinked. "Okay. This is a trade secret. It cannot be divulged, alright?"

"If it's not relevant to the murder investigation, I have no reason to divulge trade secrets."

"We were experimenting with putting the aged bourbon into barrels that had previously held other liquor. Al was partial to Scotch barrel secondary aging. I preferred the product from the Pinot Noir barrels."

"That's not a violation of the bourbon standards?"

"To be bourbon, the liquor has to be aged in new charred oak barrels for at least two years. There are no restrictions on further aging once the two-year standard is met. Premium Scotchs have been 'post-aged' in sherry and port wine casks forever. One Irish distillery even uses Caribbean rum casks. Al was experimenting with different barrels to see what trace flavors they imparted. Some are wonderful. Others are...less pleasing. Scotch lends a subtle peaty smokiness to the bourbon."

"You've sampled some of the bourbon from those barrels to know that."

After a moment of hesitation, Sophia nodded. "Alistair bottled some. I think he planned to give them to friends."

"Thanks for explaining that. I was afraid you were hiding something from us."

"Please, please, please, do not share that information outside of these walls."

"Like I said, if it's irrelevant to the investigation, it doesn't need to be mentioned again. Thanks."

I was nearly at the entrance when Charlotte's voice stopped me. "Mr. Fletcher."

I walked back to her office door. "Is there something else I need to know?"

Charlotte looked past me to make sure Sophia was going upstairs. "Please forgive Sophia. My friends talk about people who are smart in school but dumb on the bus. That describes Sophia perfectly. Alistair said she understands chemistry. On the other hand, she shows up in jeans and ratty t-shirts at customer meetings."

I read into Charlotte's comments and nodded. "Which is why you meet visitors. He wanted you to be the smiling face who met people at the door."

Charlotte smiled. "Exactly. We want to charm the visitors, not put them to sleep with a chemistry lecture."

"I think Alistair needed both of you."

"Alistair said I could sell freezers to Eskimos." Charlotte composed herself and added, "The bourbon's flavor might bring repeat business, but we need to charm customers into buying the first bottle."

"Tell me more about the bottles that are being reserved as gifts," I said.

Charlotte hesitated, weighing the confidentiality of that information. After a moment, she asked, "Do you know what a whiskey thief is?"

"That was the device Sophia was using to sample the barrels," I replied.

"In big operations, they use that sampling to decide how to best blend the barrels from different distillation batches and rickhouse locations to provide a consistent product from year to year. In the case of premium bourbon, the master distiller samples and chooses special barrels that are sold as 'single barrel' premium products." Seeing that I understood, she went on, "Mac and Carlisle reserved a couple of special barrels for our own use. Mac planned to give each employee and supplier a bottle. Mac and Carlisle planned to give the rest to special friends."

"Is there going to be an auction?"

Charlotte blushed as if caught in a lie. "Um, I don't know anything about that."

"How many bottles are we talking about?"

"Each barrel yields somewhere between 250-290 bottles."

"So, there were going to be five hundred bottles, give or take, to be given away or held for the owners. Right?" I asked.

"There are five hundred and twenty-three bottles."

"Who gets them?"

"One hundred are intended for the employees and our suppliers."

"How much is each bottle worth?"

"They're not for sale."

"Let's say you were going to auction your bottle off on eBay, how much do you think it would go for?" I asked.

"I'd never..."

"Suppose there's a less ethical employee who wants to monetize his bottle, what's it worth?"

Charlotte threw up her arms. "There's no way to know! None have hit the market."

"Would two thousand dollars be a good estimate?"

Charlotte froze, unable to answer. "I honestly don't know. Mac was planning to donate a bottle to the local American Legion. I overheard them speculating that the bidding may reach five figures."

"Ten thousand dollars?"

"At least that," Charlotte replied. "But that's the auctioneers' pre-sale estimate. That would be a charitable donation for the buyer, so no one knows how the bidding will go."

"At that price, those special reserve bottles are worth at least four million dollars."

"We really don't know what they'll sell for on the open market," Charlotte protested.

"Where are those bottles stored?"

"We have a secure room off the warehouse. They're under lock and key."

"Let me get Jill and Kristina."

"You don't really need to..." she protested as I walked to the entrance.

I explained to Kristina and Jill what I'd learned, then we returned to Charlotte, who looked flustered. "Take us there."

"Only Mac and Carlisle have keys."

I looked at Kristina. "Did you recover keys with McInnis' body?"

"I recall a watch and wallet, but not keys."

I turned to Charlotte. "Take us to the storage room."

"I don't have a key."

"Humor me," I said.

We walked through the warehouse, interrupting a forklift driver moving pallets of cardboard boxes. Charlotte led us to a double door in the back corner of the warehouse. The double doors were large enough to admit a forklift and pallet. She approached the door and grabbed the padlock, which hung open. Clearly concerned about the security breach she said, "This is supposed to be locked." She yelled to the forklift operator, "How long has this been unlocked?"

The man shrugged and resumed his work.

"Open the door," I ordered.

She opened the door and flipped on the lights, exposing two pallets wrapped in Saran wrap. One pallet's wrapper had been cut, and it appeared five boxes were missing from the top row. Charlotte groaned.

Kristina took a picture of the scene with her cell phone. "It appears you're missing about a quarter of a million dollars' worth of premium bourbon."

Charlotte rushed to the door. "We've got to review the security footage."

"We need to secure this crime scene," Kristina said, closing the door with a gloved hand. She clicked the padlock.

As we followed Charlotte back through the warehouse, I asked, "I thought Mac didn't need security cameras?"

Over her shoulder, Charlotte said, "I put my ex-husband's motion-activated game trail camera in the storage room when we placed the pallets there. I can check the activity from my phone."

It took Charlotte a few minutes to find the game camera app, log in, and retrieve the video. The first scene was of the forklift driver placing the pallets in the room. The time stamp said that had occurred two weeks ago. The next video was taken a week later, and it showed McInnis, Charlotte, and Carlisle entering the room and McInnis removing one bottle from the corner case. He handed it to Carlisle like a sommelier offering an expensive wine bottle to a restaurant customer. Carlisle inspected the label, said something that appeared to irritate McInnis. Carlisle replaced the bottle in the box. He tore away the plastic wrap and carried the entire case out of the storage room.

"What happened to that case?" Kristina asked.

"We opened one bottle in the lab. Five of us tasted the bourbon, and Sophia ran a sample through her gas chromatograph."

"How was it?" Jill asked.

The question seemed to stump Charlotte. "Um, good, I guess."

"You couldn't tell?" I asked.

"I'm not the master taster. It was smoother than off-the-shelf bourbon, but I'm really not qualified to render a judgement."

"What did Carlise, McInnis, and Sophia say?"

"As I recall, no one said anything. McInnis stared at Carlisle, waiting for his response. Carlisle didn't respond verbally. He just smiled, nodded, and capped the bottle."

"What happened to that bottle?"

"I think Carlisle took it with him along with the rest of that case. It disappeared from the lab."

"What happens next on the trail cam?" Kristina asked.

Charlotte moved to the next screen. Instead of the well-lit room, the next scene showed a light cast through the open door. An apparition wearing a hoodie moved into the unlit room and used a tool to cut the plastic wrap. Four cases were stacked on the floor and the person carried the boxes out of the room one at a time. A moment later the door closed, and the video ended.

"I think the video goes into infrared mode in the dark. That's why the light coming in the door is so intense and the person appeared ghostly," Charlotte explained.

"Did you recognize the person?"

Charlotte took a half step back and crossed her arms. Studying the screen she said, "Not wearing that hoodie. The person was trim, more like Mac, than Carlisle. That also excludes about a third of our workforce who are stockier."

"How heavy is a case of full bottles?" I asked.

"I don't know exactly. I can barely lift two of them at a time, but not four."

Jill took her phone out and punched in numbers. "The bottles contain 750 ml of bourbon, and let's say a glass bottle weighs about a pound. That totals thirty pounds a case, or so."

Charlotte nodded. "They're quite that heavy. But that's certainly in the ballpark."

"The thief removed the cases one at a time," I observed. "He or she wasn't someone willing to lift even two cases at a time."

Kristina cocked her head. "Charlotte, please run that last video again. There's something about the thief that makes me think it's a woman."

We re-watched the video. Then we had it played a third time, stopping when the thief was silhouetted in the door and when in profile.

"I agree with Kristina," I observed. "The thief's hips are a bit wider than a skinny guy and I get the impression there are breasts hiding under that hoodie."

Wrinkling her nose, Jill hesitated. "If it's a woman, she's not buxom."

"Well, we've only ruled out about three quarters of the county residents," Kristina suggested. "All the fattest and skinniest men, the buxom women, and anyone who'd likely pick up more than one case of booze at a time."

Charlotte's eyes twinkled. "You're forgetting all the Baptists. Excluding them rules out another three quarters of the remaining population."

Jill raised her hands. "Whoa. Don't rule out the Baptists. There are closet drinkers and maybe someone who'd steal the booze to pour it out."

Chuckling, I added, "Or the thief was a less strict Baptist who's not above selling a bottle of bourbon for thousands of dollars."

Kristina rolled her eyes and asked, "Charlotte, is that the last video your game camera recorded?"

She called up the recordings on her phone. "That's it."

"Please email that video file to Kristina and me," I said.

A question that had been nipping at the fringes of my consciousness finally surfaced. "The room was unlocked. Did you leave it open after pulling off the case you sampled?"

"I'm sure someone locked it."

"You didn't lock it yourself?"

Charlotte shook her head. "I didn't lock it, but I can't imagine that Mac or Robert didn't close the lock when we exited."

After making a note, Kristina summarized, "The room was either left unlocked, or the thief had a key."

"Only Mac and Robert have keys to that room."

Chapter 7

Kristina called her office and requested a technician to check for fingerprints in the storage room. After making the call, we waited with her in the parking lot. "Either they left the door unlocked, or the thief had a key."

"Charlotte was emphatic that the room was locked and that only McInnis and Carlisle had keys for the lock," I suggested. "So, one of the guys loaned his key to someone, or the killer stole the keys when he murdered McInnis. Maybe that was the motive; someone stole Mac's keys so they could get into the room and steal four cases of valuable bourbon."

Kristina considered that thought for a moment, then asked, "How hard is it to pick a lock?"

"It always looks easy on television," Jill said, smiling.

"Yeah," I replied. "Everything looks easy on television. An amateur would have a problem picking that lock. A professional would have it open in seconds."

Sighing, Kristina added, "I think lock-picking lessons are part of the prison curriculum, along with fencing stolen goods, and never talking to a cop without a lawyer present."

"What were you and Sophia whispering about earlier?" Jill asked.

"I spotted a barrel marked *Scotch* among the bourbon barrels. It made me curious. Sophia explained it's part of their aging experiments."

"I think we can put Tamsin's theory about McInnis and Sophia's affair aside."

"Yes," I agreed. "Sophia's female *partner* makes a heterosexual affair with her boss unlikely."

"Maybe Tamsin is right," Kristina replied. "McInnis was having an affair, just not with Sophia."

"I don't think he'd have an affair with Charlotte," I opined. "She has OCD. Did you notice her adjusting the position of the photo on Mac's desk? And I got a peek inside her office after you two left. Everything is perfect. I bet she alphabetizes the food in her refrigerator. People like Charlotte have a hard time sustaining relationships. Did you catch that the game camera belonged to her ex-husband?"

Jill thought about that comment for a few steps, then added, "Maybe McInnis was having an affair, but his partner didn't work for the distillery."

The crime scene tech arrived and, after showing him the lock and room, he went to work. "I snapped the lock shut, and we don't have a key," Kristina explained.

He glanced at the lock. "No problem. I've got a set of picks."

Kristina checked her phone as we walked to her SUV. "The autopsy report arrived. Give me your email addresses and I'll forward it to you."

As Jill gave Kristina her Park Service email address, I asked, "What's the condensed version of the report?"

After forwarding the email, Kristina opened it and slid her finger across the screen as she scanned the information. "McInnis drowned after blunt force blows to the head that may have rendered him unconscious. There are contusions on the back of his shoulders consistent with him being held face down in the water."

"That would explain how he drowned in a stream that's only a few inches deep," I observed. "Did the ME speculate on the type of weapon that inflicted the blows to the head?"

"Something cylindrical and slightly curved, about 2 centimeters in diameter."

"Like a three-quarter-inch pipe," I suggested.

"I think it was more like the curved part of a tire iron. Somebody swung it hard enough to fracture his skull."

Jill read the report as Kristina spoke. She stopped paging through the screens and cocked her head. "How big around was the whiskey thief Sophia was using to sample the barrels?"

"It was about an inch in diameter," I replied.

Kristina shook her head. "A whiskey thief isn't curved or heavy enough. Sophia was manipulating her whiskey thief with one hand while holding the beaker in her other hand."

"Wouldn't it be ironic if a Scottish bourbon maker had been killed by a whiskey thief?" I asked.

Wrinkling her nose, Kristina said, "I think someone has been watching too many episodes of *Midsomer Murders* and *Poirot*."

"Jill, we should be able to deduct our BritBox subscription as a business expense."

She snorted. "You're using British television shows as a source after giving me crap about quoting Sherlock Holmes."

"Sherlock Holmes was written in the nineteenth century. Poirot is at least the twentieth century and they're still writing episodes of *Midsomer Murders*."

Unlocking the SUV, Kristina said, "I'll ask how large an area they searched with a metal detector."

"Where is McInnis' body?" I asked.

"The regional ME's office is in Frankfort."

"Is that a long drive?"

"It's a three-hour round trip plus whatever time is spent there."

"Something for tomorrow?" I suggested.

"The ME may have already released the body to the family."

"I assume they don't have toxicology results yet. They wouldn't ship the body until they had test results, would they?"

"I suppose it depends on the ME and how much pressure he's getting from the State Department to cooperate with the British Consul General."

"Did you attend the postmortem?" I asked.

"No. The coroner had already removed the body by the time I got to the death scene. The ME fast-tracked the autopsy, probably because of political pressure. I was still slogging around in the stream when the ME was cutting." Kristina glanced at me as we drove into Hodgenville. "What would you expect to see?"

"I'm sure your ME is a competent and diligent doctor. However, sometimes knowing the context of the crime and crime scene gives us a different perspective on what happened to the body."

"Like knowing if a whiskey thief was found at the scene."

Jill chuckled. "Every time you say *whiskey thief*, I picture a guy rolling a barrel of whiskey out of the warehouse."

Kristina pulled into a strip mall and parked in front of a convenience store. "I'm going to call the Boyle County Sheriff's Department and ask about the rickhouse break-in. This is your chance to use a restroom or buy a can of Coke."

I paused with my hand on the door handle. "What would you like?"

"The caffeine and sugar in a can of Coke might perk me up," Kristina smiled.

* * *

After a quick trip into the store, I handed Kristina a can of Coke, sweaty from the humid air. "Thanks."

"What did you find out from Boyle County?"

"They responded to an alarm at the rickhouse. Whoever tripped the alarm was gone before they arrived. A door had been forced. Nothing was missing."

"I wonder if the burglar was looking for a free barrel of booze or information?" I asked rhetorically.

"Information?"

"McInnis and Sophia are doing some innovative things. Someone might have been more interested in what or how they're aging than in stealing a barrel of their booze," I speculated.

"The detective I spoke with said there have been a few rickhouse break-ins. The burglars usually steal a couple barrels of bourbon, as much as they can put in the bed of a pickup truck, then hightail it away before anyone realizes they've been robbed."

"What's a barrel of bourbon worth?" Jill asked.

Kristina did the math in her head. "I think they get like 250-300 bottles from one barrel of booze. The cheapest booze goes for about $15 a bottle. So, a stolen barrel of bourbon is worth at least three thousand dollars. Even if they put it into Mason jars and resell it at half price, that's a good payday for a petty thief."

"Or it'd keep them liquored up for quite a while," I suggested.

"A hell of a big party."

Kristina laughed. "Now, you've got me worried about going to my next Kentucky Derby party. What if all the mint juleps are being filled from a stolen barrel of bourbon? I could be an accessory after the fact."

"You'd have to arrest yourself for receiving stolen goods," Jill joked.

"Where are the barrels made?" I asked, thinking about Sophia's aging information.

"There's a cooperage in Lebanon, just past Hodgenville. We almost passed it on the way to your B&B."

"Let's talk to them."

Chapter 8

Milton's Cooperage was indeed only a block off of our drive to the B&B. The aging barn-like structure had multiple additions and sprawled over a city block. The firm's name had been painted many years before. In its current state of faded and chipping paint, it took some interpretation to discern the company's name.

I was hit with the strong, distinctive smell of fresh-cut oak when I opened the car door. An undercurrent of burning oak took me back to my days of camping with the scouts. Kristina led us to a door marked *VISITORS*. The noise outside of the building was loud, like chainsaws running. Inside, the din of sawing, hammers hitting metal, and the thumping of barrels was even more intense.

The office area we entered was empty aside from an unoccupied desk with a single chair and a counter. Every surface was covered with a layer of fine sawdust. The floor was tracked with wood chips and looked like it would erupt into an inferno with one match.

Kristina walked up to a counter and pushed the doorbell button mounted on the countertop. A moment later, a burly man appeared through a door behind the counter. A scarred leather apron didn't hide his considerable girth. He wore safety glasses so coated with sawdust I wondered how he could see. His sound-proof earmuffs were scratched from years of use.

"Yeah?" he asked as he pulled off the muffs.

"Take off your glasses, Uncle Ernie."

After pulling off his glasses, the man's stern expression turned into a warm smile. "Krissy, I haven't seen you since Thanksgiving. Where've you been?" The man rounded the counter and engulfed Kristina in a bear hug that covered her shirt and pants with sawdust transferred from the man's apron.

"I do have a job," Kristina teased, returning the hug.

"Y'all need to come over next Tuesday. We need a fourth for Kentucky."

"I can't keep up with your bourbon consumption and drive home after a card game."

Ernie looked at me and nodded toward Kristina. "My niece is kind of a short hitter when it comes to holding her bourbon." A frown crossed his face, then he cocked his head. "I don't believe I know you two." He held out his hand. "I'm Ernie Milton."

After introductions, Ernie nodded toward the door behind the counter. "Why don't y'all come back for the tour?"

He handed us ear plugs, then blew the sawdust off visitors' safety glasses before handing them to us. The interior of the building was filled with equipment, shelving, and an open area where three men were manually assembling barrels. Ernie gave us a loud running commentary about the barrel making process from cutting and shaping staves to fitting and assembling them, placing the bands, and finally, charring the barrel interiors with what looked like a giant torch. At the end of the tour, Milton led us back to the entrance and showed us a wastebasket for our used earplugs. "Well, are you ready to fill out an application?" he asked, exposing teeth so perfect they had to be dentures.

"I think I'll stick with the Park Service for now," I replied as I shook his hand. "Do you supply the Running Acres Distillery?"

"We supply everyone in Kentucky."

"Is there anything special about the McInnis barrels?"

Ernie's smile melted away. "I can't say exactly what specifications any of our customers have. Each has their own toasting and char requirements."

"Is the wood all the same?"

The barrel maker considered the question before answering. "To make bourbon, the barrels have to be made from American white oak."

"Not any other oak?"

"Red oak is porous when it dries, so the liquor would all evaporate. Other oaks aren't as plentiful and who knows what flavors they'd add to the bourbon."

"Is all white oak the same?"

A smile flickered on Ernie's face. "The heartwood is different from the outer layers. Some distillers prefer one over the other. Most ask us to quarter-saw the staves so they get some of each in every barrel. I can smell the difference when we toast and char the heartwood-only barrels. I suppose that's part of what makes each distiller's bourbon a little different."

"There are different species of white oak, right?"

"What are you getting at, Doug?"

"Do different distilleries use something other than common white oak?"

Ernie smiled and put his hand on my shoulder signaling the end of our conversation. He guided me to the door. "I hope the tour was informational. If you ever want a more challenging job than sitting in Krissy's cop car and chasing down speeders, come see me." Shaking my hand with both of his, he continued to smile, leaving me with the impression that I'd asked a pertinent question he couldn't answer without sharing someone's secret.

He hugged Jill briefly. Her response was more grimace than smile, and she held her arms out to the side. Kristina got another bear hug tight enough to make her gasp. Milton whispered something to her during the hug, then he waved and went back into the building.

"What did Uncle Ernie say?" I asked as we buckled in.

"He said you were a nosy Yankee who knew too much for his own good."

"What does that mean?"

"You're smart, and your questions were on the mark. The problem is, if Milton answered, he'd be divulging people's trade secrets."

"Ahh. I thought maybe there was something illegal going on."

Kristina started the Charger, then nodded. "I'd be surprised if Uncle Ernie and McInnis weren't working on some secret barrel construction. Every distillery is trying something to differentiate their high-end bourbon from the others."

From the back seat, Jill asked, "Doug, when you were drinking, could you discern the subtle differences between the different brands of booze?"

Kristina glanced at me, "You quit drinking, as in AA?"

"No AA, just poured out the booze and didn't drink hard liquor after that." I turned toward Jill and replied, "I could tell the difference between bourbon, Scotch, and

Canadian whisky. To be honest, I was drinking whatever booze they had 'on the rail' because that's what was cheapest. I didn't care for the smoky Scotch, and I tasted too much oaky flavor in the bourbon. I thought Canadian was the smoothest, so that's what I usually drank although I drank Jim Beam and Jack Daniels if someone else was buying it."

"The distilleries have tasters who have demonstrated their ability to taste and smell the subtle differences Sophia spoke about," Kristina said. "To smell and taste the caramel, vanilla, and graham cracker notes takes a refined palate. I think most buyers of high-end bourbon or Scotch know what they like and rely on their preferred brands to give them the consistently that suits their taste."

"I get the impression that there's snob appeal in the marketplace," I suggested.

"I'm sure that's a part of it. The people who are paying thousands of dollars a bottle for Pappy VanWinkle aren't buying it because they can taste the hints of dark chocolate and wet leather. They're buying it to impress their buddies."

Nodding, I added, "I'm sure there are people who can taste the differences. But, as you said, they probably can't articulate the subtle nuances of the liquor."

From the back seat, Jill said, "I suppose that's where Sophia's chemistry comes in. She can quantify the tiny bits of those flavor components. By knowing which chemicals make the good and bad flavors, she and McInnis were creating something intended to be the best of the best.”

“Measuring it is all well and good,” Kristina replied. “However, McInnis had to find ways of imparting those subtle nuances to the bourbon from the grains, yeast, and barrels. It’s not like they uncorked a bottle of graham cracker flavoring and added a couple of drops to the barrel or filtered out the bad stuff.”

I leaned back and thought. “What if McInnis was adding a bit of the flavors he wanted?”

“No,” Kristina replied. “Stop right there. If someone caught McInnis putting a drop of vanilla in a barrel, he’d be vilified. I mean, the liquor control board would shut them down and destroy all their stock. The reputation of all the distilleries rests on the knowledge there is only grain, water, and yeast going into the mash, and only charred white oak barrels being used for aging. There are no additives beyond that, period.”

“Maybe McInnis caught someone cheating,” Jill suggested. “That’d be a murder motive.”

Kristina glanced in the rearview mirror at Jill. “Wow. A scandal like that could taint the whole industry.” She paused, then added, “Yes, that would be a murder motive. But, I don’t think that it’s *this* murder’s motive. I can’t wrap my head around anyone adding something to the bourbon. I mean, most of these distilleries have generations of the same family who taste and blend the bourbon. Cheating would make your granny roll over in her grave."

Chapter 9

As we drove away from the cooperage, Kristina said, "Since you two don't have a vehicle, what are your dinner plans?"

"We get dinner at the B&B," I replied. "Bitsy told us supper is served at six and she always has sandwich makings in the kitchen, so we won't starve if we work late."

"You've got family things going on. Don't worry about us," Jill said from the back.

Kristina dropped us off at Mary's Inn. As we walked up the sidewalk, Jill said, "I really want to freshen up and change out of this shirt. It's covered with sawdust from my bear hug."

We were engulfed by a mouth-watering aroma as I opened the door. "Whatever Bitsy is cooking smells wonderful," I said, walking toward the kitchen as Jill went to our room.

Mindy was sitting at the counter reading a textbook when I walked into the kitchen. She looked up, then froze, her gaze fixed on my badge. "Uh, Bitsy ran to the store."

"Whatever you're cooking smells wonderful," I said as I walked over to a bubbling pot of what appeared to be stew. "What is it?"

"Um, it's Bitsy's version of Kentucky burgoo."

"Burgoo?"

"My family calls it roadkill stew. Mom whips it up from whatever is in the kitchen." Pointing to a recipe card, she said, "Bitsy uses a recipe. And, um, there isn't really any roadkill in it."

"What *is* in it?"

Mindy handed me the recipe. "It's mostly chicken thighs, pork roast, bacon, lamb shanks, okra, onion, and corn."

"The seasonings smell heavenly."

"Everybody has their own burgoo recipe. Bitsy seasons hers with onions, garlic, sage, rosemary, and thyme."

"May I taste it?"

Mindy gave me a tablespoon, then scooped a ladle of the stew into a bowl and handed it to me. It was steaming and obviously too hot to eat.

"What are you reading?" I asked, gesturing toward a book on the counter as I blew on a spoonful of stew to cool it.

"It's some stupid history stuff. Bitsy wants me to get my GED. She's got me enrolled in online classes."

"That sounds like a pathway to something more than cooking and cleaning."

Mindy shrugged. "Bitsy thinks it's important. I don't know what reading about some dead President is going to get me."

Bitsy walked in the back door, catching the end of the conversation. "It'll make you smarter and more interesting. You'll be able to talk about the Kennedy assassination."

Deeming the stew cool enough to sample, I slurped a taste of it. Sage, thyme, onion, and garlic burst onto my taste buds along with a cube of pork that nearly melted in my mouth. "Mmm."

Bitsy smiled. "You like my burgoo?"

"It's incredible."

"Did Mindy tell you it's called *roadkill stew*?"

"She also read me the recipe, so I know I'm not eating possum and armadillo."

Setting a shopping bag on the counter, Bitsy asked, "Do you and Jill have dinner plans other than eating with us?"

"Not really."

Removing cans from the bag, Bitsy said, "My church is having a covered-dish dinner. Everyone is welcome. Rather than eating here, why don't you and Jill join us?"

"What's a covered-dish dinner?"

"Everyone brings a homemade casserole, salad, or dessert for a communal dinner."

"In Minnesota, we call that a potluck."

Bitsy chuckled. "Potluck is a good description of what will be there. No one knows exactly what's coming, but there will be plenty of food and everything will be wholesome and tasty."

Jill walked into the kitchen, tucking her hair behind her ear. "What will be wholesome and tasty?"

"Bitsy invited us to a covered-dish dinner at her church tonight."

Sniffing my bowl of burgoo, Jill said, "If this stew is one of the covered dishes, I'm all in." She took the spoon from me and tasted it. "Yum."

"Perfect!" Bitsy replied as she checked her watch. "I'll put the pot of burgoo into a quilted sack and Doug can hold it between his feet while I drive us there."

Jill glanced at Mindy, who'd returned to reading her book. "Are you joining us?"

Mindy shook her head. "I'm not much into the holier-than-thou crowd."

Bitsy patted Mindy's shoulder as she removed a hand-made quilted shopping bag from a drawer. "Finding Jesus will be the next step of your transformation."

Mindy frowned. "If Jesus is lost, it ain't me who's finding Him."

* * *

We transported the burgoo without sloshing any of it on me. Bitsy parked in a half-full paved lot next to a stately white church. I carried the bag with the pot to a side door. We went down a few steps, arriving in a large hall with long tables set with coffee pots and pitchers of iced tea. Bitsy directed me to a counter lined with serving bowls, kettles, and crockpots. A half dozen platters at the end of the counter were covered with homemade bars and cookies. There appeared to be four or five pies closest to the end.

Two women rushed from the kitchen when they saw Bitsy. As if she were royalty, they gathered around her, asking what she'd prepared. I was directed to an empty spot on the counter, which had been reserved for the dish Bitsy was going to deliver. A hush fell over the room as I approached the reserved spot.

One of the women from the kitchen who had rushed to Bitsy stepped forward and said, "Pastor Earl is going to bless our food, then y'all can get in line."

Caught with the pot in mid-air, I paused and bowed my head for the prayer, which seemed to take five minutes, thanking everyone from the farmers who grew the corn in the corn muffins, to the pigs who'd made the ultimate sacrifice, and lastly, our heavenly Father.

Finally setting the pot in place, I helped remove the quilted bag as another woman arrived with a long-handled ladle. She sidled up to me and whispered, "Everyone loves whatever Bitsy brings. It's better than the turkey the Johnsons brought us. It was probably left over from last Thanksgiving. I saw the freezer burn."

Making a mental note to skip the turkey, wherever it was, I found myself suddenly surrounded by women who repeatedly welcomed me to the parish's covered-dish dinner. I tried to determine if they were some sort of welcoming committee or if they'd just shown up to check out the newcomer. I noticed Jill, standing near the stairs, where Pastor Earl was giving an animated monologue. Seeing the anxiety in her expression, I excused myself and made my way across the room through the forty or fifty people who were lining up for the food.

"Pastor Earl, that was an inspiring blessing," I said, trying to divert his attention from Jill.

Pastor Earl, a pudgy man with three or four chins, smiled broadly. "Thank you, son. What is your name?"

"I'm Doug Fletcher. You've been speaking with my wife, Jill."

Nodding so hard his jowls flopped, the pastor smiled, "We don't get a lot of visitors, and I don't recall any who showed up openly carrying pistols. I mean, there are people in the congregation who certainly have guns. We're strong Second Amendment supporters here. I imagine that a metal detector would be beeping like a smoke alarm if we set one up in the entrance."

"We're Park Service officers. As federal law enforcement officers, we're required to carry our firearms."

"I've got to say, it does my heart good to know that there are people like you who will put themselves on the line for us. I appreciate your service." The pastor gestured toward the line, which was moving slowly. "We should get in line before all of the pecan pies are gone. They usually go fast."

Pastor Earl led us to the line and introduced us to everyone nearby. The entire group was friendly and pleasant. "What are y'all investigatin'?" a woman asked.

"There was a death at Lincoln's Birthplace," Jill replied. "We're assisting the sheriff's department."

She nodded knowingly. "That was the Scottish guy, right? They were going to the Episcopal Church in Bardstown. There ain't many Episcopalians around here. Nope. Mostly Baptists and drunks."

Jill's eyes showed surprise at the *drunks* comment.

"Don't be shocked, honey. We know we can't save them all, isn't that right, Pastor?"

The pastor nodded his head. "We try to reach out to all people who haven't found Jesus, but not everyone is ready for God's grace." He stopped, then asked, "Are you two Baptist?"

"Episcopalian," I replied.

A woman leaned close. "That's okay. We understand that not all people embrace Jesus' teachings as tightly as we do."

"Thanks for allowing us to join your dinner," Jill interjected, hoping to move the conversation in a different direction before we were forced to reveal our marginal church attendance to this group. "Do you serve dinner every week?"

"We do! Most of the folks here are parishioners, but we get a few other community members who, unlike Pastor Earl, need a meal."

Shaking his head and patting his ample stomach, the pastor said, "I only partake for fellowship and outreach. If I was at home, I'd be eating carrot sticks and celery."

The woman wagged her finger at the pastor. "You shouldn't fib like that." She paused, then added, "I was thinking about Tamsin McInnis. We really should bring her a casserole and check in on her. She might want someone to talk to."

One of the servers grimaced. "She's a little...sharp for my tastes. I don't think we're in her social circle."

"You've met her?" I asked.

"Oh, sure. She's active in a lot of the local school and charity functions. Miz McInnis and her husband are generous with their time and donations. It's just that she's not much into socializin'. I don't think sweet tea and derby pie are her things."

Bitsy had been ahead of us in line. Seeing the group conversation with us in the middle, she excused herself and moved back to join us. "What's going on back here? Are y'all trying to convert Doug and Jill?"

"They're already Christians," Pastor Earl replied. "Although we might be able to steer them on a closer walk with Jesus than the Episcopalians." The pastor waited for me to react, then added, "I'm kidding."

Intrigued by the observations about Tamsin McInnis, Jill asked, "Was there anyone who was unhappy with Tamsin and Alistair McInnis stepping into that role?"

"Unhappy, as in ready to kill them?" A woman replied, shaking her head. "No. I mean, people around here have found their places in the social order. Some have inherited the positions left by their parents. Others, especially the politicians, feel the need to press the flesh and show up at every fundraiser with a smile and a check. I don't think Tamsin and Alistair displaced anyone. They just added to the pool of volunteers and contributors."

The woman next to Jill seemed less pleased about McInnis' contributions. "They were in a different social circle than most of us. There are cliques in school that carry over into adulthood. We Baptists bond together and socialize here with the other parishioners. Tamsin and Alistair were part of the country club set."

I reflected on Glinda Carlisle's suggestion that she and Tamsin go to the country club for lunch and bloody marys. Definitely not the Baptist social group. "Tell me about Robert and Glinda Carlisle."

The group went as silent as if I'd announced Satan had just walked into the room. Pastor Earl cleared his throat and said, "They live up nearer to Lexington. We don't see many of the *horse people* down here."

"But you know who they are?"

"Certainly," the pastor replied, "they're involved in regional charities, and they contribute generously to a number of causes."

A man snorted. "Not a penny goes to a church, but they spread a lot of money around."

Pastor Earl bit his tongue for a moment, then tried to smooth the waters. "We'd prefer to see people contributing directly to God's house. The Carlisles have said they prefer to put their money directly into good deeds instead of funneling it through a church. We don't all share the same approach, but we're all trying to show love for our neighbors."

Bitsy nudged Jill ahead. "I think we've made it to the head of the line. Make sure you get a helping of Ross Pangril's pulled pork. He makes his own barbecue sauce." Looking ahead, Bitsy added. "I think there might be a few slices of derby pie left, too."

Picking up a set of silverware and a plate, I edged close to Pastor Earl. "I sense that not everyone likes the way Robert and Glinda Carlisle make their donations."

The pastor glanced around, then whispered, "I'd prefer it if they donated as much to a church as they gambled on horses and spent on bourbon. Not that those *contributions* don't help *someone* I suppose."

With a pile of food far larger than I would be able to eat, I followed Bitsy and Jill to a table in the farthest corner of the basement. A toothless man in tattered clothes looked up at me anxiously when I set my plate down next to his.

"Everything looks wonderful," I said, hoping to make him more comfortable.

He nodded agreement but continued eating without verbalizing his response.

Bitsy smiled at the man and said, "Hubert, these are my friends, Doug and Jill Fletcher." Spreading a napkin on her lap, Bitsy turned to Jill and added, "Hubert is one of our neighbors. He joins us for every dinner."

I tried not to make Hubert uncomfortable but couldn't help wondering how he chewed his dinner without any teeth. A woman stopped between Jill and me to ask if we'd like sweet tea. Seeing no other beverage options, we accepted. Hubert held up his glass, and she topped it off.

"Do you live nearby, Hubert?" I asked.

He nodded. "I got a room in the parsonage basement."

I glanced at Bitsy, who smiled and nodded. I realized Hubert was one of the people the congregation was reaching out to. They were providing for a homeless man, giving him a place to live and meals.

Between bites of pie, Hubert glanced at me. "Are you a cop?"

"Jill and I are Park Service investigators. We're federal cops."

Hubert nodded as he thought about that. "Like revenuers?"

"I guess we're like that, although I'm not going to bust any moonshiners."

"Good. They're just trying to make a buck, too. Not many ways for a man to make a buck 'round here. I clean the church and trim the cemetery."

"Does the cemetery need a lot of care?"

"People leave flowers and don't tend them. I compost dead flowers. People think they just go away but it's me who cleans up."

"That's an important job."

Hubert nodded as he mopped up the last gravy from his plate with a roll. "Pastor Earl said I'm providing an important service for the church. No one else ever seemed to do it. He asked if I'd take care of the cemetery in return for staying in the parsonage basement. I didn't have anything else going on, so..."

"I think it's great that you and Pastor Earl came up with a plan."

"His wife is really nice. She arranged for the church ladies to bring me sandwiches, bananas, and oranges. All she asked was that I not drink in the parsonage." Hubert shrugged. "I don't need to drink anymore. So, it works out okay."

Bitsy listened to our conversation and smiled with pride as Hubert told me his story. I could hardly imagine our Texas church inviting an indigent to live in the parsonage in return for cemetery upkeep and janitorial help. I couldn't imagine any outreach we could've done that would have as much personal impact as Bitsy's church had on Hubert.

When the conversation lagged, Bitsy asked, "Do you need more socks, Hubert?"

"No, ma'am. I'm well set on socks now." Hubert slid his chair back and lifted the leg of his well-worn jeans. He showed me his white athletic sock. "Miss Bitsy thought my other socks were too holey."

Bitsy nodded. "Hubert, what do you know about the Scottish couple who run the distillery?"

"I heard that they're good folk. They're buying all their supplies locally. So, that's being right neighborly. Yes sir, they're helping Connor O'Reilly grow a new kind of corn. It's something that's old-fashioned. What did he call it? Heritage or something. Not that corn that people feed to pigs. It's a different kind of corn. My friend, Ske, told me it's really something special."

"They're growing heirloom corn?" I asked.

Hubert nodded.

"What else are they doing that's special?"

Hubert studied me for a moment, then he glanced at the badge on my belt. "Well, since you're a cop, I suppose there's no harm in telling you that they're using a special oak in their barrels."

"A special oak?"

"Yes sir. It comes from Wisconsin. Their oak grows slower so it's different from the local oak. I guess it's a little harder to cut and make into staves. Ske says it toasts differently when they char the barrels, so they expect the bourbon to have a different flavor when it's aged in those barrels."

I glanced at Jill to make sure she was listening to this revelation. Nodding, she asked, "What else are the Scots doing differently?"

"The Scots spell whiskey without an e. It's just w-h-i-s-k-y."

I smiled, surprised by Hubert's breath of knowledge. "I'd noticed that. Is there anything else interesting about what they're doing with the bourbon?"

Hubert looked around, as if he checked to make sure no one was listening to our conversation. "They use yeast from Scotland. Everyone locally leases the yeast from one of the old distillery families. All their liquor has the same flavor profile. This Scottish yeast is something different."

"Do you think the other distilleries are worried about what McInnis is making?"

Hubert shrugged. "Most of them think they're making good bourbon, and fooling around with the corn and stuff isn't going to make any difference."

"Are they right?" I asked.

"Nobody knows, do they? They're all hanging back, wondering what's going to happen when the Scot and the horse guy hand out samples of their new bourbon."

"Is there one competitor more worried about it than the others?" I asked.

"Hook and Ladder are scared shitless." Having said that, Hubert froze and looked at Bitsy. "Sorry, ma'am. I know I shouldn't swear in the church. But it wasn't really blasphemy. I didn't take the Lord's name in vain. I just used a bad word."

"Who are Hook and Ladder?" I asked.

"They started out as a micro-distillery that opened in the old Hodgenville fire hall. Initially, they sold what they called moonshine. After two years, they opened some of their barrels and started selling single barrel bourbon, which is a niche market. They moved into a pole barn near Elizabethtown when they outgrew the fire hall."

"Why are Hook and Ladder worried?"

Hubert leaned close to me and whispered, "They've got a spy."

"A spy? Inside the Running Acres Distillery?"

Hubert nodded. "He's telling them what the Scot is doing, and they're afraid they're going to get squeezed out."

"Do they have reason to be worried?" I asked.

"Their spy thinks so. Other people say the Scotch guy is going national, so it won't affect the locals like Hook and Ladder."

Two young women arrived to retrieve our empty plates. Behind them was Pastor Earl, who put his hands on Hubert and my shoulders. "Doug, I see you've met the most important person in the congregation."

Hubert shook his head. "I'm not important. I just clean up."

The pastor patted Hubert's shoulder. "Everything inside and outside of the church looks good because of Hubert. Heaven sent him to us, and we appreciate everything he does."

The comment obviously embarrassed Hubert, and he stared at the table, not knowing how to respond.

"Hubert and I had a nice conversation. I wish our Texas church had someone like Hubert to watch over things. He also seems to have his finger on the pulse of the community."

The pastor smiled. "People talk to Hubert. He's a good listener."

And he's invisible. I thought to myself. *Who would be worried about what they'd said to a toothless church janitor?*

Pastor Earl craned his neck to check the buffet line. "I see a couple pieces of derby pie, Hubert. You should help us out by finishing one of them, so it doesn't go to waste."

Hubert's gaze went immediately to the buffet table. Seeing there was indeed pie left, he pushed his chair back and moved quickly to the end of the line. He was so excited about getting another piece of pie that he ate it while standing next to the table.

Pastor Earl sat in Hubert's chair and leaned close to me. "Bless you for talking to Hubert. Most people are put off by his appearance. You willingly sat next to him and engaged him in conversation. That was neighborly of you."

I flashed back to my drinking days and to the point where I poured a half bottle of Tennessee whiskey down the drain and decided to move to Arizona to make a clean start. "There but for the grace of God go I."

"Amen, brother," the pastor said as we watched Hubert eat a second piece of pie. "Amen."

Chapter 10

We thanked Bitsy for the evening of hospitality, then walked to our room. Jill closed the door and looked at me, her forehead lined with concern. "You got quiet after your conversation with Hubert."

"He said some things that got me thinking."

"About the case?"

I reached out and pulled Jill close. "The case. My life. How lucky I am."

"Hubert made you feel lucky? Do you think you might've ended up a toothless old man living in the parsonage basement if you hadn't met me?"

"There were a lot of paths that could've led me to Hubert's situation. Meeting and marrying you probably tops the list of my good choices."

Snuggling into my embrace, Jill said, "Life is funny, isn't it?" After a moment, she asked, "I hate to break the mood, but what did Hubert say about the case?"

"He said one of the local distilleries has a spy in the Running Acres Distillery. They know what's going on, and some of the smaller distilleries are nervous."

"A spy? Do you believe him?"

"I do believe him. Hubert is the kind of person you talk to because he's invisible."

"Is Hubert credible?"

I considered her question for a moment. "Hubert is an enigma. His clothes were rags, and his personal hygiene could use an upgrade. On the other hand, he has the vocabulary of a college graduate. He told me about farmers growing heirloom corn varieties for the new distillery and how the local boutique distilleries are nervous about the new bourbon. I've never heard a street person use the words *heirloom* or *boutique*. He also told me the new distillery is using Scottish yeast, which gives their liquor a different flavor from the locals who all use the same strain of yeast."

"Interesting. How does Hubert's information change your plans?"

Chuckling, I kissed the top of her head. "I didn't know I had a plan."

"You always have a plan."

"Not a structured plan, so to speak. My plan is always based on following the leads as they emerge."

"You have new thoughts from Hubert. Where do they lead us?"

I released our hug and lay back on the bed. Using the blank ceiling to focus my thoughts, I confessed, "I'm not sure what to do about the spy information. Yes, it's illegal to steal business secrets. On the other hand, all the secrets seem to be out. McInnis was using a special strain of corn, he was fermenting with a different strain of yeast, and he had barrels made from Wisconsin white oak. That's all on the table."

Jill opened her suitcase and pulled out a pair of pajamas. "It's one thing to *know* those things. It's another to have the equipment and wherewithal to use it, crafting different bourbons."

"True. And there's also the knowledge and skill to blend the bourbon. I'm sure some barrels are better, and some complement the others, while some might clash or be objectionable."

"Don't forget the Scotch barrel. There's something more that McInnis was doing with a barrel of his family's Scotch."

I reached for the remote and turned on the TV.

"I thought we were brainstorming."

"You've got your pajamas out. I thought you were ready for bed."

"My pants are a little tight after that dinner. I thought I'd change into something more comfortable."

"Isn't that a euphemism for getting ready for romance?"

Glaring at me, she replied, "Only on television. In reality, it's exactly what I said. I'm going to change into my pajamas because they're more comfortable than my pants."

"Gee, I was getting my hopes up."

"Get your hopes back down because I'm too full to mess around, even if I was in the mood." Taking her pajamas, Jill walked into the bathroom to change. "Given Hubert's information, what would you like to do tomorrow?"

"I wonder if Hook and Ladder Distillery offers tours?"

Jill stepped out of the bathroom wearing her pajamas and picked up her phone. A moment later she said, "They open at ten o'clock and offer tours, including a bourbon tasting, starting on the hour until four o'clock."

"You can have my share of the liquor."

Snorting, Jill said, "Have you *ever* seen me sample the booze we give to Dad and Chet? I don't do brown liquor. I might drink a gin and tonic, but not straight up bourbon."

"Maybe they're still offering samples of their unaged alcohol. It's not brown."

"Get real, Fletcher. I'm not drinking moonshine, either."

"I guess Kristina will have to take one for the team and drink the samples for all three of us."

Jill nodded in a way that made it clear I'd suggested something really stupid. "Kristina weighs one-twenty, tops. I don't see her drinking three sets of bourbon samples, then driving the car."

"We need to go back to the Running Acres Distillery again, too. They need to know there might be a spy on their staff."

"How will you know the person you tell isn't the spy?"

"I can't imagine Tamsin McInnis is the spy."

Jill reached for the remote and flipped through the channels. "Go change while I find something that's not going to give me nightmares."

After taking a fresh t-shirt and boxers from my suitcase, I paused at the bathroom door. "My nightmares are from things I experienced, not things I see on TV."

Ignoring my comment, Jill continued to flip through channels. "Where do you suppose Hubert collects all that information? I doubt the Baptist congregation has discussions about the nuances of bourbon making."

"His information sounds more like the topics discussed in a bar. Hubert told me one of the conditions of his parsonage room is not drinking."

"What do people discuss at Alcoholics Anonymous meetings?"

"I've never been to an AA meeting. I've heard stories about going around the room where people introduce themselves and declare that they're alcoholics. I think the discussion beyond that is members sharing sobriety journeys and offering each other support."

* * *

Jill was watching a *Designing Women* rerun when I emerged from the bathroom. She looked up at me and frowned. "Really? You groaned?"

"Was that out loud? I thought it was in my head," I said as I pulled back the covers and slipped under the sheets. "Annie Potts is kind of cute. Are any of the others still alive?"

"Dixie Carter died a few years ago. I think the rest of them are still alive." Muting the TV, Jill asked, "Do you think Hubert is a reliable source?"

"He seems lucid and with it."

"Did you believe his comment about a spy inside the McInnis distillery?"

"He has no agenda and offered the observation without prompting. I'm more than ninety percent sure he's reliable."

"I feel sorry for him. Living in the parsonage basement and living off the charity of the church people."

Chuckling, I took the remote from Jill's hand and turned off the television. "How is that much different from the rest of us? We're living off the charity of the Park Service. If they decided they didn't need us anymore, we'd be living off someone else's charity."

"We'd be living off our pensions, and that's different."

"Our house would be up for sale, and the car would be packed for a South Dakota move within a week. Where do you think we'd live once we arrived on the ranch?"

"In..." Jill paused. "Crap, we'd be living in my old bedroom and eating my mom's cooking, wouldn't we?"

"Chet would probably give us ten acres to build a house."

Jill looked uncomfortable with the discussion. "That would be another charitable gift."

"On the other hand, we'd probably be earning our keep by running them to doctor's appointments and keeping up the house."

"That's not much different from sweeping the church and removing the dead flowers from the cemetery, is it?"

I set the remote on the nightstand and turned toward her. "Okay, tell me how you picture your retirement."

"I thought we'd..." She stopped, making me wonder if she didn't know what retirement was going to be. Or, if she didn't want to share her vision because she thought it would irritate me.

"We'd what?"

"I thought we'd ride horses and go to church potluck dinners. You could bring that chicken thing you whipped up before we left."

"Yeah, that wine sauce would be a big hit at a church dinner."

"We're not Baptist. Wine is allowed."

Jill's phone vibrated on the nightstand, and I looked at the clock as she reached for it.

"It's ten o'clock! Who's calling?"

"Hi, Mom. No, you didn't interrupt our supper. It's actually ten o'clock here." Jill put the phone on speaker and held it between us.

"Ten o'clock? I thought you were in the eastern time zone. Isn't that two hours earlier?"

"It's two hours the other direction, Mom. What's on your mind?"

"Your father looked at a map and pointed out that you're in the heart of bourbon country. His birthday is coming up and he'd really enjoy a nice bottle of bourbon."

"We're actually in a dry county here. They don't sell liquor."

"A dry county where they don't sell liquor? But they make it there, right?"

"Yes, there are several distilleries nearby. But they don't sell booze where we're staying."

"Huh. That's peculiar."

Jill held out the phone to me and whispered, "Say something. I'm out of conversation."

"We met an interesting guy at a church dinner. He's the cemetery caretaker and church janitor. He lives in the parsonage basement. I don't think he had a single tooth."

"That's so sad. Was he nice?"

"He was polite. He surprised us with a couple of tips we might be able to use in our investigation."

"Well, I hope you thanked him. Perhaps you could bring him a candy bar or a treat. He sounds like he might appreciate it."

"That's a good suggestion. We'll buy him a candy bar when we stop for gas."

"What kind of tips would the church custodian have regarding a murder investigation?" Molly prompted.

"People talk to him. They probably think he's slow and lonely, so they say things they might not share with their friends."

"How did you get introduced to the janitor at a church dinner?"

"He was sitting alone, so I took the chair next to him."

"Good for you! That's a very Christian thing to do."

"That's me. A good Christian just waiting for my chance to do another good deed."

"Jill, what is it you call him when he says stupid, sarcastic things like that?"

Jill smiled and elbowed me gently, "Smartass."

"When are you coming back home? The horses miss you."

Jill gave me a sad puppy dog look before I replied, "We're in the middle of an investigation. It'll be weeks from now. Give Joker an apple and tell him it's from me."

"He'd rather see you in person." Molly paused, then added, "You could come back for your father's birthday or the fourth of July. You didn't get to see much of the rodeo last time."

"I had my fill of rodeos for a while. We'll find another holiday or other excuse to visit. Okay?"

"Doug, think about buying Al a bottle of bourbon. He says you have good taste in booze."

"We'll find a county where they sell booze. Otherwise, there are liquor stores in Nashville if nowhere else."

I disconnected the call and handed Jill the phone.

"Mom sounded sad."

"I think that's the plight of parents whose adult children live far away. Luckily, they have my mom and Chet nearby." Sensing Jill's apprehension about our parents, I said, "We'll need to take care of them at some point. Let's cross that bridge when we get to it. Okay?"

Chapter 11

The aroma of muffins greeted us as we entered the dining room. Bitsy looked up from placing a setting at the table for breakfast. "You're the early birds. Set yourselves wherever you want." Pouring coffee, she asked, "Do you have any dietary restrictions or preferences?"

"I'm willing to eat whatever you're making," I replied.

Jill nodded. "I grew up on a ranch and we ate whatever Mom put in front of us. These days, I try to eat fewer calories and more fiber than my mom fed me."

Setting the carafe aside, Bitsy thought for a second, then said, "I've got some berries and cinnamon rolls to start. How do you prefer your eggs?"

"Over easy," I said.

"I'd prefer mine scrambled."

Bitsy disappeared into the kitchen as Jill and I spread cloth napkins on our laps. Jill whispered, "I'm not accustomed to eating this much for breakfast."

Bitsy swept into the room carrying a tray. Setting small bowls of berries and a plate with a warm cinnamon roll in front of each of us, she asked, "Is bacon okay with your eggs? Whole wheat toast with homemade strawberry jam?"

Chuckling, Jill looked at the generous portion of berries and the cinnamon roll. "I really don't need any more than this." After pausing for a second, she added, "Although the devil just whispered in my ear that some bacon would taste really good."

"I doubt it's the devil who whispered that, dear," Bitsy said as she disappeared into the kitchen.

Jill ate a spoonful of berries as I peeled off a piece of roll and popped it into my mouth. "Are you serious about touring that little distillery that might have a spy?"

"That's a thought, although I don't see them as murderers. I wonder what Kristina has planned for today?"

"Mmm. This roll might be better than Mom makes." Licking her fingers, Jill added, "Tamsin and Glinda were going to the country club. I wonder what it looks like?"

Bitsy walked in carrying plates with eggs, bacon, and whole wheat toast. "The country club looks like a fancy restaurant with a golf course and tennis courts."

"Were you eavesdropping, Bitsy?" I asked.

Smiling, she replied, "A good hostess anticipates her guests' needs."

Setting her plate aside, Jill turned to face Bitsy. "What have you heard about the McInnis murder?"

"I don't recall anything."

"Is that the other part of being a good hostess, you conveniently forget what you've overheard?"

I pulled a chair out and nodded toward it. "Why don't you sit down and have a cup of coffee while we eat."

"I really need to..."

"Bitsy, please join us for a moment before your other guests come down."

"You two are my only guests. It's the off-season." Bitsy sat. "Am I going to get the third degree?"

"We lack local knowledge," I replied. "That's often what helps us understand the context of the crimes we're investigating. Our job is assisting local law enforcement people. There are times when they're too close to see the forest for the trees."

Bitsy stared at the table and dabbed at a crumb that had fallen from my roll. "What trees do you expect to see?"

"That's the problem," Jill explained. "We are outsiders here. We don't know which trees we should be looking at."

Meeting Jill's eyes, Bitsy paused. "You said you grew up on a ranch. So, you know how small-town people react to outsiders."

"We were polite but watched what we said around them."

Bitsy nodded. "Many of the families here have deep roots. They consider anyone whose grandparents aren't buried here to be outsiders. The polite folks will smile at you and treat you with kindness. As soon as they close the door, their smiles disappear, and they say what they're really thinking."

"What are they really thinking about the McInnis murder?" I asked.

"I haven't heard much. I assume they're talking among themselves about the snooty foreigner and his social-climbing wife. I imagine not too many people are deeply upset that he's dead."

"He's just an outsider and wasn't welcome anyway?" Jill asked.

Bitsy appeared as if she was composing her thoughts before replying. "Please don't misunderstand what I'm saying. We're good Christian folk who know that murder is breaking a commandment. On the other hand, McInnis dying is like taking a scoop of water out of the bucket—the water closes up around the hole and it's hard to see that anything has changed."

"Life goes back to what it was," Jill said.

"Order has been restored," I countered.

Cocking her head, Bitsy considered our comments. "I suppose order is being restored. McInnis was causing ripples."

"Other distilleries have opened. Did they cause ripples?" I asked.

"Local folks or families opened them. They used local labor and local suppliers. Those weren't really ripples. It was more like they added a bit of water to the bucket."

"How was that different from what McInnis was doing?" Jill asked.

"He has this horsey partner who used carpenters from Lexington, and lawyers from Louisville who drew up contracts when a handshake would've been sufficient."

"Was McInnis the problem, or was it Robert Carlisle who was making waves?"

"It was both of them. Robert was causing the ripples and McInnis wasn't smart enough to realize there were ripples." Bitsy paused, "That's not right. McInnis was smart, but he wasn't savvy. He knew business and distilling. He rarely went to the local hamburger shop to have a burger and sweet tea with the people who make these towns work."

"Would that have made someone angry enough to kill him?" Jill asked.

"None of the Christian folks would've killed him over that social gaffe. Nope."

I was struck by what Bitsy wasn't saying. "Whoever killed him was either moved by the devil or wasn't a believer."

"Or they were more of the Old Testament type who believe in fire, brimstone, and dealing in-kind when their ox is gored."

I was about to ask for clarification when Jill raised one finger to stop me. "Most of the people here can't afford an ox."

Bitsy raised her eyebrows, but didn't speak.

The front door opened, and Kristina stepped in. "Can a girl get a cup of coffee here?"

Bitsy stood and pulled her chair back for Kristina. "You most certainly can! Have a seat while I get a fresh pot of coffee."

Jill followed Bitsy into the kitchen as Kristina sat next to me and surveyed our dirty dishes. "Wow, it looks like you ate enough to feed the entire neighborhood."

"What's your plan for today?"

"It depends. Have you spoken with the crime scene tech about the break in?" I asked.

"There were prints, but none where the burglary occurred. The lock and door were clean, like someone had worn gloves. Same with the plastic wrapping peeled back from the cases."

I nodded. "Finding the burglar's prints would've been too easy."

"I think we should talk to a couple of McInnis' suppliers. I have the names of his corn, barley, and rye farmers. They're all around today and have agreed to talk to us."

"That might give us some interesting insight into Mac's dealings with his suppliers," I suggested.

"They all seemed sad about Mac's passing, so I doubt they're the killer. On the other hand, they might be able to steer us to someone who is less pleased with the new distillery opening."

"We heard the Hook and Ladder distillery has a spy inside the McInnis operation."

"I know the owners. They're concerned about the impact McInnis might have on their operation, but realistically, they're not marketing to the same people. Hook and Ladder sell almost all of the bourbon out of their tasting room or to regional buyers. McInnis was aiming much higher."

"They might want to understand how to tap into the high-end marketplace," I countered.

Kristina snorted. "They're good ole boys who are making more money than they've ever had. They don't have the...flair required to go after the high-end buyers. They're 'Aw shucks' guys who wear flannel and blue jeans. McInnis knew that and so do the owners of Hook and Ladder. I wouldn't waste our time talking to them."

Bitsy returned with a cup of coffee in one hand and a small plate with a cinnamon roll in the other for Kristina. "You need some meat on your bones, dear."

"I need to stay trim to chase down bad guys, Miss Bitsy. But I don't refuse many freshly baked rolls."

A moment later, Jill carried in a fresh carafe of coffee while wearing a wide grin. Jill patted my stomach. "Doug's foot pursuit days are behind him."

Bitsy considered Jill's trim figure for a moment. "I think you'd be right beside Kristina if there was a foot pursuit."

"Not after that huge breakfast! I'm about ready for a nap."

We all laughed and sipped coffee while Bitsy filled Kristina in on what she'd missed by not attending the church's covered-dish dinner. Resisting Bitsy's attempted proselytizing, Kristina said she was perfectly happy with her Christmas and Easter attendance at her Presbyterian church. Bitsy clucked her tongue but conceded that as long as Kristina was baptized and had accepted Jesus, she'd be going to Heaven.

With that resolved, Bitsy turned to Jill and me. "Which church do you attend?"

I hesitated a second too long and Jill's mind was obviously elsewhere.

"You acted like church people last night. You even willingly sat at the table with Pastor Earl. Unchurched people run from him as if he were a demon."

Jill's attention returned to the conversation, and she patted my arm. "Don't worry, I'm pulling Doug into Heaven on my coattails despite his evil ways. We attend the Episcopal Church where we were married."

Feeling the need to rescue us from whatever conversion Bitsy was about to attempt, Kristina set aside the last half of her roll and wiped her fingers. "I hate to break up this revival meeting, but there's a corn farmer waiting for us."

Walking to Kristina's cruiser, I thanked her for rescuing me. "Bitsy was just about ready to take me to her church's baptismal font."

"Bitsy's church takes you to the river and baptizes by immersion. Pastor Earl holds sinners under the water as long as he thinks it will take to wash away the sins. Since you're a cop, he might think you'll need to be reborn."

"Which means he'll hold me under for a full second or two?"

Kristina chuckled as she unlocked the car. "Pastor Earl might have the EMTs on hand to revive you after you've drowned."

Jill snorted as she climbed into the back seat. "Doug would probably come around swearing up a blue streak. The pastor would have to repeat the baptism."

"Tell us about this corn farmer," I suggested, hoping to redirect the conversation.

"Connor O'Reilly runs a small operation. A few years ago, he realized the opportunity in switching from bulk feed corn to planting organic heirloom varieties. He worked with the university to find some older strains of corn that had fallen out of favor when farmers switched to high-yield hybrids used for animal feed and automotive ethanol. For a few years, Connor sold all his corn as seed, which was far more profitable than growing hybrids. McInnis made some bourbon from a couple of Connor's heirloom strains and realized they made a mash with different flavors than those made from hybrid corns. The rumor mill says Connor stands to be one of the big losers with McInnis dead."

"Don't you think the other distilleries will be interested in O'Reilly's corn?"

"Some of them do small batches of specialty bourbons. Most are huge operations and the limited volume of corn that O'Reilly grows isn't enough to make a difference to them."

Kristina turned onto a gravel road that ran alongside a field of red dirt. The first sprouts of corn were just visible.

"O'Reilly can't use chemical fertilizers or weed killers if he's growing organic corn," Jill said from the back.

"I don't know all the details. I do know that most of his neighbors consider him a kook. He grows a buffer of hay around his corn fields, so the neighbor's pollen and chemicals don't drift into his corn." Kristina turned into a driveway leading to a dilapidated farmhouse with a barn whose roof had been redone with galvanized steel. "Connor is a bit...volatile. One of his neighbors said O'Reilly's 'Irish' comes through every now and again. He goes off on tirades when things don't go his way."

A man emerged from the barn as we parked. His once red hair was brassy and mixed with gray. His clothing looked like it might've come from the dumpster behind a thrift store. A smear of grease on his cheek made it appear he'd been working on his equipment.

Ignoring the women, O'Reilly walked up to me and offered his greasy, dirty hand.

"Connor O'Reilly. You must be the Texas cop Kristina warned me about."

"I'm Doug Fletcher," I said, matching O'Reilly's firm handshake.

"You're okay, Fletcher," O'Reilly said as he pulled a filthy rag from his back pocket and wiped his hands with it. "You didn't even balk when I shook your hand."

"I never balk when I shake the hand of a man who's making an honest living."

Pleased by that comment, O'Reilly handed me the rag and offered his semi-clean hand to Jill. She smiled and shook his hand.

O'Reilly smiled at Kristina who held up her hands, avoiding the handshake ritual. "I'm a city girl. Nice to see you, Mr. O'Reilly."

Addressing Jill and me, O'Reilly said, "Kristina says you're looking into McInnis' murder. It's a dirty shame, that was. He was a prince among men."

"That's high praise," I replied.

"He understood the value of my corn and was willing to pay what it's worth. Most of the people who come here are trying to get a deal. McInnis asked for a sample and told me if it worked out, he'd be back. No bullshitting around, just business-like. When he came back, he brought a bottle of good Scotch. We sat down at my kitchen table, discussed his plans, and I told him what my corn was worth. We shook hands and the next day, a truck showed up to buy a storage bin of my corn. McInnis handed me a check and asked if I could supply twice as much the next year."

"That's impressive in this day and age," I opined.

"It is. His check didn't bounce, and I made plans to provide him with twice as much corn the next year. He showed up the next fall with two trucks, another bottle of good Scotch, and an even bigger check."

"So, you had no problems with McInnis?" I asked.

O'Reilly shook his head. "I trusted him more than my kids. He was a true gentleman."

"Was there anyone who felt otherwise?"

Snorting, O'Reilly blew his nose into the rag he'd used to wipe his hand. Jill grimaced. "A lot of people thought McInnis was a fool. I don't think they disliked him. They just couldn't see his vision. I don't know of anyone who'd kill him."

"What happens to you now that McInnis is dead?"

O'Reilly shrugged. "That next chapter is yet to be written. If his bourbon release goes well, I assume whoever takes the helm at the distillery will want my corn."

"Robert Carlisle?" Jill asked.

O'Reilly spat on the ground. "Carlisle is an ass. All he knows about are horses and jerking people's finances around. He's the opposite of McInnis, and I doubt he'll take over. He can't tell the difference between fine bourbon and moonshine."

We spoke with O'Reilly for a few more minutes, but didn't learn anything new. As we prepared to leave, he nodded toward the house. "I've got some of that good Scotch that McInnis left here. I'd share a dram with you."

I saw Kristina glance at her watch, perhaps signaling it was too early to start drinking.

"I'm honored by your offer," I said, "but there was a time when I liked whiskey too well. I haven't touched a drop in nearly a decade. I sincerely appreciate your offer."

I shook his hand again and he nodded his understanding. "I like a man with principles, Fletcher. Good luck finding Mac's killer."

After taking a step, I paused and turned. "Did you taste the new McInnis bourbon?"

O'Reilly's lip twitched in what approached a smile. It disappeared as fast as it had appeared. "I can't really say."

"You haven't tasted it, or are you sworn to secrecy?"

"Does it make any difference?" O'Reilly asked.

"If it was really good or really bad, we'd have a different set of suspects."

"I suppose that's true."

"Mr. O'Reilly, you haven't answered my question."

O'Reilly grimaced, accentuating the wrinkles in his fair skin. Studying his face made me realize that I couldn't tell if he was fifty or eighty. "No, I guess I haven't."

Intrigued by O'Reilly's reluctance to answer the question, Kristina joined me. "Mr. O'Reilly, this is serious. If you know something that would direct us to one set of suspects over a different pool, we need to know it."

O'Reilly's face colored and I wondered if he was embarrassed, or if he was about to explode. "Mac was my friend, and I made a promise to him. You can't force me to break it."

I tried to de-escalate the discussion. "If Mac was your friend, you would want to do all you can to help us find his killer."

The man studied me while considering my statement. "Let's say his bourbon was unique. I wouldn't say it was better or worse. There are people out there who seek out the unusual."

"We should focus on people who'd be losers if his bourbon were a success," I summarized.

O'Reilly looked past us, into the field. "A lot of people unassociated with the bourbon business disliked Mac. Like a politician, he had a way of polarizing people."

"Give me an example."

"He told a Baptist minister they should've been using the King James version of the Bible. A lot of people disagreed with that."

"I doubt he was killed because of his Bible choice," I replied.

Raising his eyebrows, O'Reilly smiled. "You're not Baptist, are you?"

"No."

O'Reilly made an *oh well* shrug, then turned and walked back to his barn.

I walked with Jill and Kristina to her squad. "Really? Someone might kill in a disagreement over which version of the Bible should be read?"

Kristina started the engine before answering, "Some militant religious folks think they're practicing the only true religion. They don't suffer atheists or heretics well."

From the back seat, Jill added, "We've just added a whole new set of suspects."

"How many hard-core Baptists live in this area?"

"There's a church every mile, and nine out of ten are Baptist."

"Every mile?" Jill asked. "They're all Baptists! Can't they consolidate?"

Chuckling, Kristina said, "They're Baptists, but not all Baptists are created equal. There are Southern Baptists, Separate Baptists, unaffiliated Baptists, Original Free-will Baptists, and others. Each has a little different take on the Bible and their own beliefs."

"Do they agree on anything?" Jill asked.

Glancing at Jill in the mirror, Kristina said, "None of them drink liquor, swear, play cards, or dance. Beyond that theological agreement, I think any of them will argue the color of the sky."

"And Mac pissed off someone by criticizing their version of the Bible," I summarized.

"I doubt someone would kill him over that. They might pray for him or suggest that he's bound for hell, but they wouldn't violate a commandment."

"Let's assume our killer isn't playing with a full deck," I suggested. "He's already upset with this outsider coming into town and threatening to change things. Would Mac's religion be enough to push him over the edge?"

Kristina glanced at me. "You're assuming the killer is a man."

"It's someone who held Mac's face underwater. I think that would take a man's strength."

Jill chuckled in the back seat. "Maybe it was a baptism gone wrong. Bitsy said her minister adjusted his baptismal immersion time based on the amount of sin that needed to be cleansed."

"Nah," Kristina replied, shaking her head. "Most of the churches do immersion baptisms. The creek in Lincoln's birthplace is only a few inches deep. You couldn't immerse a nightcrawler in that creek for half of the year."

"Think of this as a crime of opportunity. Maybe Mac insulted someone's religion or blasphemed. The killer took it upon himself to cleanse Mac of his immorality and got carried away."

"Let's shelve that thought," Kristina said as she turned into a driveway. "Here's where Mac's barley grower lives."

Chapter 12

All of the farms showed the same degree of disrepair. Bill Brown's barn needed paint. The entire exterior was bare boards except for a faded red band under the eaves. Like Connor O'Reilly, Bill's shirt, pants, and jacket were threadbare and patched. Folding a pocket knife he'd been using to clean his nails, Bill looked up but made no move from his rocking chair on the front porch.

"He could be Uncle Chet's brother," I whispered to Jill as we approached the house.

"Why, because he's gray-haired, has a belly that hangs over his belt, and is wearing jeans and a plaid shirt?"

Overhearing us, Kristina added, "I bet he invites us in for a shot of moonshine poured from a Mason jar." She led us up the creaking steps and offered her hand to Bill. "I'm Kristina. These folks are Jill and Doug Fletcher."

With considerable effort, Bill hoisted himself from the rocking chair. After a moment's hesitation, he shook Kristina's hand. "Mornin', Miss Kristina." He looked over her shoulder at me, then glanced at Jill, his eyes pausing on the badge on her belt. "Feds?"

Ignoring the contempt in Bill's voice, Jill smiled and offered her hand. "We work for the National Park Service. We're not your everyday feds."

Reluctantly, Bill shook Jill's hand, using only his fingertips. He nodded to me and made no effort to shake my hand. "You're looking into the McInnis murder?"

"We're assisting Deputy Blake with her investigation."

"I can save you some time and breath. I didn't kill Mac. I liked him."

Kristina took out a notebook and pen, then said, "What had you been doing for Mr. McInnis?"

"I'm his barley supplier."

Kristina waited, hoping for more information. When it was clear he was through, she asked, "What kind of barley do you grow for him?"

The question distressed Brown. With a furrowed brow, he replied, "I can't tell you that."

"Why not?" I asked.

The farmer drew a deep breath and blew it out. "There are different strains of barley. Each has its own flavors, both before and after malting. Mac supplied me with the seed he wanted me to grow."

"You don't know which barley you're growing?" Jill asked.

"It's not that. I'm not at liberty to discuss which barley he's using."

"It's a secret," Kristina stated.

"Yeah. A secret."

"You said you liked Mr. McInnis. Do you know anyone who disliked him?"

"I said Mac was a friend. That's a step beyond liking someone. Mac and I sat at my table and sipped Scotch while we negotiated. Our contract was a handshake. He was an upstanding man, and I was pleased to call him my friend."

"Who disliked him?" I asked.

Brown lifted his cap and scratched his greasy gray hair. "Mac didn't suffer fools very well. When some stupid shit started spouting off about what made a bourbon good and gave it certain flavors, Mac didn't hesitate to put him in his place."

"Did that happen often?" I asked.

"It doesn't have to happen often for a few people to be pissed off."

Kristina readied her pen. "Do you have names?"

Brown snorted. "I don't know a lot of those snot-nosed bubbas who mouth off about shit they don't know. And I don't want to know them."

"Was there someone in particular McInnis offended?" I asked.

"Nah, he just put a few people in their places. He did it in a way that showed them the error of their opinions without making them want to step outside to settle the dispute."

"So, he educated them rather than arguing with them?" Jill asked.

Brown nodded. "That was it. Mac was smart. He knew the bourbon business, and when he corrected someone, they got a lesson along with the correction. I saw him correct some guy who got pissed. Mac brought him to the bar and bought a round of shots for the hothead. Mac explained what gave each of the shots its unique flavor, then they drank together. The guy cooled down, and he actually thanked Mac."

"But there were others who didn't cool down?" I asked.

"There are people who like to argue for the sake of arguing. There's nothing you can say to one of them. There's an old Kentucky saying, 'If you wrestle with a pig, the pig's going to enjoy it and you're going to get dirty.' That's illustrative of arguing with a know-nothing idiot."

"Names, please," Kristina urged.

"Bubba. Fatso. Jerkwater."

"Proper names?"

Brown shrugged off the question, "I don't know what their given names are. They just call each other by their nicknames."

"When and where did this happen?"

"In every E-town drinking establishment on any Friday or Saturday night."

"McInnis was drinking in a bar every weekend?" I asked.

Brown got a sly smile. "Mac was selling. Every person in the bar got one of his cards. People will be lined up to buy his bourbon."

"Have you sampled his bourbon?"

"I can't say."

"Was it as wonderful as he was making it sound?"

Brown got a dreamy look. "Have you heard of 'the Kentucky hug?'"

"That's the warm feeling you get after you've taken a shot," Kristina explained.

"Mac told people they'd get a Scotch kiss with their Kentucky hug."

"Did you?" Jill asked.

Brown's sly smile returned. "I might've." He paused, then added, "If I'd ever tasted his bourbon."

"Who is going to be the big loser when the McInnis bourbon is released?" Kristina asked.

"Nobody loses when a new bourbon comes out. No one."

"How about his competition?" I asked.

"Everyone wins. There'll be a resurgence of interest in bourbon. People will want to sample other bourbons to compare them with Mac's release. People all over the world will be pouring bourbon. Everyone wins."

"Do you really think it'll be that big?" Kristina asked.

Brown puffed up like a proud father. "I've leased four hundred extra acres for growing Mac's barley. And I'm not sure that'll be enough."

"We went to the cooperage yesterday," I added.

Brown let out a whistle. "You're getting the whole bourbon experience, aren't you?"

"We're getting everything except a motive for his murder."

"You're barking up the wrong tree, son. Whatever happened had nothing to do with bourbon."

Kristina frowned as she put away her notebook. "How can you be sure about that?"

"The bourbon people are a tight-knit group. We're families who've been working together and helping each other for generations. When Heaven Hill distillery burned down, all of the other distilleries in Bardstown and Louisville pitched in and gave them still time and helped them fill barrels and bottles. Farmers sold them corn and barley below their cost. Nobody took credit for that. We just did it."

"McInnis came from Scotland," I countered.

"Mac spoke the same distiller's language, and he treated everyone with respect. No one who knew him well disliked him."

"Like I said, someone disliked him."

As Connor O'Reilly had, Bill Brown looked past us into his field. "This isn't about bourbon."

"Bitsy suggested looking at the country club," Jill added.

Brown's dreamy look turned into a sour grimace. "That bunch..."

"What about that bunch?" Kristina asked.

Brown shook his head. "I've got no words to describe how I feel about those uppity social climbers," then walked into his house.

"He was a bit touchy about the country club," Jill said as she buckled herself into the back seat.

"There are social strata. Most folks are hard-working, go-to-church-on-Sunday folks. There's the after-work drinkers and the hair-of-the-dog morning drinkers. There's a meth-cooking, drug dealing group. Then, there's *the country club*."

"What do you know about the country club?"

Kristina turned to me and smiled. "I've never been invited there, so I have no opinion."

Smiling, Jill said, "I'm sure you have an opinion."

After a deep sigh, Kristina replied, "I think it's full of stuck-up snobs who don't want to mix with the hard-working people who make money for them. The bankers, horse owners, and social climbers belong to the country club."

"We have a Texas friend who was a debutante."

"If there are people like that, they'd belong to the country club." Driving out of Brown's driveway, she added, "Lester Bailey isn't a country club guy either. He grows rye for the distillery."

* * *

Bailey's farm was a bit more upscale than his neighbors. His barn had a fresh coat of paint, and the lawn was manicured. "It appears Mr. Bailey is better off than O'Reilly or Brown," I observed.

"I don't know about any of their financial situations," Kristina replied as she parked on a concrete slab next to the house. "Most folks around here live hand to mouth. I'd be guessing if I said Bailey had any more than anyone else."

Lester Bailey waved to us as we parked. He was slender, with a touch of gray in his hair. Like the buildings, his clothes were newer with no patches. After introductions, he invited us into the kitchen and took coffee mugs out of the cupboard. "Are you like most cops, who drink their coffee black?"

We all nodded, and he poured from a coffee machine on the counter.

"I heard you're investigating Mac's murder," he said as he set steaming mugs in front of us. "I'm not sure there's much I can tell you." He repeated much of what we'd

180

heard from the corn and barley farmers. Everyone liked McInnis.

"You're wasting time talking to O'Reilly, Brown, and me."

"I can count on one hand the number of killers I've arrested who weren't known to the victim, Mr. Bailey."

"It wasn't one of the bourbon people. I think you'd be more successful looking in a different direction."

"Are you suggesting the horse or country club people?"

"There's a big overlap in those two groups."

"Do you have anyone specific in mind?"

Bailey stared at his shoes. "There's a lot of betting going on. There are bettors who have a lot more at stake than any of us farmers."

"Horse betting?" I asked.

"A lot of money will be changing hands when those first bottles of Mac's bourbon are released."

"People are placing bets on the bourbon?"

"People are paying to be in line to purchase a bottle or two."

"I thought it was going to be a set price."

"There are people who claim there are some special bottles that are being held back for the owners. Mac said they're intended to be gifts to people like us suppliers. Robert

Carlisle has a reputation for monetizing everything. Even his 'gifts' come at a price."

I shook Bailey's hand. "We'll take a closer look at Mr. Carlisle."

"Look at both Carlisles. They're taking bids on special bottles of the first release."

As we drove away, I asked Kristina, "Is it legal for a distillery to auction off bottles of bourbon?"

Kristina frowned. "Not unless they're running a charity auction."

"Bailey didn't say it was legal... The country club came up again."

Jill leaned against the back of the seat. "How do we get into the country club?"

Kristina looked at Jill's image in the mirror. "We won't get past the front door by flashing our badges."

"You must know someone..."

"I could have the sheriff ask for a favor. I'm sure he knows someone who belongs there. Of course, once I tell him we want to question the members, he'll tell me to think again."

"We could call Robert Carlisle," I suggested.

Jill sighed. "I'm sure that would go over as well as Kristina making a request to the sheriff. 'Gee, Mr. Carlisle, we'd like an invitation to the country club so we can question your friends.'"

I handed my phone to Jill. "You're the diplomat. Charm him."

Kristina glanced at me to see if I was being serious. She eased the car onto the shoulder when she realized Jill was entering Carlisle's phone number. "I've got to hear this."

Jill made a *zip your lips* gesture as the phone rang. "Mr. Carlisle, this is Jill Fletcher. We'd like to update you on the McInnis investigation. Is there any chance we could meet you for lunch tomorrow at the country club? I overheard your wife talking about the great food and bloody marys, and I thought it would be nice to experience the place."

Kristina gave me a look as if to say *does that approach really work?*

Jill scowled at us, then said, "A late lunch, after your golf match would be perfect. We'll see you at one o'clock."

Kristina gestured, pointing to herself and mouthing *me too.*

"Would it be okay if we brought Detective Blake?" Jill nodded, then said, "Super, we'll see you tomorrow."

Kristina was excited as she drove us back to the B&B. "I wonder if I should warn the sheriff that we're going to the country club?"

"That depends on how your sheriff handles irate calls from influential people," I replied.

"You're right. This will be one of those *asking forgiveness not permission* operations."

"I'm not sure what country club attire is," Jill commented.

I tried to hide my sly grin. "Wear your white tennis shorts and sweater."

"Fletcher, you are such a smartass. I was wondering more about wearing our uniforms instead of khaki pants and a golf shirt. What's your plan, Kristina?"

The question caught Kristina by surprise. "I suppose I'll wear dress pants and a button-down shirt."

Chuckling, I said, "Kristina, do you have any white-collar criminals we can arrest tomorrow without getting our pants dirty?"

"You know how that goes—the best laid plans..."

"We're a lot smarter about what's going on behind the scenes. It'd be interesting to ask Carlisle to explain exactly who was getting those special bottles and if he's taking orders for them."

* * *

The inn seemed empty when we walked in. We were at the foot of the stairs when Bitsy showed up. "Did you arrest anyone today?"

"You know how it goes," I replied. "The investigation is ongoing."

"Are you two willing to go out for supper?"

I glanced at Jill who shrugged and said, "Sure."

"I was thinking about going to a BBQ place that has the best smoky barbecue brisket in the county. Would you like to join me?"

"That sounds like an offer we can't refuse," I replied. "Can you give us a minute to clean up?"

"The car is ready whenever you are."

"We're treating Bitsy to supper," I said as we climbed the stairs.

"You're darn right we are."

Bitsy was sitting in the dining room reading a newspaper when we came downstairs. She nodded toward the side door as we walked in.

"This place isn't much to look at, but the food is darned good."

"It'll feel like I'm back home," Jill said as Bitsy drove through town. "My parents know every out-of-the-way eatery in the Black Hills. I didn't know what the inside of a McDonald's restaurant looked like until I went to college."

The waitress waved at us and pointed to a recently vacated booth. She was back with a tray and a rag before we were seated. "Nice to see you, Miss Bitsy," the young waitress said as she bussed and wiped the table. "Sweet tea, like usual?"

Bitsy nodded. Jill and I ordered unsweetened tea. The menu was a chalkboard on the wall. A pulled pork sandwich and fries were the special, followed by rib tips, and a burger. The prices were amazingly affordable. Dozens of conversations buzzed around us, and I caught snippets about farming, politics, the weather, and the price of gas.

Pastor Earl was at a nearby table and immediately walked over. "I see Miss Bitsy brought you into town to experience the local culture." The pastor gestured to the dining room. "These people are what make Kentucky work."

"I don't suppose one of them might be able to solve our crime," I replied.

The pastor laughed like that was the funniest joke of the year. "I doubt you'll find your killer among these people." He touched my shoulder, then went back to his table.

Jill watched him walk away. "If that were any other person, I'd swear he was running for office."

"Pastor is always trying to enlist the votes of his congregation."

The waitress rushed over with our glasses. After setting them in front of us and pulling straws from her apron, she pulled out her pad. "Are y'all ready to order?"

We all ordered pulled pork sandwiches. Jill substituted a side salad for her fries. Our conversation was interrupted when one of the male parishioners we'd met the previous night walked over and whispered to me. "It's kinda noisy in here. Can I have a word with you outside?"

He held the door for an elderly couple shuffling in. "What's up?" I asked.

He looked at the parking lot and sucked his teeth before answering. "There's something you need to know about the murder of that Scottish guy."

"What would that be?"

After nervously checking around again, he said, "McInnis wasn't the saint everyone says he was."

"What unsaintly thing was he doing?" I asked, half expecting a punch line rather than an answer.

"He'd broken the seventh commandment."

Not being a biblical scholar, I tried to count through the ten and gave up. "Which is number seven?"

"Thou shalt not commit adultery."

"Who was his partner?"

Looking nervous, my informant pulled a pack of cigarettes from his pocket and shook one out and offered it to me. When I refused, he lit it, inhaled deeply, then blew the smoke over his shoulder. "I don't want to be the one casting stones...you know, glass houses and all. I saw him walking into an E-town motel room with a blonde."

"E-town is Elizabethtown?"

The man took another hit off his cigarette and nodded. "They were in that little place on the outskirts run by Mel and Cindy Jones. All the rooms are accessible from the outside."

"Which night was that and did you recognize the woman?"

"It was like two weeks before Mac was killed. I didn't get a good look at the woman, but she was driving one of those jacked-up Ford pickups. You've seen teens with too much money on their hands driving them."

"Remind me of your name."

Dropping his cigarette and rubbing it out with his toe, the man shook his head, "My name isn't important."

"Humor me."

"Kicker Moran."

"Kicker?"

"It's a high school nickname that's stuck. I was the punter on the football team since like seventh grade. My first name is Winston, like the cigarettes. My mom said I should be glad my dad didn't smoke Chesterfields."

I chuckled. "Thanks, Winston. I'll check this out. Where can I contact you?"

"Bitsy knows how to reach me. I'm on her calling tree."

"Calling tree?"

"When something happens at church, there are people who make calls. Those people call others who have assigned lists of contacts. It's more organized than word of mouth."

I returned to the table where Jill and Bitsy were eating their sandwiches.

"What did Winston want with you?" Bitsy asked.

"He had a thought about our investigation," I replied as I tucked a paper napkin into the neck of my shirt.

"And?" Bitsy asked.

I bit into my sandwich, so Jill answered, "And he can't comment on an ongoing investigation."

I lost track of the conversation for a moment as the smoky pork and molasses sweetness in the sauce filled my mouth.

Bitsy smiled as she saw me react. "I told you this was the best barbeque."

I nodded, then asked, "How far away is the Jones Motel?"

Bitsy frowned. "Are you moving out? If you are, that's not the place I would recommend."

"I might want to talk to the motel's owners," I replied.

Bitsy's sour look said all I needed to know. "They don't cater much to serious travelers. I've heard they rent by the hour, not the night, and aren't too particular about writing down names of the occupants." Connecting my question to the conversation with Winston, she asked, "Will you be asking the coroner if the water in McInnis' lung was from the creek or a motel bathtub?"

"He probably already knows that answer. I'll be asking other questions."

Bitsy closed one eye and squinted with the other. "You two are absolutely worthless when it comes to sharing good rumors."

"Do you know any pretty blondes with a jacked-up pickup?"

Bitsy stared at me with a fry halfway to her mouth. After a moment of thought, she replied, "That wouldn't be anyone from our congregation. I can't say I know any blondes who drive a vehicle like that."

I was wiping my hands on a napkin after finishing the last of my fries when our waitress delivered three slices of pie. "Compliments of Pastor Earl," she said.

Jill closed her eyes and sighed.

"What's wrong, child?" Bitsy asked.

"I barely had room for my sandwich."

"It's derby pie. It'll find places in the gaps."

I savored a bite of chocolate pecan pie. "If you run out of gaps, I'll finish yours."

After taking a bite, Jill smiled. "On second thought, I might have room for most of this."

Chapter 13

Kristina arrived as we were finishing breakfast the next morning. Bitsy invited her to the table and poured her a cup of coffee. "Miss Kristina, you look like you're going to a party."

Kristina, dressed in a button-down shirt and dress pants, had curled her hair and put on a touch of makeup. She smiled, acknowledging the compliment, then looked at Jill. "You decided against wearing your uniform to the country club?"

"We talked about it and decided uniforms would be the wrong look. We want this to be informal and comfortable."

Bitsy stopped with my plate in her hand. "You're going to the country club? Are you going to arrest someone?"

"No, we're going to have lunch with Mr. Carlisle," I replied.

Bitsy paused, then sighed. "I had some unchristian thoughts about that country club bunch, but I suppose they're just another group of sinners awaiting redemption."

"What's that Bible quote about it being easier for a camel to go through the eye of a needle than for a rich man to get into Heaven?" I asked.

We all looked at Bitsy, who considered my comment. "Like I said, they're just a bunch of people in need of redemption. All they have to do is take Jesus as their personal savior and ask for forgiveness. Amen." She paused, then added, "I stopped by the church to bring Hubert a sandwich and a piece of pie. He asked about you, Doug. He said he'd like to talk to you again."

Kristina frowned. "Who's Hubert?"

"He's the janitor at Bitsy's church," I replied. "He and I had a long talk after the church dinner."

"Hubert Jackson, the homeless guy?" Kristina asked.

"He's probably homeless because he can't deal with the structure of a traditional job."

Bitsy put her hands on her hips and frowned. "He's a little slow, but his heart's in the right place. He just needs a helping hand now and again."

Kristina snorted, "The last time I saw him, Hubert was drunk and needed a hand getting out of the dumpster he'd crawled into."

"Miss Kristina, he's made some bad choices, but it's time we turned the other cheek and let him get his life back on track. He's doing the Lord's work now."

"We'll talk to Hubert tonight," I said, ending the conversation.

Bitsy nodded. "I'll wrap up a sandwich and a can of Coke for you to bring him."

In the car, Kristina looked at me. "What do you hope to get out of a conversation with the village idiot?"

"He sees and hears things other people miss."

Jill added, "He's invisible to people, so they're more candid around him. We've received some assistance from intellectually disabled individuals in our past cases."

Kristina started the car and pulled away from the curb while considering that comment. "I just hope you don't expect to bring him in front of a jury. Everyone here knows Hubert and will dismiss his testimony."

"When we used a man called Gunner in Arizona, he gave us the links that led us to the killer. He never needed to testify. He just supplied the missing puzzle pieces."

"Good luck with that. Hubert has a few pieces missing, and I'm not sure what puzzle he's a part of."

We pulled into the distillery parking lot as five workers arrived for their shift. A few of them gave Kristina a look like they were seeing her for the first time as an attractive woman rather than as a cop.

A younger redheaded man whistled at her. "What are you doing later, Kris?"

"I'm busy, Rusty, but you're welcome to come over and babysit my kids."

"I take it that you know most of those guys," Jill said, smiling.

"Went to school with half of them and ticketed or arrested the other half. Being a cop in a small town isn't all it's cracked up to be."

Hearing our voices, the administrative assistant came out of the office. "Hey, Kristina and friends. What can I do for you today?"

"Tell us about Robert Carlisle taking bids on bottles of bourbon."

Charlotte froze. "I didn't know that was happening. As a business, we would never sanction that. Mac would've put an end to it quickly."

I looked at Kristina, who nodded. "Are there other things that Mac and Robert Carlisle fought about?"

Charlotte froze again. "I didn't mean to say they would've come to blows over something like that. It's just that sometimes Robert got...over enthusiastic. Mac had to talk him back from the brink of doing something stupid."

"Give us another example," I urged.

Crossing her arms, Charlotte shook her head. "Nothing specific comes to mind."

Kristina glanced at her watch. "We need to head for our lunch appointment at the country club."

Charlotte feigned being impressed. "Ooh, lunch at the country club. You're moving up in the world. How did you wrangle an invitation there?"

"We're meeting Robert Carlisle," I replied.

"Drink expensive booze and eat lobster," Charlotte suggested as she escorted us to the door.

"We have to pay for our own meals," I explained.

"Not at the country club. No cash or credit cards are accepted. All charges go to the members who settle up at the end of the month. Carlisle is treating you...not that your free lunch won't come without a cost."

In the car, Kristina scowled. "Crap, we can't accept lunch from a suspect."

"It sounds like we don't have an option," I replied.

Jill leaned on the back of the seat. "We need to make it clear that lunch is not a get out of jail free card."

"Based on my experience with influential people, they assume that they're getting a get out of jail free card from their social position. They believe that right until you hook the cuffs on them. And some of them continue to display a smug smile right up until they're sentenced."

"You make it sound like Carlisle is one of our prime suspects," Kristina said as she pulled onto the highway.

"Isn't he? Do you have anyone higher up the list than Carlisle?"

"I'm thinking of this as a multiple-choice question. My answer is *none of the above.*"

* * *

I'd never been to a country club, so I was unsure of what to expect. We drove past fields and barns for miles. At some point, the farms went from corn crops to barbed wire enclosures with beef cattle. Following that were horse pastures enclosed with acres of white fences. One fence ended abruptly at a manicured fairway where four men were chipping onto a green with their golf carts parked nearby.

"I think we've arrived at the country club," Jill observed from the back.

A half mile farther down the road was the stone monument displaying the sign for the Elizabethtown Country Club. The concrete driveway wound past fairways, tee boxes, sand traps, and ponds for half a mile before we reached the clubhouse, which was sandwiched between a pool and tennis courts. A sign directed us to valet parking.

"No," Kristina said before pulling her squad car in between two large SUVs. "I'm not handing the car keys to a pimple-faced teenage kid."

Concerned that we'd missed the sign, a young man dressed in a red vest trotted over to the squad car and met Kristina at her door. "Ma'am, you should've just pulled up to the front. We'll park for you."

Kristina smiled and showed the teen her credentials. "I can't allow a valet to drive a police vehicle."

The teen stepped back and looked at the plain Dodge Charger, then inspected the flashers hidden inside the front grille. "Cool. I've never driven a cop car."

"And today won't be your first time," she replied as she locked the doors. "We're meeting someone for lunch. Where is the dining room?"

The teen led us to the heavy front doors, opening the right-hand one. "Go straight back to the bar. Someone will seat you." He hesitated, then asked, "Who are you meeting?"

"Mr. Carlisle," Kristina replied.

The teen nodded. "I just saw his golf cart drive past. He'll probably shower before he meets you."

A smiling middle-aged woman met us at the hostess stand. While aware we weren't members, she politely asked whom we were meeting. Hearing Carlisle's name, her smile became less formal and more genuine. "Yes, Mr. Carlisle asked for a table near the tennis courts. Follow me."

We passed a dozen tables where casually dressed men and women were eating or drinking. All wore golf shirts and dress pants, or white tennis outfits. Each looked up and smiled politely as we passed.

The hostess held the chairs out for Jill and Kristina, then assured us our waitress would be over shortly to take our beverage order. Kristina unfolded her linen napkin and leaned close to Jill. "I didn't realize there were so many beautiful people in this county."

"I think they all hang out here with their *tribe*."

I watched a tennis coach hit shots to a woman practicing her backhand. "Is that Glinda Carlisle?"

Kristina and Jill looked at the tennis players. "The coach is really giving Glinda a workout. It takes a lot of stamina to hit twenty or thirty shots that quickly."

"And nearly all of her return shots appear to be landing inside the lines," Jill observed.

After finishing the five-gallon bucket of tennis balls, the coach walked to the net and praised Glinda, who glistened with sweat. After a moment, the coach reached across the net and rubbed Glinda's back.

Kristina shuddered. "I can't stand having people touch me like that."

Jill cocked her head, deep in thought. "That's a very intimate move. They must know each other very well."

A middle-aged woman wearing a white golf shirt and black shorts scurried over to us with a pitcher of water. As she poured, she asked, "What would you like from the bar?" She leaned close and whispered something that made Kristina smile.

"Just water for me, thanks," Kristina replied. I ordered Diet Coke, and Jill ordered unsweetened iced tea.

The girl raised her eyebrows. "Are you sure I couldn't tempt you with one of our award-winning bloody marys?"

"No, thanks," we replied in unison.

I looked at Kristina as the server left. "Someone you know, or someone you've arrested?"

After making sure no one could hear her, Kristina whispered, "Maggie is a high school friend. She got pregnant, then married, which led her down a very traditional career path."

"I assume the tips are better here than at the barbecue place," I suggested.

"I hope so, for Maggie's sake. She was a nice kid with few prospects."

Jill watched a server interact with the people at a nearby table. "I suppose this is like a lot of rural areas. Women who don't go to college or a trade school don't have a lot of options."

Sighing, Kristina replied, "Yeah, if you don't join the military or get a job in a distillery, you either stay home and raise kids or you get a service industry job."

Our beverages arrived just as Carlisle appeared. He walked to the table, his hair damp from the shower but nicely combed. I stood to shake his hand, but he gestured for all of us to remain seated. Surveying our beverage choices, he seemed disappointed.

"You're missing your chance to have the best bloody marys in central Kentucky."

"We're still officially on duty," Kristina replied.

"I don't think the sheriff would mind if you had just one."

The waitress rushed back with a tall glass whose rim was crusted with seasoned salt. A wooden skewer garnished with a jumbo shrimp, olive, and pickle stuck out of the top. "Here's your usual, Mr. Carlisle."

"Thanks, Magnolia. Could we have menus?"

"Certainly!"

As she left, Carlisle ate the shrimp and explained, "All of the members know the menu, so the waitstaff don't usually bring menus. Personally, I recommend the French dip sandwich with a side salad. The chef hand-carves the prime rib."

Magnolia returned and handed menus to Jill, Kristina, and me.

After ordering, Carlisle asked Jill, "What inspired you to suggest lunch at the country club?" His voice was controlled, but I caught the slight slurring of his words, indicating he might've had a few drinks during his round of golf.

"We'd been told the country club had the best chef in the county, and that the only way we could get in was to finagle an invitation from a member."

Carlisle's smile spread. "I'm pleased to be your designated host." He studied

Kristina while taking a sip, then added, "And I've never seen this side of Detective Kristina. You look lovely."

Although smiling, I sensed that Kristina didn't appreciate the compliment. "I have to admit, we have an ulterior motive. Four cases of your special reserve bourbon were stolen from the distillery the night Mac was killed."

The smile melted from Carlisle's face, and he choked on the olive he'd popped into his mouth. Once he caught his breath, he asked, "Four cases were stolen? Have you caught the thief?"

"Charlotte said you and McInnis had the only keys to the storage room. Do you have your key?"

Carlisle patted his pocket, as if checking to make sure he had the keyring. He removed it from his pocket and sorted through the keys until he held up a small brass key. "This is it!"

"Someone must've stolen Mac's keys when they killed him," Kristina suggested.

Carlise stared over my head as he thought. "Four cases. Forty-eight bottles. That's a lot of bourbon hitting the market when we're preparing for our first release."

"If the bidding gets hot, I suppose that might be a quarter million dollars going up on the internet."

Carlisle set down his glass and rubbed his forehead like he'd developed a sudden headache. "Shit." Looking up at Kristina, then Jill, he apologized. "Sorry, ladies."

"You took a case when you tasted it. What did you do with it?" I asked.

"It's under my bar at home. A couple dear friends have sampled the open bottle, but most of it is still intact."

"Is it as wonderful as you'd hoped?"

Carlisle's smile returned. "Mac didn't let me down. I'll leave it at that."

Magnolia and the male server arrived with our lunches, and we ate.

After everyone had taken a few bites, Carlisle asked, "Is everything to your satisfaction?"

"This is wonderful," Kristina replied.

"You haven't asked if we've arrested Mac's killer," I commented.

Carlisle chewed while considering his answer. After wiping the corners of his mouth, he replied, "All of the television cops use the same line, 'we can't comment on an ongoing investigation.' I assume you'd have the courtesy to inform Tamsin and me before we read about an arrest on the internet."

Kristina nodded her agreement.

I decided to push Carlisle a bit. "Virtually all killers are known to their victims. The most likely suspects are family members and business associates."

Without missing a beat, Carlisle replied, "Eliminating Tamsin and me must make your investigation more complicated. And I can't imagine anyone at the distillery killing Mac. He was well-liked."

I looked at Kristina, hoping she'd take the lead. "Everyone we've spoken to thought of McInnis as a well-respected friend. A confidential informant suggested one of your investors or someone who might make money from the release of your special reserve was the killer."

"We haven't even announced the release date of the special reserve," Carlisle protested. "There's no one lined up to get any of that bottling."

"We heard you've committed a bottle to an American Legion fundraising auction. Have you promised bottles to other charities or individuals as well?"

Magnolia rushed to the table and whispered something to Carlisle before he could answer. His face turned red as he processed what he was hearing. He folded his napkin, set it on top of his sandwich, and stood. "There's been some sort of accident at the distillery."

Kristina was out of her chair like a shot. "Ride with us. Lights and siren."

I got a glimpse of two women in white tennis outfits standing in front of the women's locker room as we hustled through the lobby. Carlisle waved at Glinda, who appeared to be having a serious discussion with her tennis coach.

"Emergency at the distillery," Carlisle shouted to his wife.

Glinda nodded her understanding as we rushed past. Her coach darted into the locker room.

* * *

There weren't any emergency vehicles in the distillery parking lot. Charlotte was standing outside the door, wringing her hands. Kristina parked, blocking the main sidewalk.

"Someone got into the storage room!" Charlotte said as she led us to the warehouse.

Alcohol fumes were nearing flammable levels in the warehouse. As we neared the storage room, I saw bourbon streaming from the open storage room and running into a floor drain. Carlisle pushed aside a worker who was throwing sodden cardboard and broken glass into a steel drum. He froze, and we pushed into the storage room beside him. The pallets of special reserve bottles lay in a heap, crushed flat and leaking by a pallet of barrels.

"What happened?" Carlisle demanded.

Charlotte continued to wring her hands. "One of the workers noticed bourbon running out of the storage room door. He called me, and I called you."

"Can we salvage anything?" Carlisle asked.

"We're clearing some broken boxes out of the way so we can remove the pallet of

204

barrels. At this point, it looks like a total loss."

Kristina tapped Carlisle's arm. "You have to step out. This is a crime scene."

"But we need to know if anything is…"

"Mr. Carlisle, please step back. Nothing more is going to be ruined if we wait. I'll get a forensics team to check for evidence."

I walked to the door and inspected the lock. It was still intact, but the hasp had been ripped from the door. I turned to Charlotte. "Show us the security camera feed."

Carlisle was still in shock with Jill at his side. She nodded to acknowledge that we were leaving to look at the video. "I'll stay here and keep the scene secure."

Carlisle looked at me and mumbled, "Those stolen bottles just went up in value by about one thousand percent."

Chapter 14

Kristina dialed dispatch from Charlotte's office. After identifying herself, she requested a crime scene team at the distillery. A moment later, she was explaining the situation to the sheriff, who sounded disgusted.

Charlotte logged onto the website that loaded the game camera video to the internet cloud. Carlisle watched over her shoulder, frowning. "When did we get a security camera?"

"It's my second ex-husband's game camera. I thought we should keep an eye on the room where we are storing the bottled bourbon."

"Who authorized that?"

Charlotte turned her head and glared at Carlisle. "I did. Do you have a problem with that?"

Carlisle backed down and shook his head. "Next time, ask first."

"Ask who? You and Mac are never here. In case you missed the memo, Mac left me in charge while you two were off schmoozing people, racing horses, and drinking bloody marys. Someone needs to be on site to make decisions."

Carlisle glanced at Jill, Kristina, and me, who were all awaiting his response to Charlotte's challenge. "We'll talk about this later."

"Like hell we will," Charlotte snapped. "If you don't like the way Mac had things set up, say so now, with witnesses. Unless you're planning to come in every day to sign for loads, check timecards, make payroll decisions, hire and fire people, and answer the damn phone, I'm all you've got. Do you want me to resign? Fine. I quit."

Carlisle turned red and stammered. "No. No, you're doing fine. I was just unaware of the situation here."

Charlotte looked at Kristina. "Do you want to look at the video while Robert is here, or do you want to wait?"

Carlisle snorted. "You make it sound like I might be the person who vandalized the bourbon."

"Are you?" Kristina asked.

"Hell, no!" Carlisle pointed at the computer. "Charlotte, play the damn video."

Charlotte turned back to her computer and punched a few keys. "By the way, if I'm going to do both my job and Mac's, I want a raise."

Carlisle waved off her comment. "Whatever."

Charlotte fast-forwarded past the previous videos, then paused when she reached the newest recording. "The time stamp says 3:24 AM." She started the video, which began with one side of the door opening, then the other. A shadowy figure entered the room and flipped the light switch.

"Pause that!" Kristina commanded. "Do you recognize that person, Charlotte?"

With the video frozen, Charlotte leaned back and crossed her arms. "He's wearing our coveralls with the distillery logo on the back, but I didn't see enough of his face under his baseball cap to identify him."

When the replay restarted, the person disappeared from the room, and the video stopped. The video restarted when a forklift transported a load of barrels into the room. The forklift driver was mostly hidden behind the raised pallet loaded with barrels. At first, he familiarized himself with the forklift's controls, raising, lowering, and tilting the load. It appeared he was going to set the pallet of barrels atop one of the pallets of bottles. Instead, the load of barrels was lowered violently, almost dropped, from several feet above the cases of bottles.

Carlisle gasped. "Did he do that on purpose? What kind of idiot..."

Before crushing this load, we watched the forklift driver remove two cases from the other pallet, which he set next to the door. The crushing process was repeated until both pallets were nothing but wet cardboard and broken glass.

Carlisle groaned as if in pain, then waved his arms. "Did you see that? The thief pulls two cases off because he knows how valuable they will be."

"Or, he was thirsty," Kristina suggested.

Carlisle glared at her. "What? Someone would steal two cases of incredibly valuable bourbon so he could drink it?"

"Some people don't appreciate good bourbon," I said. "To them, it's just something to mix with Coke."

Carlisle's eyes widened. "No, please tell me the thief wouldn't dilute that fine bourbon with Coke. It's sipping whiskey."

Kristina gestured for me to step out of the office. "It's stupid that they didn't have more security here. It's a small town, but not without crime. One of our murder investigations was solved when the local police got security camera video from a nearby gas station showing the killer's car. I'll have some uniformed deputies canvass the neighborhood. Someone might have a doorbell camera."

"How many roads lead out of this area?" I asked.

"The road going past the distillery is a county road that intersects with other county roads a mile in each direction. This area is a little run down, but the tractor dealer has a booming repair business, so there's a fair amount of traffic. One of the neighbors might have been intrigued by a strange car driving around at night."

Carlisle and Charlotte were having a hushed but intense discussion inside the office. Carlisle looked drained when he emerged ahead of Charlotte. She had a smug smile. Running his fingers through his hair, Carlisle said, "I know this is closing the gate after the horses escaped, but Charlotte convinced me to hire a security company to set up cameras and alarms. We still have a rickhouse full of aging bourbon, and we'll bottle some of that to replace what was destroyed."

Kristina nodded, showing her agreement with the plan. "If you're willing to pay for an off-duty deputy to guard the distillery until the security system is installed, I can get someone here tonight."

"Yes, please," Charlotte replied.

Carlisle appeared ready to challenge that decision, but one glance at Charlotte made him change his mind. The power dynamic had changed during their discussion in the office, and Carlisle was willing to defer to Charlotte.

"Have you discussed what you're going to do with the case you removed from the storage room?" I asked.

Carlisle looked at Charlotte. "I'd planned to pass those bottles out to my friends."

Charlotte looked like she couldn't believe what she'd just heard. "It would be prudent to delay your gifting to the good ole' boys until we have spare inventory. That case may be the only bourbon we'll have in time for the release party."

"But there are only eleven bottles..."

Charlotte looked among us, then focused on Carlisle. "Those eleven bottles might be worth as much as the whole two pallets that were destroyed. Between Mac's death and the destruction of most of our inventory, we may have created a unicorn—something extremely rare and worthy of collecting instead of drinking." She paused, then added, "You'd better bring back the rest of that bottle we tasted. That way we won't have to open another bottle at the release party."

Carlisle was suddenly sheepish. "Too late. It's gone."

"Gone?" Charlotte gasped.

"It was really good. I drank it."

Sophia had emerged from the lab and overheard the hallway discussion. She held up a strip of paper. "You guys need to see this."

We followed her into the lab where she'd spread several strips of paper on a bench top, each labelled with a code that meant nothing to me. Pointing halfway down the paper, she said, "This peak is unique to the heirloom corn Mac started using the second year. This later peak is from the malted barley we smoked. This peak at the end is from the Monongahela rye."

Carlisle shook his head. "What are you telling us?"

A smile flickered on Sophia's lips. "Mac created a flavor profile that no one else has. He added elements to the flavor chemistry that give our bourbon the best of bourbon, rye whiskey, and Scotch, without the harshness. Like Charlotte said, Mac invented a unicorn. We either have blended the best damn bourbon in the world, or we've created a whole new category of whiskey."

Carlisle became so excited he could hardly get his question out, "How many more barrels of this do we have?"

Sophia bit her lip. "Mac blended those two barrels after sampling all of the six and seven-year-old bourbon. They were the best of the best. We've got a couple hundred more of the seven-year-old. Mac said they were good, but inferior to what we bottled up. We won't have anything as good as this until we blend them with the next year's barrels."

Carlisle turned to Kristina. "You've got to find the two cases that guy took."

"I'll do my best. If the thief is savvy enough, he'll sell them to private collectors. They're not going to show up on eBay."

Charlotte turned to Carlisle. "Where is the case you took when we sampled in the QC lab?"

"I...um...have it in my garage."

"You're storing a case of rare bourbon in your *garage*?" Charlotte fumed. "I'll arrange for an armored car to pick it up and deliver it to the secure room. Considering the poor state of our *secure room*, I should talk to the banker and have him put those bottles into the bank's vault!"

"Let's not get overly dramatic," Carlisle protested. "I'll bring the rest of the case back to the distillery tomorrow."

"No," Charlotte said. "I'll follow you home and pick it up right now."

Carlisle bristled. "Listen, I'm the owner..."

"And you're paying me to make sure we do the right thing. I'll pick it up right now."

Seeing an opportunity to redirect the investigation back to the murder, I jumped in. "Jill would like to see your racehorse operation. Maybe Kristina can drive us to your farm. We'll pick up the bourbon."

Kristina's glare would've melted ice. She stepped beside me and whispered, "The sheriff's department isn't running a secure delivery service."

Jill stepped alongside Kristina so she could be part of our whispered conversation. "I don't think this is the time to be *checking out* the horse operation."

"Forget the bourbon thief for a minute." I waited until Kristina nodded her understanding. "Who hears more about what's going on than anyone in a stable? Let's see what the grooms taking care of Carlisle's horses have overheard about the McInnis murder."

Kristina's icy glare faded. "Do you think Carlisle will actually go for that?"

I looked up at Robert Carlisle. "Is your wife home? It'd be great if she could show Jill around the stables."

After an eye roll, Carlisle said, "She's probably at the country club." He took out his cell phone and punched in a number. "Hey, dear, the female park investigator would like to see our stables. They need to pick up the bourbon I'm storing, and this would be the perfect opportunity."

We couldn't hear much of what Glinda Carlisle said, but her raised voice and the few bits of her unhappy response were audible before Robert stepped into Charlotte's office.

Charlotte stepped over to us and whispered, "Mrs. Carlisle, Glinda, isn't...um...flexible. This will probably conflict with her bridge game, art class, or charity work."

Intrigued by Charlotte's comments, I asked, "How well do you know Mrs. Carlisle?"

Charlotte looked at the door to make sure Carlisle was still on his phone call. "She's never been to the distillery. The only time I've met her is at social events. Personally, I think Glinda has an addictive personality. Robert says she gets into things whole hog. The word *moderation* isn't part of her vocabulary."

"She might have OCD," Jill suggested.

Charlotte shrugged. "There's a whole alphabet of things that could be going on with Glinda Carlisle. I'm sure her weekly 'therapist' visits are helping her work through them."

The conversation ended when Robert Carlisle emerged from the office. His face was red, like he was either very angry or embarrassed. "Glinda is tied up right now. She suggested I have Jill get a stable tour from our head groom while I give Doug and Kristina a tour of the grounds. Glinda will stop over if she gets free from her...commitment."

I nodded and smiled. "That sounds perfect! We can get a tour without inconveniencing your wife."

Jill entered Carlisle's address into her mapping app. "We'll meet you at the farm."

Chapter 15

We'd driven alongside a mile of pasture enclosed by white wooden fences before reaching the Carlisles' driveway. The entrance was flanked by two life-size bronze horse statues.

"Wow," Kristina said as she turned into the paved driveway. "I should buy stock in the company that sells white paint."

The house that loomed in front of us, with barns alongside it, reminded me of something I'd seen in the movie *Secretariat*. An upper balcony was supported by a row of two-story-high white columns. "I think they used as much paint on the house and barn as they did on the fence."

Kristina parked on the loop that circled in front of the house. As we stepped out of the squad car, she commented, "I half expected the butler to race out and open the car doors for us."

"He's probably busy polishing the silver," I replied.

Ignoring us, Jill climbed the steps and crossed the porch. She was about to push the doorbell button when the 10-foot-tall door opened, and Carlisle's smiling face greeted us. "Come in. Pedro, our head groom will be here momentarily to give Jill a tour." He paused, then asked, "Would you two like to see the barns too, or would you prefer to see the house and grounds?"

Kristina spoke up first, "I'm not much of a horse person, so I'd prefer a house tour."

"I'm not a horse person either. My motivation was more aimed at getting Jill alone with the head groom than it was my lack of interest in horses."

A Hispanic man jogged to the house and raced up the steps. Barely five feet tall, and built like a jockey, Pedro smiled and introduced himself in perfect, unaccented English. He wore a black cap with the same logo as the bourbon distillery and looked like he was ready for a race.

Smiling, Jill stepped away from us and joined Pedro on the porch. "I'll see you two later." They walked away toward the barn.

The interior of Carlisles' house was as impressive as the exterior. Robert Carlisle's office was filled with trophies, ribbons, and pictures of him with a variety of people, most of them unfamiliar to me. He gestured toward a picture taken with a horse and mud-splattered jockey. "That's *Hero Worship's* last race before we retired him to stud service."

"Was he your biggest winner?" I asked.

"Yes. His syndication fees are what pay for this operation and the distillery."

"Syndication?"

"We sell shares in the breeding stallion. Each syndicate member has the right to breed one mare per year."

"I suppose asking how much a syndicate share costs would be akin to asking for the balance of your stock portfolio," I joked.

Carlisle smiled. "Let's just say, millions."

"I assume the syndicate has quite a few members?"

Carlisle ignored the question and led us to his dining room, with a table that could seat twenty people. "Glinda enjoys entertaining." This room also had pictures. Instead of horses, Robert and Glinda were standing next to groups of people including one past president and several senators. I also recognized one man who was now in a federal prison for running an investment Ponzi scheme.

Carlisle hustled us through the industrial-sized kitchen where two cooks were busy preparing food, and out to a gazebo where a table was set with two sweating pitchers and glasses. Robert gestured for us to take seats.

"What triggered your interest in partnering with McInnis in a distillery?" I asked. "It seems like you've got plenty to do with the horses."

The horse topic was comfortable for him. Carlisle leaned back in his chair and stared into the distance. "The horse operation is run by the experts I've hired. Pedro runs the stables and takes care of the horses. I have a CPA who handles the syndicate. I have a trainer who handles the young horses and decides which to sell as yearlings and which ones we keep in hopes of having the next Secretariat. To be honest, it's become boring. The distillery is interesting and gets me in touch with groups other than just the horse people."

"The distillery seems like a money pit," Kristina suggested.

I watched with interest as Robert shifted from breeder to money man. "Not a money pit as much as a long-term investment. Once we start selling the aged bourbon, the distillery will pay for itself. Within a few years, Mac thinks...thought we'd be making a tidy profit. If we're successful, one of the big liquor companies will buy us out and we'll struggle to find space to store all the money they'll pay us."

"So, your ultimate plan isn't to continue operating the distillery?" I asked. "You plan to sell it?"

"Not immediately. The value will be in the history of producing extraordinary bourbon. Right now, all the value is in the building and a rickhouse full of barrels that are unproven as of now."

"I suppose those barrels are somewhat like a yearling prospect," I speculated. "They have potential, but you really won't know what they'll become until sometime in the future."

Carlisle continued to watch his horses grazing. "I'd never thought of the bourbon in those terms. But, yes, we just won't know until we sample the aged product. We have great hope, but it's unproven."

Kristina finished her sweet tea and looked toward the six-stall garage. "Did you really store the bourbon in your garage?"

"No, it's in the game room closet, near the bar. Would you like to move it to the trunk of your car?"

Standing, Kristina said, "Sure, let's get that done now. Then, it'll be ready for your armed guards to transport it back to the distillery," she made a motion toward us with her thumb.

Carlisle chuckled as he led us back into the house. "I hadn't thought about the great security around this transport. The bourbon will have three armed guards."

The game room included billiards and foosball tables. A bar ran the width of the room opposite the windows. Carlisle opened a closet, exposing the bourbon box. We carried it to the bar, which was stocked with every premium liquor I'd ever seen.

"I told Charlotte a white lie." He stepped behind the bar, then set a half-full bottle of dark liquor on the bar along with three Glencairn glasses. "Would you like to taste a sample of our limited release bourbon?"

"None for me," I said as he pulled the cork and prepared to pour.

"You don't drink?" Carlisle asked as he poured.

"I quit years ago."

"Not one drink in all those years?" Carlisle asked.

"Not even one. I'm scared of it."

Kristina glanced at me, then took a breath. "Just as an investigative background, I'll try a sip."

Carlisle poured a half-inch of liquor into two glasses and slid one to Kristina. The two of them swirled the liquor in their glasses, then inhaled. Kristina's eyes lit up, and then she held the glass out to me. "Just smell this."

Inhaling brought back memories of cop bars, cheap booze, and hangovers. Following that came a vision of the NCO club in Iraq and drunken soldiers. I handed the glass back to her. "It's lovely," I lied.

Carlisle was swishing bourbon in his mouth as if tasting a fine wine. Kristina took a small sip, then closed her eyes. After swallowing, she said, "Wow. I mean, there are no words to describe that flavor. It's bourbon, but...more."

Carlisle's smug smile spread. "That's it, isn't it? It's everything and more." He patted the carton of bourbon. "To our future," he said before drinking the rest of the liquor in his glass. He pushed the empty glass toward me. "You're absolutely certain you don't want to sample this?"

"Thank you, but no." I paused, thinking about Jill's ranch. "I wish Jill's father and Uncle were here. They love Gentleman Jack and other good whiskeys. They would appreciate this."

Carlisle patted the carton again. "Maybe you'll have to bid at the charity auction."

"I'm sure the bidding will quickly surpass my price point."

Kristina handed her half-full glass back to Carlisle. "Thanks for the opportunity to sample this, but I'm not going to drink more than one sip."

Carlisle accepted the glass and drank the remaining bourbon. "It's over one hundred proof. I'm not concerned about your germs."

Voices in the hallway preceded Pedro and Jill's entry into the bar. I saw Jill's concern when she saw the partial bottle of bourbon and three empty glasses. I shook my head in response, indicating that I hadn't taken a drink.

"I just poured a sample for Kristina. Would you like one, Jill?"

"I'm more of a wine drinker. Good booze would be wasted on me."

"Robert suggested we bid on a bottle of the reserve bourbon at the charity auction. I'm sure your father and uncle would be elated. They've been known to finish a bottle of whiskey in one sitting."

Jill snorted. "I'd have to take out a loan."

"Who's finishing off a bottle in one sitting?" a woman's voice asked from the door. Glinda Carlisle walked in, still wearing her white tennis outfit. Although she'd been playing tennis recently, she looked ready to slip into a cocktail dress and host a party.

"I just offered samples of my special bottle."

Glinda Carlisle wrinkled her nose. "I don't do brown liquor. Give me a bloody mary or a vodka martini and I'll be happy." I caught a slight slurring of her words, making me think that she'd already had a few and probably shouldn't have driven herself home from the country club.

With a practiced hostess smile, Glinda turned to Jill. "How was your barn tour?"

"It was great. Your horses are impressive."

After a nod, Robert changed the topic. "Let's carry this box to Kristina's car. Y'all will want to deliver this to the distillery and get home for supper."

Glinda bid us goodbye from the steps. Jill and I walked a step behind Kristina and Robert, who carried the carton of booze. "Did you learn anything from the groom?"

"Glinda has drinking and gambling problems," Jill whispered. "She owes a lot of money. A lot."

"Sounds like a murder motive."

Jill shrugged. "I don't know how Mac's death or the destruction of the bourbon would solve her gambling debt."

* * *

On the drive back to the distillery, Kristina glanced at me. "Carlisle asked me if he needed police protection in light of all that's happened."

"What did you tell him?"

"I said that decision was entirely his. We don't know who killed McInnis or what motive the killer had, and we don't know if the thefts are anything more than petty thieves taking advantage of their poor security."

"Are there a lot of petty thefts in this county?"

"What's a lot? We've always had some opportunistic thieves. They usually do something stupid, and we catch them. It got worse during the methamphetamine boom, then slowed down a bit when the government limited sales of cold medicine and other precursors for cooking meth."

"Are there a lot of burglaries right now?"

"Not a ton. I mean, there are a few. I don't think there's an organized ring working the area. We'd be seeing more."

"Who benefits the most from destroying the bourbon?" Jill asked.

"I suppose the person who stole the boxes before crushing the rest. He or she might have created a gold mine by making a limited release even rarer."

I considered that in silence as we left the area of white fences and switched to plowed

224

fields and pastures of grazing cattle. "If these thieves are smart, they'll have private buyers who'll keep their mouth shut."

"This is rural Kentucky, Doug. We're more likely to catch them selling the booze off the tailgate of their pickup."

"Or on eBay!" Jill added.

"We've got a deputy who checks eBay, pawn shops, and other on-line sales for stolen goods. I'll make sure he adds this bourbon to his list."

As we approached the distillery, I saw a sheriff's department SUV backed into the loading dock with a second sheriff's vehicle blocking the distillery driveway. That deputy backed up to let us enter. There was only one civilian car in the parking lot.

Charlotte, looking haggard, held the door for Kristina, who'd insisted on carrying in the liquor despite my attempt at chivalry. "How many bottles are left? Tell me Carlisle didn't drink them all."

"There are eleven sealed bottles in the carton," Kristina replied. "Carlisle showed us the open bottle and that was still half full, too."

"Thank God for small favors," Charlotte said leading Kristina to her office. "I'm going to put that case into the bottom drawer of my file cabinet, then we'll lock the office."

"I assume the sheriff's vehicle at the loading dock is the forensic team?" I asked.

Charlotte hustled us out of the office, turned off the lights, then locked the door.

"Yes, there are two forensics people checking for fingerprints all over the warehouse. They're going to have a time of it separating the employees' prints from the others."

"Go home, Charlotte," Kristina said. "There'll be a deputy at the gate all night. Everything here is under control."

Biting her bottom lip, Charlotte nodded. "We're locking the barn after the horse ran off. On the other hand, Sophia has all her analytical information and how it relates to the mash recipe and aging. That's where our future lies." Charlotte looked at Jill and me. "Don't get me wrong, losing the bourbon is a kick in the shins. Our future lies in the know-how that went into making that bourbon."

After seeing Charlotte out of the door, we walked back to the warehouse where one forensic technician was dusting the forklift for fingerprints. A second tech was vacuuming under the storage racks.

"Hey, Camilla, are you making any headway?" Kristina asked.

The fingerprint specialist looked away from her sampling. "I've rarely had a crime scene this large. We're focusing on the storage room, this forklift, and the load of barrels, but there are fingerprints on every surface," she looked around the room, "of the entire warehouse. We'll need exclusion prints from all the employees so we can find the outliers."

"Our prints are in AFIS," I offered.

"That's two down and like twenty to go."

"Is there anything we can do to help?" I asked.

Camilla's sour expression answered the question. "You're feds, right? Unless you've got a dozen forensics techs in the car, the best thing you can do is leave my crime scene."

Kristina gestured to the door, and we left as Camilla went back to her fingerprinting. As we walked to the car, I commented, "Camilla gave me the impression her previous *help* from federal agencies has been less than pleasant?"

"I assume that's a rhetorical question," Kristina replied as she unlocked the car.

Chuckling, Jill added, "Call it rhetorical, facetious, or smartass Doug's the master."

I asked Kristina to drop us at a convenience store near the Baptist Church. Jill followed me into the store and watched me take a pre-made sandwich from the cooler. "Bitsy is going to feed us in an hour," she said as I chose a jumbo bottle of Coke from a different cooler.

"We're bringing supper to Hubert at the church."

Nodding her understanding, Jill chose a party-size bag of chips and a candy bar from shelves near the checkout counter and an apple from a table display.

I looked at the apple. "Hubert doesn't have any teeth. Did you see bananas anywhere?"

Jill nodded and returned the apple. A minute later she returned with a banana. "I feel sorry for Hubert."

"He either made some bad choices or got dealt a bad hand by the Almighty. Bitsy's church is taking care of him now."

We carried our bag the two blocks to the church. Walking to the back of the parsonage, I found the door leading to the basement where I'd last seen Hubert. Announcing ourselves and calling his name, we stood at the door. The sound of a chair scraping on the floor preceded the appearance of Hubert's face at the bottom of the stairs.

"Ranger Doug?"

I held up the bag and said, "We brought you supper."

Hubert seemed confused. "Miss Bitsy already brought my dinner."

"Do you have a refrigerator where you can store this until you're hungry?"

"I guess." He walked upstairs and accepted the bag.

"Do you have time to talk?" I asked.

"Got nothing but time." He glanced down the stairs, then looked past me at Jill. "I've never had a woman except Miss Bitsy visit me. It might be best if we stayed outside. I don't want people talking."

"I see a picnic table. Can we sit there without people talking?"

Hubert accepted the bag at the table and looked through the contents. He took out the banana and considered it carefully. "I appreciate the banana. My teeth aren't so good anymore."

"Can you help us with a problem?" I asked.

"Maybe so. Maybe not. What's your problem?"

"Someone stole bourbon from the Running Acres Distillery's warehouse. We're trying to find out who took it."

Hubert was more interested in the contents of our bag than the question and I wondered if he had problems focusing on more than one thing at a time. After a few moments, Hubert took the Coke and chips from the bag. He twisted the cap off the bottle, then pulled the chip bag open. After eating a handful of chips and taking a drink of Coke, he looked at us like he'd just realized we were there.

"Which time?" he asked.

"You know that there have been two break-ins?"

Hubert nodded as he took another handful of chips from the bag. Realizing that Jill was watching him eat, Hubert paused and offered the bag to her.

After glancing at Hubert's dirty fingernails, Jill declined the offer. "Those are for you. Miss Bitsy is feeding us later."

Returning his focus to me, Hubert nodded. "Everyone knows there have been two break-ins."

"Let's talk about the first one."

Hubert shrugged. "Okay."

Realizing he needed prompting, I asked, "Do you know who broke in?"

"Not by name."

"What do you know about the person who stole the bourbon?"

"He was selling it in town."

"Selling it from his car?" I asked.

Hubert shook his head emphatically, "Naw. He had a pickup."

"Can you describe the pickup?"

"Not really."

Realizing I needed to ask the right question to get an answer, I thought for a second, then asked, "What can you tell me about the truck or the man who was selling the stolen bourbon?"

"His pickup was full of wood chips."

"Wood chips?" I asked. "Was he delivering wood chips from a sawmill?"

"I don't think so. I just think they were there. You know, from cutting down trees."

"So, the person who was driving the truck cuts down trees?"

Hubert cocked his head. "Of course he does. That's what Bowman's tree company does."

"Was Mr. Bowman driving the pickup truck?"

"I don't know what his name is. I see him in that truck all the time." Hubert was nearing the bottom of the chip bag. It appeared that a substantial portion of the contents were scattered on the picnic table and on Hubert's shirt and fingers.

Jill stepped away from the table and pulled out her phone. She mouthed, "Calling Kristina," to me before turning her back to us.

"What do you know about Mr. Bowman, Hubert?"

"Not much. People know he's been in jail. They want him to cut their trees because he's cheap, but no one lets him into their house. He likes to be paid in cash, so he doesn't have to share it with the government."

"And you're sure he was selling the stolen bourbon?"

Hubert nodded. "Do you want to see the bottle I bought from him?"

"Do you have it in the basement?"

Hubert hung his head. "I'm not supposed to have liquor in the church or parsonage." He paused, then asked, "Am I in trouble for buying stolen booze?"

"Trust me, Hubert, you're not in trouble about the bourbon. Because that bottle was stolen, I need to return it to the police."

"I paid twenty dollars for it. I thought I might be able to sell it for twenty-five."

I pulled out my wallet and removed two twenty-dollar bills. "I'll pay you forty dollars for it."

Hubert stammered, "I only paid twenty."

"That's okay. I'm happy to give you forty. Let's get it."

"It's in the cemetery," he said as we stepped away from the picnic table.

I signaled to Jill that I'd be back shortly, then followed Hubert to a corner of the graveyard. He removed leaves from a niche broken from a headstone and was about to reach into the hole when I stopped him and pulled on a pair of purple gloves.

"Let me pull it out, okay?" As promised, I removed a 750 ml bottle of Running Acres bourbon. The unopened bottle was covered with dirty leaf litter, which I was sure Camilla would love because it had protected the underlying fingerprints on the bottle's surface. I gave the cash to Hubert, who jammed it into his front pocket.

As Jill approached, I held up the bottle for her to see. She smirked but didn't say anything.

"Hubert, that helps with the first burglary. Who broke into the distillery the second time?"

Without hesitation, he replied, "That country club woman."

"Which country club woman?" Jill asked, thinking she'd missed something.

"I don't know her name. People just call her that country club woman."

"Glinda Carlisle?" Jill asked.

Hubert shrugged. "I don't know her name. She's just that country club woman. People talk about her."

"Does she own horses?" Jill asked.

"I don't know anything about horses. I think she plays tennis at the country club."

Jill put her hand on Hubert's arm. "Thanks, Hubert. You've been a huge help."

Staring at Jill's hand, he froze and his face flushed. "I've got to take my sandwich to the refrigerator," he finally said. He scooped up the bag and walked to the basement door. Pausing at the door, he glanced at Jill, then darted inside.

"Kristina is on the way," Jill said, still smirking.

"Should I be jealous of your new boyfriend?"

"Yeah, right."

Chapter 16

Kristina arrived five minutes later. She'd changed into jeans and a blue Kentucky Wildcats sweatshirt. I held up the bottle as she rolled to a stop in front of the church. Shaking her head as she approached, she said, "For heaven's sake, you're in front of a Baptist church, keep that bottle under your shirt."

As she opened an evidence bag, I said, "Hubert bought it from Mr. Bowman, who runs the tree-cutting service. He didn't know their value because he was selling them for twenty bucks each."

Kristina sealed the bag and signed it before placing it into her trunk. "Every patrol car in the county is watching for Bowman's pickup. I spoke with his parole officer and Bowman's not allowed to have liquor. He's driving to the parolee's house now."

Jill took the front seat, and I sat in the back as we pulled away from the church. Jill explained, "Hubert stashed a bottle in the cemetery."

Kristina blew out a breath. "I hope Bowman didn't sell many bottles. I'd like to recover a few of them."

"It'd be even better if he told us who bought the ones he's sold," Jill suggested.

I snorted. "If he's been in prison, he's not going to say anything except asking for a lawyer."

"It'll be interesting to see the dynamic between Bowman and his parole officer. A parole violation gives us leverage."

* * *

Bowman's home was a tiny shotgun-style structure with the front and back doors at either end of a hallway that ran along the right side of the house. The shotgun house description came from the observation that someone could fire a shotgun from the front door and hit someone standing at the back door. The foundation appeared to be constructed from the same gray shale slabs used in the nearby fences. The poorly maintained yard sat among a string of one-acre lots that had probably been carved out of a farm at some point in the distant past. A brown pickup with Bowman's name and phone number painted on the driver's door was parked alongside the house. Parked ahead of it was a beat-up Pontiac. A Ford Taurus, that looked like it had been a squad car in an earlier life, blocked the driveway.

A burly man with a two-day beard stepped out of the Ford. He smiled and nodded to Kristina as we got out of the squad. "Hey, Kris."

Kristina introduced us to Ken Blackburn. I explained the recovery of the bottle from Hubert and the explanation of how he'd acquired it.

"It sounds like Ole Billy has violated his parole," Blackburn gestured toward the house, then led us to the front door. He pounded on the door. "Billy, open up. It's Blackburn, your parole officer."

I heard the sound of a TV in the house, followed by the sound of someone scurrying around inside. Blackburn twisted the doorknob and, surprisingly, pushed open the unlocked door. He gestured for Kristina, who'd put on a sheriff's department bulletproof vest, to take the lead.

"Sheriff's department! Come out with your hands where I can see them!"

Jill and I pulled our pistols and held them alongside our legs as we followed Kristina and Blackburn. She checked each empty room as she walked down the narrow hallway. Her pace picked up when we heard sounds from the kitchen.

We raced ahead and interrupted Bill Bowman as he poured a bottle of Running Acres bourbon into the sink. "Stop!" Kristina yelled as she lunged forward and took the nearly empty bottle from Bowman's hand.

Blackburn stepped forward, holding a pair of handcuffs. "Bill, I'm arresting you for a parole violation."

Bowman, who sneered at us, put out his wrists. His long gray beard was flecked with wood chips, food, and Copenhagen snuff. His grizzled look was completed with a tattered plaid shirt and denim bib overalls.

Blackburn shook his head. "Turn around." With the cuffs snapped into place, Blackburn searched the old man, removing a key ring, wallet, can of Copenhagen, and dirty red bandana from his pockets.

With gloved hands, Kristina capped the bourbon bottle and asked, "Where's the rest of the bourbon you stole?"

"I want a lawyer," Bowman replied.

"That's fine, you're under arrest for burglary," Kristina replied. Then she read the Miranda card in her pocket.

Blackburn turned Bowman and sat him on a kitchen chair. "You'll get a lawyer. You don't have to say a thing until your lawyer arrives. On the other hand, the judge might be more lenient if you told us where the rest of the stolen bourbon is."

"I don't know nothin' about no stolen bourbon."

"How long will you have to serve for a parole violation?" Blackburn asked. "What was left on your sentence, like another thirty months?"

"Twenty-seven."

"I'll contact the parole board and get a warrant. They'll hold a hearing. Because you violated the no alcohol condition of your parole, they will probably reinstate your original sentence as well as time added for the burglary."

"I didn't burgle anything. I just bought a bottle of booze. No crime in that."

"Just to be clear, the terms of your parole specifically say no drugs or alcohol. The bottle you were pouring out was a clear violation of that condition. It was also stolen from the distillery. You'll be charged and tried for burglary."

"We'll add possession of stolen property and destruction of evidence to the theft charge for pouring the booze down the drain," Kristina added. "It's a shame you were selling these bottles for twenty bucks." Kristina held up the bottle and swirled the remaining brown liquor before she put it into an evidence bag. "We think that the remaining bottles are going to sell for several thousand dollars each."

Bowman's head snapped up and he glared at Kristina. "The hell you say, a thousand dollars...each?"

"Maybe more."

Blackburn pulled eight twenty-dollar bills from Bowman's wallet. "It appears you sold eight bottles. You were pouring one out. That leaves three bottles from one case left, plus three other cases. We're missing thirty-nine bottles of bourbon."

Kristina nodded toward the door. "Put Bowman into the back of your car and take him to jail. Making an arrest in a two-hundred-thousand-dollar burglary is going to look good on my monthly statistics."

"What two-hundred-thousand dollars? It was just a couple cases of bourbon," Bowman protested as the parole officer guided him down the hall.

Blackburn stopped at the end of the hallway, and Kristina glanced over her shoulder. "You know, if you help us recover the three unopened cases, the judge might take pity on you and only charge you for the ones you sold."

"I'm telling you, it was just a few bottles of cheap bourbon. What in hell you talkin' 'bout?"

"Who bought the bottles you sold, and where is the rest?" Kristina asked.

"I don't know who they were! They just came up to me in the parking lot and handed me twenty bucks for a bottle. They were just folks I've seen around."

I smiled at Kristina, who'd just got the admission she needed. She nodded.

"Where are the other three cases, Billy?" Blackburn asked. "The judge might take pity on you if you told us."

Kristina held a cupboard door open and said, "We'll tear this place apart and find them eventually."

Bowman glared at her. "Look under the tarp in the back corner of the shed."

Kristina pulled the keys out of Bowman's belongings and gestured toward the back of the house. "Doug and Jill, can you give me a hand with the evidence?"

She tried three keys before finding the one that opened the padlock on the shed. As expected, we found the cases of Running Acres bourbon under a tarp in the back of the shed. Kristina took pictures of the boxes where we'd found them, then we carried them to her squad car.

"I suppose these will have to remain in your evidence room until after Bowman's trial," I offered as we carried the boxes.

Kristina sighed and nodded. "That'll kill Charlotte and Carlisle. They'll want them ASAP, but it's evidence required for Bowman's trial."

"It'll be worth much more in a year or two," Jill suggested. "You might be doing them a favor by keeping it in secure storage."

"If your district attorney is as busy as most, he'll work out a plea deal and you can return the bourbon to the distillery in a couple of months," I suggested.

With the boxes stowed, we stood behind the squad, and Blackburn joined us. Kristina looked off into the distance. "There's something off about Billy's house."

"Off?" Blackburn asked.

I nodded my agreement, sniffing the outside air. "There was a smell in the kitchen besides old garbage."

"Did you search any of the rooms as we went through? I checked to see if there was anyone else there, but something wasn't right." Blackburn, Jill and I all shook our heads. "Let's walk though again."

We walked into Bowman's living room, which faced the street. The TV was still on, showing a game show. The lone piece of furniture was a threadbare couch, which was set directly in front of the television. I put on a pair of gloves and turned off the TV. "Nothing much to see here. Bowman lived a spartan life."

Jill ran her gloved hands into the recesses of the couch as Kristina removed the couch cushions. "I found a quarter, dime, and popcorn."

"Let's look at the bedrooms," Kristina said leading us into the hallway.

The first bedroom contained a single bed and a chest of drawers. The bed was unmade and there were men's clothes strewn around the floor. The second bedroom had a double bed and a dresser with a mirror. That bed was also unmade, but aside from the messy bed, the room was neat. Jill walked into the room and picked up a plastic disc from the nightstand. "Unless Bowman is taking birth control pills, there's a woman living here, too."

Kristina opened the top drawers of the dresser. "Panties and bras in here. She held up a bra and cocked her head. "I'd say his partner is well endowed."

Blackburn looked at a pair of pants hanging in the closet. "These are size 20. I'd say his girlfriend is chunky," he chuckled.

"Were you aware he was living with someone?" Kristina asked Blackburn.

"As far as I knew, he was living here alone."

"Are there any stipulations about roommates in his parole conditions?" I asked.

Blackburn shook his head. "He can't be in contact with any known felons. If he has a girlfriend who's never been in prison, he's okay."

"Uh oh," Jill said after pulling out the nightstand drawer. "There's a half box of 9mm ammo in here."

Blackburn sighed. "That's a problem. He can't possess a firearm either."

Pulling the drawer out farther, Jill bent down. "There's no pistol in here, but there are a few more loose cartridges and a bottle of personal lubricant."

Kristina searched the remaining dresser drawers as Blackburn went through the closet. Jill and I lifted the mattress and checked under the bed, finding nothing but dust bunnies and a pair of worn-out women's slippers.

Blackburn stepped to the door. "I'll ask Billy about his roommate and the ammo. Will you guys search the rest of the house?" He left without waiting for a reply.

Kristina smirked. "I'll flip a coin to see who has to search his wastebaskets."

"I'm sorry," I replied. "We have no jurisdiction here. I think you have to do the wastebaskets."

Stopping at the door, Kristina put her hands on her hips. "Wow! After all I've done for you, you're going to pull the *no jurisdiction* card?"

"We'll check the other bedroom and bathroom," Jill offered.

"Unless there's something really disgusting in the bathroom," I replied. "I'd hate to disturb your crime scene if there's anything bloody in the bathroom wastebasket."

Kristina glared at me. "Yeah, if there's a tampon in there, be sure to leave it for me."

Jill and I quickly went through the other bedroom, finding nothing but a few clean clothes in the chest of drawers and dirty clothes on the floor. I pulled a shoebox off a shelf in the closet while Jill felt under the mattress and looked under the bed.

"Ah, geez!" she uttered while I was still in the closet. I stuck my head out to see what had disgusted her. "There's a stack of pornographic magazines under the bed. He'd folded a couple of them open to his favorite page."

"Legal porn?"

"Yeah, I think so," she replied as she pushed the pile back under the bed. "All of the models are tattooed and look well past eighteen."

There was a medicine chest behind the bathroom mirror. Besides the expected Motrin and Tylenol, there were three prescription bottles. "Bowman was taking meds for blood pressure and cholesterol. A woman named Lynnette Qualley was taking Omeperazole." I removed that bottle as Jill looked through the linen closet. "Now we know his girlfriend's name."

"I found a stash of feminine supplies under the sink."

We found Kristina searching the kitchen cupboards. "His girlfriend is Lynette Qualley. Is she known to you?"

After closing the last cupboard, Kristina took the prescription bottle from me and read the label. "Her name is familiar but she's not someone I've arrested." She sniffed the kitchen air. "That's not garbage I smell." She looked around the kitchen. "Did you see a mouse in a trap?"

I sniffed the air again. "Yeah, something died. I wonder if there's a dead racoon under the house."

"Was there a water heater in the bathroom?" Kristina asked.

"No, there's a linen closet, but no water heater." I looked around the kitchen for a basement door. Seeing none, I said, "I suppose it's in the basement or crawlspace."

Kristina hung her head. "I don't suppose you want to be gentlemanly and offer to climb into the spider infested crawlspace?"

"Not our..."

"Yeah, yeah. It's not in your jurisdiction." She led us out the back. "Let's find the door."

The rusty metal door was nearly flush with the ground. The hinges groaned as the door opened. Inside was a set of cement block steps leading into a space that appeared to be about four feet high. Kristina took out her flashlight and eased down the steps slowly, keeping her hand on the butt of her gun. She stopped and sniffed the air again. "The stink is stronger here." She took two steps down, then paused and said, "If a rabid racoon attacks me, shoot it."

"Gladly," I replied as she ducked her head to enter the crawlspace.

Jill looked at me and shook her head. "You could've done the gentlemanly thing."

"If there's contraband down there, it's better if she discovers it. I don't want to fly back to testify in a trial."

"NOOOOO!" Kristina yelled before we heard a heavy thump.

I rushed to the door, drew my pistol, and climbed down the steps. A bat fluttered out of the basement, causing me to jerk to the side as it passed. "Kristina? What's going on?"

Jill bumped into me when I stopped just into the crawlspace. My eyes couldn't adjust to the darkness beyond the door. "What can you see?" she asked.

"Nothing. I need a flashlight."

"Kristina, are you okay?" I called out, finally seeing the light of Kristina's flashlight shining on the opposite side of the space.

"Uh," Kristina groaned.

Moving ahead slowly with my left hand on the wall, I approached the origin of her flashlight beam. "Kristina? Talk to me. What's going on?"

"I...uh..." she replied as I edged ahead, not sure of what had happened and if there was something threatening ahead of me. My head bumped into a pipe that thrummed after being struck. A foot farther, my head hit a bigger pipe. "Ouch, dammit."

Kristina groaned in response to my oath. I moved ahead using my right hand to reach out for unseen pipes and floor joists ahead of me. My foot hit something soft about two feet away from the flashlight beam.

"Is that you, Kristina?"

"Yeah," her voice came from a few feet farther ahead. I probed ahead with my foot and determined whatever was in my path was soft, so not a wall, and heavier than five or ten pounds.

A flashlight beam came on behind me and probed the darkness. It stopped, shining on my back. "Are you okay, Doug? Did you find Kristina?"

"Where did you find a flashlight?"

"Our phones have flashlights," Jill replied.

Not wanting to admit I'd forgotten that, and not willing to let go of the wall and overhead floor joist, I said, "Shine the light on my feet. I'm tripping on something."

The beam quickly swept down my legs and shone on dirty denim. Jill slowly shone the beam left and right, illuminating legs, dirty tennis shoes, a torso wearing a gray sweatshirt, and arms. Whoever it was, had fallen facing away from me.

"Kristina?"

"Yeah, watch your step."

"Jill, come over here with the flashlight."

With Jill alongside me, she shined the light farther ahead and lit Kristina who was sitting on the floor with her arms resting on her knees. A gash on the back of her head was oozing blood. I reached down and touched the wrist of the body at my feet and realized the person's skin was as cold as the crawlspace. I sniffed and got a whiff of the sickly sweetness of a body that was starting to decay. Stepping over the body, I knelt next to Kristina. When I touched her arm, she recoiled from my cold fingers.

"Talk to me."

"Damn you, Fletcher."

I sighed in relief. "Jill, call an ambulance."

"No," Kristina said as she blinked. "I don't want EMTs shining lights in my eyes and half the sheriff's department staring at me. Just give me a second."

"What happened?" I asked.

After picking up her flashlight, Kristina shone the light on the body. "Is that a dead person?"

"It appears to be."

"Well, shit."

"What happened to you?"

Kristina touched the back of her head. "I hit my head on something." She shined her light on the floor joists and pipes. "Damn they're hard."

"How did you hit the back of your head?"

"I tripped on something, then something flew by and brushed my face. I must've jerked my head back and hit a pipe or something." After brushing spider webs out of her forehead and hair, she looked up at me.

"A bat flew out of the basement just after you screamed."

"I DID NOT SCREAM." She paused as if in thought. "I might've sworn, but I didn't scream."

"I'm sure the bat startled you."

Kristina shivered involuntarily. "I hate bats and rats." That said, she glared at me. "If you tell anyone about this, I *will* kill you."

Jill snorted behind me and Kristina leaned to look past me. "That goes for you, too. You'll both be..." Kristina froze, and her eyes went wide. "Oh, shit, there really is a dead body down here."

"I think you've got a concussion," I said. "You should be seen."

"Not happening."

Kristina turned her flashlight to illuminate the person's face, which was a mottled purple, indicating the victim had been dead for several days. She moved the beam around and stopped while focused on the victim's long brown hair.

"I suppose this is Lynette," Jill suggested.

I helped Kristina get to her feet, and we skirted around the body as we duck-walked to the stairs. "We've messed up this crime scene," Kristina said as she climbed the steps."

Once outside of the crawlspace, we all stood and stretched as Blackburn approached us. "What have you guys been up to?"

Kristina brushed dirt from her pants and shirt. "Bill has…had a girlfriend. We think she's in the crawlspace, dead."

He cocked his head. "Kris, why are you covered in…"

She cut off the question. "Can you call this in? We need the coroner and the crime scene techs."

As we followed Blackburn to the cars, Kristina pulled Jill aside. "How bad am I bleeding?"

Jill looked at the back of her head. "It was oozing. I think the bleeding has stopped."

"When we get to the car, I'll pull out my first aid kit. Clean up my hair before anyone else shows up. I've got a baseball cap in the trunk. Okay?"

I took her arm and stopped them. "You might have a concussion. You should go to the ER."

"Screw that! There's no way I'm going to do that. I'm already on the sheriff's shit list. I don't need a workman's comp claim on my record."

"I'm serious."

"That is not happening," she hissed.

"Fine. It's your call. But you and Jill are attached at the hip for the next few hours. If you get dizzy or sleepy, you'll be on the way to the hospital without further discussion. Understood?"

"Fine." Kristina looked at Jill. "Remind me of your name again."

Jill's eyes went wide, and she looked at me.

"I'm just pulling your leg," Kristina said.

"That was NOT funny," Jill replied.

Kristina grinned. "I probably shouldn't be joking at a death scene." She turned to me. "Did you get any sense of what happened to that poor woman?"

"I didn't see any blood or wounds. Maybe an overdose or strangulation?"

Blackburn met us at Kristina's squad as Jill swabbed the blood out of her hair. Looking concerned, he asked, "Are you okay?"

"Yeah. I bumped my head on a pipe in the crawlspace."

He nodded, then gestured toward his car, where Billy was seated. "I mentioned the dead body in the crawlspace to our prisoner. He got very quiet."

"I assume he asked for his lawyer again."

"No, he actually teared up and said it was an accident. Lynnette shot up with some fentanyl laced shit. After he slid the body into the crawlspace, Billy burned all the drugs and paraphernalia in the barrel out back. We can probably recover the needles and spoon."

"I suppose he panicked because it was a parole violation, so he dumped her in the basement," I surmised.

Jill nodded. "And later, he realized she was too heavy for him to lift out of the crawlspace."

Kristina stared at the house. "I wonder what his plan B was? Maybe he would've burned down the house in hopes of destroying the body and evidence."

"That doesn't usually work," I said.

Blackburn chuckled, "Billy isn't a rocket scientist. I doubt he had a plan."

We hung around until the crime scene techs and coroner arrived, then I put out my hand to Kristina. "Keys."

"Say what?"

"I'm driving until we're sure your bump on the head isn't serious."

"I'm fine."

"Give me your keys, or I'll call the dispatcher and speak with the sheriff."

She slapped the keys into my hand. "Fine."

I pulled Jill aside and whispered, "Keep her talking. I want to make sure she doesn't nod off or have a brain bleed of some kind."

As I pulled away from the curb, Jill asked, "What does your husband do?"

"He's a freelance computer programmer."

"He works from home?"

Kristina nodded. "He's working on crew staffing software for Southwest Airlines. He's been fine-tuning the glitches for almost two years."

"So, he's around if something comes up with the kids?"

"Sort of. I mean, he's there, but when he's focused, getting him to pay attention is impossible. He's able to focus and tune out the world."

"But if the kids are sick, you don't need to take time off?"

"No, Hank is home with them. The kids have orders not to go into his office unless there's something urgent going on."

Jill looked at me in the mirror, and mouthed *enough?* I made a gesture to keep going.

"Are your kids old enough to grasp the concept of what's really important?"

"For the most part. My son is in seventh grade. He's good about taking care of himself. My daughter is a sixth grader who knows where all of her brother's buttons are and she doesn't hesitate to push them."

"I imagine it's tough being a cop's kid."

Kristina sighed. "I guess so. The kids don't complain about being picked on. It probably helps that my son is the tallest kid in his class."

"Does he play basketball?" Jill asked.

"He's a nerd, like his parents. He prefers gaming on his computer to competitive sports. My daughter is the class clown, which has its own set of issues." Kristina looked at me in the rearview mirror. "Are we through with the interrogation yet? I'm awake, coherent, and capable of reason."

"No headache, vision, or speech problems?"

"My head hurts where I banged it, but I don't have a headache per se."

I turned toward Mary's Inn at the next corner. "If you're really okay, we'll jump out at the inn and let you drive yourself home."

We drove in silence until we reached the inn. I handed the keys to Kristina counted them as if making sure I hadn't taken any. "About your jurisdiction comment."

"Yeah. What about it."

She got a sly smile and said, "You're feds. You have jurisdiction anywhere in the United States."

"Huh. I guess I'd forgotten that."

Kristina turned to Jill. "Is he always a smart aleck?"

"Most of the time."

We were about to step away when Kristina stopped us. "Thanks for checking on me. Most cops would've let me drive myself home or would've sent me off in an ambulance."

"We've been trying to tell you; we're not most cops."

"I'll see you in the morning."

Jill waved. "You might as well plan on having breakfast with us. Bitsy is going to feed you whether you're hungry or not."

* * *

Bitsy surmised we'd made a breakthrough in the case, saying we seemed more relaxed. She was polite enough not to press us for information about the days' events. As we turned to go up the stairs, she said, "There's no need for you to tell me about your investigation. Hubert will know all the details when I bring him supper."

As we climbed the steps, Jill whispered, "I hope Hubert doesn't say anything about the dead woman in Bowman's basement."

"Getting information out of Hubert is like pulling teeth. Unless Bitsy asks precisely the correct questions, she won't get useful answers."

"Doug, Bitsy has known Hubert for years. I think she knows how to get answers out of him."

Chapter 17

There was an extra place setting at the table when we came down for breakfast. Bitsy swept out of the kitchen with coffee and a tray of sweet rolls.

"I didn't hear you greet a new lodger last night," I said as Bitsy poured coffee.

Smiling, she replied, "As I said, it's quiet this time of year. I suppose Miss Kristina might just as well stay here. I'm probably seeing more of her than her family does."

The front door opened as Bitsy returned to the kitchen. A moment later, Kristina walked into the dining room. She stopped at the head of the table and started at the extra silverware and napkin. "Is there another guest?"

"It's for you," Jill replied. "Bitsy suggested you move in since she's seeing so much of you."

Kristina, who was again dressed up and wearing makeup as she had for her country club luncheon, sat and spread the napkin on her lap. "Sadly, that's the truth. I was out of the house before the kids finished breakfast. My husband kidded me and asked if I was having an affair with *that park service ranger*. I explained that there were two of you, and that second one was named Jill, a woman. That ended the discussion."

I studied Kristina as she spread her napkin and poured herself coffee. We'd progressed to a more personal relationship.

"How's your head?" Jill whispered.

"I've got a bump, but no headache or concussion symptoms."

"Good."

Bitsy appeared with two bowls of grits. She set them in front of Jill and Kristina. "Doug, your high cholesterol eggs and bacon will be up in a moment with toast dripping butter."

Snickering, Kristina glanced at me. "She's got you pegged." Then she looked at Bitsy. "You don't need to feed me."

Bitsy looked at Kristina's trim figure and then at the grits. "Honey child, you need to put some meat on those bones. A bowl of grits is the least I can do to carry you over until you get a decent lunch."

When Bitsy left, Kristina whispered, "I checked the country club website. They have pages for golf, tennis, the restaurant, and social activities. The tennis page has dozens of pictures of tennis players socializing, in tournaments, and taking lessons. Glinda Carlisle is in about a quarter of the photos. She's a fixture in the club. On the other hand, there are at least another twenty women in the pictures, including Tamsin McInnis in tennis whites."

"We're basing our suspicions about Glinda being 'that country club woman' on hearsay evidence from a less than stellar source," Jill added.

Bitsy returned with my breakfast, then stepped back. "Miss Jill, you've got raisins and brown sugar. Miss Kristina has traditional red-eye gravy for her grits. Mr. Doug has greasy bacon and eggs with toast dripping butter. Does anyone need anything else, or should I disappear again so you can continue your confidential police discussion?"

Smirking, Jill asked, "Do you have a hidden microphone and camera in this dining room?"

"No, I've just learned how to read people," Bitsy replied. "I'll take my leave now."

"She's incredible," I said as I spread strawberry jam on my toast.

"How do you plan to approach Glinda Carlisle?" Jill asked.

"I thought we'd go to their house. My cover story is that we're there to tell Mr. Carlisle we've made an arrest and recovered some of the stolen bourbon. I thought we'd ask Glinda to join us before the revelation. If she's got a guilty conscience, she might flinch when I say we've solved one of the burglaries."

I considered Kristina's suggestion, then offered, "I think Glinda is as hard as one of Tasmin's glass sculptures. I doubt that she'll react to the news. If she does, she'll cover it up quickly."

"Do you have a better approach?"

"No, your idea is good. I just think what she does after she hears the news will be telling. Mention having a lead in the second burglary. If she's involved, she'll be on the phone to her accomplice."

Jill paused and stirred her grits absently. "Let's tell a white lie. Tell the Carlisles we've got a suspect in the second burglary, and a judge has approved a tap of the suspect's phone. That will force her to meet with her co-conspirator."

Kristina grimaced.

"Let's roll the dice on this," I suggested as I pushed my empty plate away. "Since we think the link is at the country club, let's drop Jill there when we go to the Carlisles' house. She'll be in place to see what happens after we talk to Robert and Glinda."

Jill frowned. "First of all, I'd need an invitation to get inside. Secondly, what am I going to do for the hours between you dropping me off and Glinda rushing in to flush out her co-conspirator?"

"You're going to use your badge to get inside. Tell them you're meeting Glinda Carlisle."

Kristina nodded. "Do you have a white tennis outfit?"

"No. I didn't bring my golf clubs either."

"Then go to the bar and sit where you can see the tennis courts."

"Don't you think me sitting at the bar for several hours will look suspicious?"

Kristina reached out and touched Jill's arm. "You've never hung out in a bar during the day, have you? There are barflies who show up to get their *eye opener* as soon as they unlock the doors. Another group will show up at ten o'clock to get an early start on their three-martini lunch. About noon, the golfers will start circulating through to settle their bets and have a beer after finishing their morning rounds."

"I'll look very suspicious sitting at the bar and not drinking."

"Order a virgin bloody mary," I suggested. "You'll fit right in with the early birds who drink their breakfasts."

Kristina started laughing. "Your biggest problem will be fighting off all the propositions you'll get."

"Really? No." Jill replied, rolling her eyes.

"I worked undercover surveillance in a bar for a week. I've never been hit on so many times in my life. Every horny guy who walked in saw me as a lonely heartbroken woman who might be willing to go back to his place."

"You're making me ill," Jill replied, pushing her bowl of grits aside. "I might need to drink real bloody marys."

"Are we ready to roll?" Kristina asked.

"I think Jill should wear a bit of lipstick and..."

Jill cut me off. "Forget it, Fletcher. I'm not there to encourage the barflies."

* * *

We delivered an Egg McMuffin to Hubert, who was apparently not a morning person. I waited patiently at the parsonage's basement door with the McDonald's bag in hand while listening to scraping sounds and mumbling from behind the door. Based on Hubert's appearance, I thought he probably slept in his clothes. He stared at me with bleary eyes, not speaking.

"I brought you breakfast," I said, holding out the bag.

Hubert stared at it for a moment. "I don't usually eat breakfast."

I pushed the bag into his hand. "Consider it a special treat, okay?"

He nodded, then stepped back, preparing to close the door.

"Hubert, where do you hear all of the information about the country club?"

He cocked his head while considering the question. "Just around."

"Where do you spend the day?"

"I clean the church first thing."

"And after that?"

"One of the church ladies usually brings me a sandwich and I eat."

"What do you do in the afternoon?"

"I usually trim the cemetery bushes or mow. You know, that's my job."

"Where do you meet the people who tell you about events in town?"

Closing his eyes, Hubert rubbed the whiskers on his chin. "Around."

"Do you walk around town or go to a bar?"

At the word *bar* he flinched. "I don't go to any bars. I told you, Pastor doesn't want me to drink." He paused then added, "Demon alcohol is what got me in trouble to begin with."

"How long have you been sober?" I asked.

Hubert dug his hand into his pocket and handed me a bronze coin with the Roman numerals *IV* embossed on it.

Like someone had turned on the light in a dark room, I suddenly realized that Hubert attended Alcoholics Anonymous meetings. I handed the coin back to him and said, "I'm really proud of you. It takes a lot of character to admit you have an alcohol problem and to become engaged in AA. How often do you attend meetings?"

"There are meetings most nights. If there's a church dinner, I skip my meeting that night."

"Where are you meeting tonight?"

Hubert tipped his head back and closed his eyes. "If today is Tuesday, we're meeting in the Episcopal Church."

"It's actually Wednesday."

"Oh, sure. Wednesdays we meet at the school." As if suddenly aware of me, he asked, "Do you belong to AA?"

"I've never attended meetings, but I quit drinking hard liquor after my divorce."

"Our Wednesday meetings are open. Would you like to come as my guest?"

A vision of me sitting with a circle of people who were discussing their alcoholism flashed through my mind. My first instinct was to recoil. Then, I realized that Hubert was offering me an opportunity to join his social circle, the people who discussed town politics and passed rumors.

"Should I meet you here, or at the school?"

"I walk to the school at six-forty-five for our seven o'clock meeting. Afterwards, we sit around drinking coffee and eating snacks or go out for coffee. If you're extra, we'll need to bring extra snacks. People like cookies."

"I'll meet you here at six-forty-five and I'll have cookies."

Hubert started closing the door, then pushed it back open. "We're not picky. Store bought cookies are okay."

"Thanks for the tip."

Kristina appeared irritated when I got into the squad. "Did you have to wait around while Hubert ate his Egg McMuffin?"

"I found out where Hubert gets all his inside information about the comings and goings of Hodgenville. He's in AA."

"What does that have to do with the rumor mill?"

"He attends a meeting every night of the week. After their meeting, the members drink coffee and socialize. I think it's part of the twelve-step program, moving away from the social groups associated with your alcoholism. The AA members bond with each other and reinforce their sobriety. Hubert invited me to tonight's meeting."

Jill laughed. "You're finally going to fess up that you have an alcohol problem and join AA?"

"I'm going as Hubert's guest. I'm more interested in his group of friends and what they have to say about the country club, McInnises, and Carlisles."

"Isn't that unethical?" Kristina asked. "Aren't the people in AA supposed to remain anonymous? What's said in AA, stays in AA."

"I think they only announce their first names when they talk. I won't identify any of the members or divulge their stories. However, if they're socializing after the meeting and providing information pertaining to people outside of the group, I'll listen."

Looking pained, Kristina glared at me. "I don't like it."

"I won't misrepresent myself. If people wish to remain anonymous, I'll honor that. I won't do anything illegal."

"There's a fine line between illegal and immoral," Kristina replied.

"I won't coerce information or lie about who I am or how I'm going to use what I hear."

Kristina wrinkled her nose. "You may get a lot of dubious hearsay information."

"I agree. That dubious information won't provide grounds for a search warrant. On the other hand, it may offer lines of inquiry we hadn't considered."

Hearing chuckling from the backseat, I turned to face Jill. "What?"

"I am picturing you, sitting in a folding chair, cup of coffee in hand. 'My name is Doug and I'm an alcoholic. I've been sober since I had a beer with pizza last week.'"

"As I understand it, guests are welcome. It's perfectly acceptable to listen to their sobriety stories while considering your own situation. Sharing is optional."

Kristina glanced at me and asked, "Have you considered Hubert a suspect? He seems to know a lot of inside information about the murder, crime scene, and victim."

"What motive would he have? He has nothing to gain from McInnis' death."

"I'm just saying, let's not ignore the possibility that Hubert is somehow involved."

"Hubert's not bright. But he's smart enough not to tell a cop details about a murder he's committed."

* * *

264

We dropped Jill at the country club and talked to the parking valet until we were certain she wasn't going to be thrown out for showing up without an escorting member. After that, Kristina and I drove to Carlisle's farm, chatting about Texas, our South Dakota horses, and the circumstances that delivered my suburban mother to a ranch in the Black Hills.

The Carlisles' front door opened before we exited the car. Robert met us on the top step looking concerned. "Is something wrong? Is there a problem at the distillery?"

I let Kristina take the lead. "Could we talk inside? I'd like to give you and Mrs. Carlisle an update on one of the distillery break-in cases."

"Glinda is in the barn. I'll page Pedro and ask him to send her to the house." He held the door for us and led us to a breakfast nook in the kitchen. After starting a pot of coffee in a machine that looked like it might be nuclear powered and cost as much as my house, he punched a number into his cell phone and spoke to Pedro. After disconnecting, he said, "She's with the farrier. Pedro's going to ask her to come in."

Following a hiss of steam, the coffee machine played a few musical notes, announcing the completion of the brew cycle. Carlisle retrieved coffee mugs decorated with the Running Acres Distillery logo and set out four of them. "Glinda designed the logo," he explained.

I inspected the running horse logo which consisted of four white streaks that somehow created a running horse. "That's a very clever design. I would've guessed the logo had been created by an advertising firm."

"Glinda is very artistic. We met in college when she was a graphic arts major. Now she dabbles in painting, sculpture, and blowing glass."

"And horses," Kristina suggested.

Carlisle sighed. "Yes, and horses. And tennis."

"You don't seem pleased about her involvement in the stable," I observed.

"I've got Pedro running the operation, a trainer, and a bevy of grooms, riders, and other horse people."

"What's the problem?"

Carlisle looked at the door as if making sure Glinda wasn't walking in. "She interferes. I've got the best of the best, and Glinda is constantly injecting herself into decisions. I spend as much time smoothing ruffled feathers as I do..." The door opened and Glinda stepped in. "...golfing."

Glinda nodded to us as she pulled off her boots and set them next to the door. "Be a dear and pour me a cup," she said to Robert.

As he poured coffee for his wife, Carlisle asked, "Why are you making the big reveal in person? A phone call would've been sufficient."

"It's a big break," Kristina replied. "I wanted you, the distillery owner, to be the first to hear it. I brought Investigator Fletcher along because it was his shrewd plan that broke the case."

Carlisle frowned as he sat. "Where is your partner, Mr. Fletcher?"

"She's pursuing a different part of the investigation. We hope to pull together more of the pieces in the coming days."

Carlisle leaned back and considered Kristina and me. "If I didn't know better, I'd think you were setting up a *Columbo* kind of scene. One of you is the good cop, the other is the bad cop. After grilling me, one of you will pause as you walk to the door and will say, 'Ah, just one more thing.'"

I chuckled and replied, "I wish I was as good as *Columbo*. He solved every crime in ninety minutes. I have cases that have been open for decades."

A smirk flickered on Carlisle's lips. "I sincerely doubt that Mr. Fletcher. You strike me as a skilled investigator. Why else would the US Park Service send you here from Texas to investigate something as common as a simple murder?"

"My boss likes to keep me busy. Besides, I get tired of tracking down cold cases. Working a fresh murder case with someone as skilled as Detective Baker is a thrill."

I stood as Glinda sat down. Without makeup, Glinda looked twenty years older than the last time I'd seen her. Her eyes were puffy with dark rings underneath, like she had a hangover. The crow's feet at the corners of her eyes made her appear closer to sixty than thirty. She took a sip from the mug her husband handed her and leaned back. "What's going on?"

I looked at Kristina who said, "We made an arrest in the burglary last night."

I watched Glinda, who flinched. She quickly recovered without saying anything. Her husband's reaction was more expressive. "Damn!" he said, having been burned by the hot coffee spilled on his hand.

"Grab a towel out of the second drawer," Glinda said, watching him shaking his burned hand and cursing. She made no move to help.

We waited for Carlisle to sop up the spilled coffee. He rubbed the burn as he sat. "How many bottles did you recover? Who had it? I hope you throw the book at the sonofabitch."

Kristina waited patiently for him to stop ranting. "We recovered most of it, but several bottles are missing and were likely sold."

Without letting Kristina finish Carlisle stood. "When can we pick it up?"

"Please sit down," I said. "The bourbon is evidence in the burglary, and it has to remain in police custody for now."

Carlisle sat, then ran his fingers through his hair. "Shit. We need those bottles. Can I drop the charges and get the booze back?"

I watched Glinda. I expected her to react to her husband's histrionics. Instead, she checked her watch.

"You *can not* drop the charges and get the bottles back. The McInnis murder is still under investigation and the thieves may be involved in that crime," Kristina explained.

Carlisle seemed to deflate as he reasoned through Kristina's explanation. "Oh. Yes. Of course. Solving Mac's murder is the big issue here. What's going to happen?"

"At Investigator Fletcher's suggestion, we've requested warrants to tap several phones and monitor cell phones and text messages from several involved parties. We hope to identify the additional people involved in both the burglary and murder."

Carlisle nodded. I glanced at Glinda and watched the color drain from her face. She wobbled for a second and I placed my hand on her arm. "Are you okay?"

Quickly composing herself, Glinda nodded. "Sorry. I think my blood sugar is crashing."

Carlisle rushed to the refrigerator. "I'll get you some orange juice." As he poured, he added, "Didn't you eat after your insulin?"

"No, the farrier arrived, and I went right out to the barn." She accepted a small glass of orange juice and drank it down and then looked at her watch again. "Please excuse me. I've got a tennis lesson, and I need to change."

Carlisle looked disgusted. "You could skip one damn lesson. The world wouldn't end."

Dismissing his comments with a wave, Glinda took a final sip of juice and walked out of the kitchen.

"She's got lessons two and three times a week. You'd think she'd be ready for Wimbledon pretty soon, wouldn't you?"

"That's all we had," Kristina said, standing. "We wanted to update you."

Carlisle reached out and pumped Kristina's hand. "Thank you. This is the first hopeful news I've had since Mac's death. Please keep me updated." He turned to me and repeated his thanks.

A red Range Rover was racing out of the driveway when we exited the house. When we got in the squad car, Kristina smiled. "Looks like Glinda recovered from her blood sugar crash and got changed rather quickly."

I took out my cell phone and punched in Jill's number. "Glinda is on her way to the country club. She should be there in fifteen minutes."

I heard Jill excuse herself, then waited until she found a secure spot to speak. "Thank God. Has anyone ever died of tomato juice poisoning? I'll never drink another bloody mary again."

"You could sip them slowly," I replied, chuckling.

"Are you kidding? There are three lined up in front of me. Every unaccompanied guy who's walked into the bar has bought me a drink. I've been hit on more times than I was in high school and college combined," Jill hissed.

"Glinda went for the bait. She was as white as a ghost when Kristina announced the phone taps and cell phone monitoring. She rushed off to her tennis lesson."

"How did Mr. Carlisle react?"

"His reactions ran the gamut. Happy. Angry. *When can I get the bourbon back*? He even offered to drop the burglary charges if he could recover the bottles immediately."

"He wasn't concerned about solving the McInnis murder?"

"Not until we reminded him that was our primary focus."

"It sounds like we can check him off the suspect list." Jill paused and spoke with a man in the background. I overheard a comment about finishing their drinks and then checking out his backyard hot tub. Jill politely declined, then came back on the phone. "Get me out of here! This place is Sodom and Gomorrah filled with creepy middle-aged men."

"If the country club is her destination, Glinda should be there any time now. See who she meets and try to catch their conversation. We're on our way."

"Whoa! Change of plans. The tennis instructor just flew out of the ladies' locker room and is running to her car."

"Get a description of the car and a license number if you can."

"What's going on?" Kristina asked.

"Lights and siren," I replied. "The tennis coach just ran out of the country club. She headed for her car."

I was pushed back in my seat as Kristina accelerated and activated her unmarked car's lights and siren. She broadcast a description of Glinda's red Range Rover and asked for anyone seeing it to pull her over.

Jill was breathing hard when she next spoke. "The tennis instructor's car is a little blue thing, maybe a Mazda Miata convertible. A little two-seater. The license number is ten-Sierra-November-Echo-One."

I repeated the license number to Kristina.

"You're kidding. Really?"

"What?"

"10SNE1. You don't get it? Ten-S-N-E-One." When I shook my head she said, "Tennis anyone?"

I sighed. "Just radio it in."

After relaying the license number to her dispatcher, Kristina took a turn with the squad's tires squealing.

"Where are we going? This isn't the road to the country club."

"If Glinda and her coach are going to meet somewhere away from the country club, they're probably going toward E-town.

This is a crossroads that cuts between the club and town."

"We're no longer enroute to the club. We are attempting to intercept the meeting between Glenda and her coach. Talk to the club manager and get the coach's name and home address."

"Gladly. Anything to get me away from the bar."

"Find someone who'll give you a ride to the sheriff's office. Or call an Uber."

"I'll figure it out. Catch them!"

Chapter 18

Kristina's route cut through farmland with very little traffic. Stone fences defined the edges of the road, leaving no shoulders. The one car we met pulled over and let us pass. A few miles later, we slowed, and Kristina turned off the siren as we approached a crossroads.

We stopped one hundred yards short of the intersection. "Come on tennis coach, where are you?" Kristina asked rhetorically as she tapped her fingers on the steering wheel.

"Is there somewhere they could've met between the country club and here?"

"Not unless they pulled up to someone's house. There's nothing in between there and here except for a dollar store. If she doesn't drive past in the next minute or two, I'll backtrack her likely route."

A blue speck appeared on the crossroad, approaching us from the direction of the country club. It streaked past and Kristina accelerated.

"Don't you just love it when a plan works out?" she said, smiling.

"Don't gloat yet."

"She's got to be going over a hundred miles an hour," Kristina observed as she turned the corner and sped up to keep the Miata in sight.

"Luckily, you've got about four times the horsepower of that little sports car. I just hope we don't come over the hill and find her wrapped around a tree. She's probably unaccustomed to high-speed driving."

Focused on the rolling road ahead, Kristina commented, "Sadly, about half of our chases seem to end in a crash. Everyone thinks they can outrun a cop car. They don't know how their vehicle handles at high speeds. We spend weeks training for chases."

"That last sign said Elizabethtown two miles. She's got to slow down."

Kristina's nervous chuckle was chilling. "She'll either have to slow down or she's going to be an ornament in the town square. This road ends in a T at the courthouse."

We closed the gap between us and the Miata as the speed limit dropped to forty, then thirty. We were now a block behind the Miata when we slowed to twenty-five. Sidewalks and brick commercial buildings lined both sides of the city street. Matching the Miata's speed, Kristina followed, hoping not to be spotted. "Come on, tennis lady, where are you meeting Glinda?"

The Miata stopped to allow a car to back out of a parking spot across from the old courthouse. The Miata zipped into the vacated spot. The tennis coach got out and walked down the sidewalk.

"There's no other parking spot here," I said. "Let me out and I'll follow her."

"Take it easy, Fletcher, the traffic isn't moving any faster than the pedestrians and her tennis whites stand out like a neon sign. You'd might as well ride until she steps into a shop or turns down a side street. Besides, if you're following her on foot, she might sprint to get away. What was it Jill said this morning? Your foot chasing days are over."

As Kristina predicted, the coach glanced around to see if anyone on the sidewalk was following her, then she darted around a corner. "Get ready to bail out if she disappears or walks into a store." Kristina turned the corner as the coach opened the passenger door of a white car parallel-parked along the street. The door was barely closed when the car darted out of the parking spot, nearly sideswiped by the aging Buick ahead of us. The white Infiniti accelerated but was trapped in the slow mid-morning traffic.

"Did you see the driver?" I asked.

"I had the impression it was a man. But I really didn't see enough of his face to identify him." We followed as the Infiniti tried to find a gap in the oncoming traffic so he could pass the slow pickup in front of him.

"He's going to make a break for it as soon as he gets past that pickup."

"Yes, and half the cars in Kentucky are white, which will make it hard to follow him if he gets too far ahead of us," Kristina observed.

The words were hardly out of her mouth when the Infiniti pulled out to pass the pickup. The oncoming car veered to the right, nearly hitting a woman pushing a shopping cart. The Infiniti's driver cut back into the traffic lane, where our view of him was hidden by the slow-moving pickup. Kristina activated her flashers and siren, which caused the pickup to stop in the street. The driver looked at us in the rearview mirror and threw up his hands. Kristina gestured for him to pull ahead. He eventually found an alley and let us pass. By then, the Infiniti was out of sight.

We drove out of town, Kristina switched off her siren as we checked for the Infiniti down each side street and in every parking lot. Ahead, I saw yellow flashing lights mounted on a school-zone sign.

"He must've slowed down here."

Kristina glanced at me. "Yeah, it's well known that fleeing felons slow down for school-zones. We routinely try to chase criminals into school zones to arrest them."

"Smartass."

We were passing the school building when I looked ahead, hoping to see the Infiniti racing down a side street. "Wait! The tennis courts!"

Kristina turned hard, jumping the curb and pulling into the school parking lot. Cruising slowly down the row of parked cars, we approached the Infiniti which was parked next to a red Range Rover. Two women and a man were having a heated discussion, oblivious to our approach. Glinda waved her arms wildly and was getting into the face of the man giving back as much as he was getting. The tennis coach watched with her hands on her hips.

"Can you read lips?" Kristina asked as she rolled to a stop, blocking the two vehicles.

"I don't need to read lips to know that every other word starts with an F."

We left the squad's doors open and approached the threesome, our hands on the butts of our pistols. I briefly thought about the bulletproof vest in Kristina's trunk.

"Glinda Carlisle!" Kristina shouted to be heard over the argument.

Glinda spun to face us, fire in her eyes. "What the fuck do you want?" As soon as the words were out of her mouth, she froze.

The man, who wore sunglasses and a baseball cap, turned toward us as the tennis coach spun around. His golf shirt and khaki pants would've fit into any American workplace. Noticing Kristina's hand on the butt of her gun, he froze. He glanced at me, momentarily weighing his chances of pushing past me and jumping into the Infiniti. Then, he realized his car was blocked by Kristina's squad. Composing himself while Glinda seethed, he held out his hands to show he wasn't a threat.

The tennis coach looked at me, then at Kristina. As if we were irrelevant, she walked toward the Infiniti's passenger door.

"Please stop," I said.

"Get out of my way," she spat. "I'm leaving."

I put my left hand on the Infiniti's door, blocking her access. "Not right now. We're going to have a discussion."

She stopped at the front fender and glared at me. "I don't know what you think is going on, but I'm not a party to it."

A cell phone started playing an unfamiliar song and the man glanced at his pants pocket.

"Do you need to get that?" Kristina asked, smiling.

"Um, they'll leave a message."

"Are you sure? They might need to place their bet before the next race at Keeneland."

"I don't know what you're talking about," the man replied.

I squatted down to look inside the Infiniti. "Are there any weapons or drugs in the car?" The tennis coach looked at the man with fear. "Would you give us permission to search your car?" I added.

"I definitely will *not* give you permission to search my car."

I looked at Glinda. "How about you, Mrs. Carlisle. May I search your vehicle?"

She blinked as if taking a mental inventory of the Range Rover's contents but didn't reply.

"Actually, I can just look in the windows and see whatever you have. Unless you have an unregistered gun or drugs under the seat."

Indignant, Glinda replied, "I don't have a gun *or* any drugs."

I walked to the Range Rover's door and looked inside, shielding my eyes from the sun's glare. "I don't suppose the insulated cup in your console is a bloody mary."

Glinda closed her eyes, then turned to the man. "Well, Reggie."

"Well, what?" he asked.

"What do you plan to do?"

"I plan to tell these officers they don't have probable cause to search my vehicle or to detain me. I plan to drive away." He started walking toward the Infiniti.

"No," Kristina said. "I see a bulge under your golf shirt that looks suspiciously like a pistol in a holster."

"I have a concealed carry permit."

"Wonderful!" Kristina replied. "Please slowly remove your wallet and show me your permit."

"I...ah...keep it in my glove compartment."

"Perfect!" Kristina replied. "Investigator Fletcher can retrieve it for you."

"Um, no. I'll get it myself."

I eased my pistol from the holster and held it alongside my leg. "That's not happening unless I verify there isn't a firearm or something dangerous inside the car first."

Glinda was fed up. "I'm calling Robert. He'll get in touch with his lawyer, and we'll get all of this cleared up."

"Sir, what is your name?" Kristina asked.

The man smiled, trying to look harmless. "Why do you need my name? I'm just an innocent person having a conversation with my wife and her friend."

The man looked familiar, and I recalled where I'd seen him. "Actually, we met Reggie when he was with Mr. Carlisle and his attorney. Unless I'm mistaken, Abigail is Glinda's tennis coach and is married to Reggie." The same ringtone played on the man's cell phone again. I smiled and asked, "Are you sure you don't need to answer that?"

"It's fine. I'll get back to them."

The tune had hardly finished when it restarted. Reggie clenched his jaw and glared at me. "I have an investment business to run. Am I being arrested, or am I free to leave?"

"Actually," I replied, "I'd like to know why you have overalls from the distillery in your backseat."

"I have no idea what you're talking about. If there's some...overall in my backseat, I have no idea how it got there."

Keeping my eyes on the trio, I walked behind the Infiniti and made a show of sniffing the air. I leaned over and sniffed around the trunk's seams, like a drug-sniffing dog. "If I'm not mistaken, I detect the aroma of Running Acres bourbon. Kristina, I think there's a broken bottle in the trunk. We need to seize this car until you can get a search warrant."

Glinda went ballistic and pointed at the man. "You stupid shit! You're driving around with half a million worth of booze in the trunk of your car?"

The man spun to face Glinda. "Shut up! That cop is baiting you."

The tennis coach looked like she was ready to faint. The color drained from her face, and she put one hand on the car's fender to steady herself. "What's wrong?" Kristina asked.

The tennis coach's mouth moved like a goldfish, but didn't make a sound.

Glinda flapped her arms. "Abigail, where *is* the bourbon? Is it still in your Miata or is it in the Infiniti?"

The man held his hands out at waist level and started taking backward steps. "Everyone. Stop. Talking. Now. This is bullshit. The cops are baiting you. Stop talking!"

"Which one of you killed McInnis?" I asked, focusing on Reggie who appeared ready to sprint away.

Kristina moved to her left, cutting off a path that led between the tennis courts. "Sir, stop walking and put your hands behind your head."

"This is a misunderstanding," he protested. "We can sort this all out."

Glinda dug in her pocket, presumably for her cell phone. "Mrs. Carlisle, remove your hand from your pocket!" I ordered.

"No. I have to call Robert's attorney."

While I focused on Glinda, Kristina had drawn her gun. She yelled at Reggie, "Use your left hand to remove the pistol, then drop it on the ground."

I realized Abigail was screaming with her hands clamped over her ears. I looked at Reggie, who was removing his pistol with two fingers from his left hand. Once clear of his holster, Reggie dropped the gun at his feet.

Kristina skirted around him and kicked his pistol farther away. "Doug! Call for backup!"

I pulled out my cell phone and dialed 911.

Chapter 19

Abagail was being interviewed by Hardin County deputies. Meanwhile, Glinda and Reggie were seated in the backseat of two squads while other deputies verified that they had permits for their pistols. Kristina and I supervised the loading of both the Range Rover and Infiniti onto flatbed tow trucks for transport to a secure garage. Kristina nudged my arm as another police vehicle turned into the parking lot. "Straighten up, the sheriff's here."

Jill emerged from the passenger door as the sheriff stepped from the driver's side. Both of them looked solemn as they approached. Half a step behind the sheriff, Jill flashed a thumbs up sign to me.

The sheriff stopped next to me and shook his head. "Helluva thing."

"Yep."

The sheriff gestured toward the tennis courts, and I followed him. Jill hung back, aware of the upcoming conversation. "Kristina said you spotted the distillery coveralls in the back of Reggie's car."

"I saw something that looked like distillery coveralls," I bluffed. I paused, then asked, "I assume Reggie is known to you?"

Looking at Reggie seated in a nearby car, the sheriff nodded. "He's a local financial advisor. I didn't know he was running a betting ring from his phone."

"Between tennis lessons, Abigail handles his bets at the country club. Glinda Carlisle was their biggest customer and biggest loser."

The sheriff looked at Glinda, who turned her head. "I wonder how deep she is and what she might be willing to do to pay off her debt?"

"I wonder which of them cooked up the scheme to steal the bourbon and smash the rest to drive up the price of the remaining bottles?"

The sheriff glanced at me, then back at the scene. "Once Abigail hires a lawyer, I assume she'll paint Glinda as a loser desperate to cover her losses, and Reggie as the predator who took advantage of her desperation."

"I can't see Glinda killing McInnis."

"That must've been Reggie. Although, I can't figure out how he lured McInnis to the park or why he killed him."

"Let me try out a scenario for you. There'd been a break-in at the rickhouse, but nothing was stolen. I wonder if it was Reggie who broke in to try and understand what McInnis was up to."

The sheriff raised his eyebrows. "That's a theory."

"I wonder how much money Robert Carlisle has invested with Reggie?"

The sheriff cocked his head. "Do you think Robert Carlisle was in on it too?"

"If it was my case, I'd ask a judge for a warrant to see Reggie's client list and Carlisle's investments. I think he had a lot of money invested in aging bourbon and Reggie was concerned he wasn't getting a financial advisor's percentage of that investment. I'd also look at the cash flow from Carlisle's stud syndicate. I wonder if it's as profitable as he tells people it is? He's got a lot of people on his farm and distillery payrolls."

The sheriff turned and stared at the school. "Do you think the motive is as simple as Reggie missing out on a percentage of Carlisle's investment income?"

"I don't know how large of an investment portfolio the Carlisles have, but if Reggie gets a percent or two a year of whatever he's managing for them, he's probably unhappy about Carlisle's investment in the distillery."

"A financial advisor gets one or two percent of the portfolio *every year*?" the sheriff asked.

"I think that's common," I replied. "Advisors are usually adamant about diversified portfolios. I bet Reggie urged Robert to diversify, not anticipating that he would invest a big chunk of money in a risky start-up distillery that wouldn't yield any profit for seven years."

The sheriff nodded. "That's a real Kentucky kind of investment, more based in pride than good sense."

"We've received some great tips from Hubert, the church janitor. I suggested that Kristina bring him a treat once a week. He's got his finger on the pulse of what's happening around town. He's invisible to people. They open up to him and say things they assume he doesn't understand and won't repeat."

"Hubert? The church janitor?" the sheriff asked, frowning. "He's only about half there."

"Hubert is smarter than people give him credit for. And he's a good listener."

* * *

Kristina dropped us at the B&B. Bitsy was reading a magazine at the dining room table when we walked in. "Which one of you arrested Glinda Carlisle?" she asked, smiling.

I smiled back. "As you know, we can't comment about an ongoing investigation."

"I know," she admitted. "But knowing doesn't stop me from asking the question. Why don't you two freshen up? We're having a light supper tonight."

Jill took a shower while I laid out fresh clothes. She found me lying on the bed and

287

staring at the ceiling. "What are you thinking?"

"We've got three suspects. They're guilty of gambling and a burglary but I don't think any of them killed McInnis."

"Okay, who does that leave?"

Sitting up and gathering my clothes, I replied, "Mac's unidentified mistress."

"Fine. What's her motive and how are we going to identify her?"

I stood under the shower with hot water pounding my back while pondering the questions of motive, means, and opportunity? *Tamsin McInnis wanted to move back to Scotland. She claims her husband was having an affair. Was she unhappy enough to kill her husband?*

I rushed out of the bathroom as Jill pulled a shirt over her head. "Let's assume Tamsin, homesick and fed up with Kentucky, confronted Alistair and threatened to go back to Scotland. McInnis meets with his mistress and announces that he's not going to leave his wife and is returning to Scotland with her."

"Sure, the woman scorned. How many times have we heard about a cheating husband who's promised his mistress he's going to get a divorce so he could marry her? Like ninety percent of the time the divorce doesn't happen. Or, if there is a divorce, the cheating husband finds a different mistress to cheat with on the previous mistress."

"That's true," I replied, "and most mistresses end up bitter and broken. We need to find one who has enough resilience to say, 'screw you, buddy. You may be dumping me, but this is not my end, this is *your* end.'"

"I suppose Alistair's mistress could be any woman in Hodgenville or E-town."

Closing my eyes for a second, I thought. "It's not some random woman he met in a bar. He's been working closely with his suppliers and potential customers. The wife of one of the farmers?"

"Charlotte!" Jill exclaimed. "She and McInnis spent many evenings with potential customers. What if McInnis promised to marry her, then broke it off? She would've been on the brink of being married to a guy who owns half of a potentially profitable distillery. She finds out the guy she's been sleeping with isn't going to leave his wife and now she's not going to own part of the distillery she's helping build."

"Wow. From Charlotte's point of view, the world revolves around her."

"When we were looking at the game camera video, she told Carlisle she and McInnis had been running the show. But Mac was busy schmoozing potential customers. Charlotte thinks she's steering the ship."

The pieces continued to fall into place in my mind. "Yes, she told us the game camera belonged to her second ex. She's been grooming Alistair to be husband number three."

* * *

Bitsy fed us salads and sandwiches. At six-fifteen, I glanced at my watch and excused myself. "I have a meeting to attend."

Bitsy frowned. "At this time of night?"

Smirking, Jill said, "Doug's going to an Alcoholics Anonymous meeting with Hubert."

"I didn't realize you were in the program."

"I had a problem. I'll never forget when liquor controlled my life."

"Good for you! I applaud anyone who can turn their back on demon rum." Bitsy turned to Jill. "I've got a Bible study group tonight if you'd like to fill your evening."

Jill's smirk disappeared, "Um, thanks for the offer, but I need to work on my report."

"Surely your report will wait until after the Bible study," Bitsy urged.

Seeing another possible opportunity for gathering information, I asked, "How much time do you spend discussing the Bible vs. socializing?"

"Depending on the group, it's probably fifty-fifty. We'll be drinking sweet tea and eating cookies, too."

The cookie comment fired a memory. "Bitsy, I'm supposed to bring cookies to my meeting. I forgot to stop at the store."

"Follow me. We'll put a dozen in a Tupperware container. You promise to bring my container back, right?"

* * *

Hubert was standing in front of the parsonage as I approached. He looked like a hobo, with tattered clothes, hunched shoulders, and the downtrodden demeanor of someone down on their luck. With his hands in his pockets, he waited patiently.

"I wasn't sure you were serious," he said as we walked together.

"I'm looking forward to the meeting. I've heard about AA meetings, but I've never attended one."

"You told me you quit drinking. Cold turkey?"

"Cold turkey. One night, I realized I needed to crawl out of the booze bottle and get my life together."

Hubert's head bobbed. "I guess that's how all of us get there. Some people can do it on their own. Some can't manage to kick the bottle even with help."

"I know a few people who went through treatment after getting ticketed for a DUI. Some of them stuck with the program."

"Lots don't," Hubert replied. "You've got to want to make it work. Lots of people are forced into rehab. It really doesn't work unless you're convinced you need it."

We walked in silence the rest of the way to the school. Hubert led me to a side door, then around a corner into a classroom where a dozen chairs were arranged in a circle. A coffee pot gurgled on a nearby counter where several plates and trays of baked goods were placed. Everyone in the room stopped talking and stared at me, the newcomer. I brought my Tupperware to the counter and removed the lid.

A white-haired man wearing a pin declaring him a Vietnam veteran approached me. "Welcome to the Wednesday evening group."

"Hubert invited me. He said this is an open group."

"It is. Anyone is welcome. Where are you in your addiction journey?"

"I'm a couple of years sober. I've never been to an AA meeting, but I have immense respect for what you do and the discipline you have to stick with it."

"Everyone is concerned about your badge."

I unclipped the badge from my belt and put it into my pocket. "I understand what's said here, stays here."

"Welcome. Take a seat. You can share if you want to. Otherwise, listen and understand that you're not facing anything unique. We've all been down and now we're celebrating our sobriety and the success that comes with it."

A man and woman walked in as we took our seats. The group ranged from a woman who appeared to be in her twenties to the white-haired vet who'd greeted me. As the evening progressed, the members introduced themselves by first name only, said they were recovering alcoholics, and shared stories about what was working for them, and the struggles that continued.

When they got to me, I said, "I'm Doug, who's just visiting." No one had a problem with that. And the introductions moved on.

After an hour, a guy with a graying ponytail and wire-rim glasses introduced himself as Ske. He said he was an alcoholic who now worked as an addiction counselor at the county jail. He'd been divorced and now lived with his dog. After Ske spoke, the Vietnam Vet named Jerry announced a break and everyone got in line for coffee.

A burly man stood alongside me and offered his hand. "I'm Gene."

"Nice to meet you."

"You're a cop?"

"I'm actually a Park Service investigator."

"Your drinking didn't end your career?"

"This is my second career. I quit drinking in between a previous job, a divorce, and a life reset."

We poured coffee and took a cookie each before Gene directed me to a corner. "I've done a lot of things over the years, from driving a semi to driving a school bus. I met some good cops and a few bad ones."

"There are good and bad people, regardless of your occupation. I've tried to be fair with people who treated me well."

Gene nodded, obviously in thought. "Did you hear the joke about..." He proceeded to tell me an involved joke about a highway patrolman and an annoying fly.

I laughed at the punchline, and Gene smiled.

"A cop ticketed me for a DUI despite my hard luck story." He paused and looked around the room. "That was my watershed moment. It was my second DUI, and I'd been in denial about my drinking. That cop told me he was giving me a ticket and he hoped it was the kick in the butt I needed to get my shit together. I was ready to punch him. But something about the way he said it made me think. When he showed up in court for my hearing, he wasn't a jerk or a shit. He walked up to me like a fellow human and said, 'Gene, for your own sake, I hope this is a wake-up call. Join AA and get your shit together. I genuinely hope I never pull you over again."

"And that did it?"

"Oh, hell. I've slipped a couple of times, but that was the start."

"Good for you! It's not easy."

Gene laughed. "Especially here! Every time I drive past a rickhouse, I smell the bourbon and my mouth waters."

Hubert joined us, and Gene threw his arm over Hubert's shoulder. "How are you doing, Hubert?"

"Good."

"Hubert's a man of few words. Because of that, people listen when he speaks. What's the good word tonight?"

"Tupperware."

Gene frowned and cocked his head. "Tupperware?"

"Yup. If Doug doesn't remember to return Miss Bitsy's Tupperware, she'll have his head."

"Oh, geez!" I said. "Is it empty? I should grab it before I forget again."

Ske walked up to me as I snapped the lid on the empty Tupperware container. "A group of us are going over to the Waffle Express for coffee and lies. Would you like to join us?"

"Yeah, I'd like that a lot."

Six of us, including Hubert, Gene, and Jerry, walked three blocks to the restaurant. They had a usual table in the back corner, and we threaded our way past the half dozen other patrons.

After coffee was poured, making me wonder if I'd get to sleep after all the late-night caffeine, Gene told a story about a winter trip through Minnesota and encountering his first blizzard. After we all laughed, he asked, "Are you in Kentucky working or vacationing?"

"I'm investigating the death of the bourbon maker who was found in Lincoln's Birthplace."

"Helluva thing," Jerry declared. "You aren't safe even in a national park!"

"The parks get the same criminals you find anywhere else," I explained.

"Really?" Gene asked. "I always thought they were safe, like Disneyland."

"That's a problem. Most people think they're safe, and they let their guard down."

"Who killed that guy?" Ske asked.

I looked at Hubert, who was silently drinking coffee, and thought about how he absorbed information from these conversations. "We don't know. We're still investigating."

"Huh," Gene interjected. "I thought you always arrested the spouse. I know for a fact that if something happened to my ex-wife, the sheriff would be pounding on my door before she was cold." Everyone laughed but nodded.

"It's rare for someone to be killed by a stranger," I explained.

"But you haven't arrested that Scottish guy's wife?" Jerry asked.

"I've got no evidence that she killed him."

The table went silent, and the others looked back and forth at each other. Ske finally said, "You know he was screwing his secretary, right?"

"I wasn't aware of that."

"He drives that green Jag, right?" Several heads nodded, and Ske went on, "Well, I saw someone standing next to that Jag swapping spit with a hot blonde in a skirt. As I recall, his wife is a redhead."

Jerry laughed. "You've got to be careful around those redheads. They've got short fuses."

"Like your second wife?" Ske asked. "Wasn't she the one who superglued your junk to your leg?"

Jerry held up his hands. "That was a great lesson about not going to bed angry."

The guys laughed and someone added, "Or pass out naked when your angry redheaded wife has a tube of superglue in her hand."

When the laughter died down, I asked, "Does McInnis' redheaded wife know about his affair with the secretary?"

Gene nudged my elbow. "In this town? Are you kidding? She probably knew every time he farted! She'd probably even figured out that they were getting together at that Lincoln park."

"They were having their affair in the park?"

"The owner of that green Jag was either a real history buff, or he was meeting someone there. I've seen him turn in there three or four times. You know, there's a whole string of empty cabins there."

"Are you stalking him?" I asked, attempting to sound like I was kidding. "Why would you see him turning into the park that many times?"

Gene chuckled. "Did you forget that I drive the school bus? I go past the park every afternoon at 3:30."

Ske nudged my other elbow. "Your biggest problem is figuring out whether the secretary killed him because he wouldn't leave his wife, or if the wife killed him because he was going to leave her for the secretary."

I glanced at Hubert as the others laughed. He was nodding in agreement.

As the last of the other customers left, our server returned to top off our coffee cups. Out of curiosity, I asked the middle-aged waitress, "Are these guys big tippers who deserve your bottomless cups of coffee and great service?"

A few chuckles came from the guys. She shook her head as she looked at each of the guys. "Let's say they tip slightly better than empty tables. More than anything, they make the quiet evenings pass more quickly."

I handed her a $20 bill and said I was buying the coffee. She nodded her thanks and slipped the money into her apron.

Gene elbowed me as the waitress walked away. "That's a bit overboard. She probably thinks you're hitting on her."

She stopped halfway to the cash register and turned. "I think your new friend is a gentleman, unlike the rest of you cheapskates."

Her comment brought a round of laughter from the guys. Ske spoke up, "You probably got hit on a lot more when you worked at the country club."

The waitress snorted. "I got hit on, groped, and outright propositioned. You guys are amateurs compared to that crowd."

"The country club sounds like a hotbed of cheating husbands," I said, hoping to open a discussion.

Jerry jumped in, "They're a different social group."

"Are there many social groups in town?"

Ske started counting off the groups on his fingers, "There's the Baptist dinner group, the Baptist choir group, the Free Church holy rollers, the country club, Ollie's Bar, and there are at least a couple of AA groups every night of the week."

"There's more than one AA group every night of the week?" I asked.

Ske nodded. "I think that has something to do with us living in bourbon central."

"I thought having dry counties and lots of teetotalling Baptists would minimize the number of AA groups."

"As much as the Baptists and holy rollers would like to believe that abstinence results in sobriety, I think the opposite is true. None of us ever learned to be social drinkers. I mean, there's no moderation models. If you drank, you drove to a different county where you could buy a bottle of booze, then you'd drink the whole thing that night."

Gene nodded, "Or you and a buddy would go in to buy a bigger bottle and the two of you would drink the whole thing."

"It seems like the country club folks would be learning to drink socially," I suggested, hoping to get back to more discussion about that setting.

"Nah," Gene replied. "They drink just as much. They pretend to be social, but they're just a higher class of drunks. The women are just as bad as the men. There are always a few cars in the country club parking lot when I drive by on the morning bus route. And you can't tell me those are cars with dead batteries."

Ske laughed. "That's why we sometimes call it the *divorce club*. It seems like every month, someone is either getting a divorce or leaving their spouse."

Jerry stood, ending the discussion. "I've got to work in the morning," he said as he set $5 on the table. The others got up, each throwing a dollar or two onto the pile.

Ske scooped up the money and carried it to the server as the group walked past the cash register. He winked at her and said, "I gathered the cash up so you wouldn't have to walk over."

She snorted as she sorted the cash. "You gathered it up so I wouldn't see that you didn't contribute to the pile."

I'd watched him throw in $2, so I knew he'd put in his share, but it seemed like the tips were a running joke among the guys and the server. He smiled and replied, "Next week I'll put in twice as much."

As we walked out of the door, she retorted, "Two times zero is still zero!"

Ske sidled up to me as we walked away. "We feel for her. Both of her ex-husbands beat her and left her with a kid. Those kids are both adults now, living with her. She supports them while they 'get on their feet.' Thanks for throwing the $20 in. It really means a lot to her."

Gene put his hand on my shoulder. "If you're around tomorrow, you should join our group at the community center. Megan always brings bars or cupcakes, which helps with attendance." He turned and added, "Isn't that right, Hubert?"

Hubert was lagging behind the group, enjoying their camaraderie without speaking. He nodded. "I like Megan's cupcakes."

We stopped at Gene's pickup, and he shook my hand. "Do you have a business card?"

I handed him my card. "Are you going to call me with a hot tip?"

He removed a pen from his pocket and scrawled a phone number on the back of my card before handing it back to me. "We all have our slips. If you're on the brink of having a drink, call me."

"I don't know how much longer we're going to be in Hodgenville."

"It doesn't make any difference where you are. Sometimes we just need to talk to someone else who's been there and can remind us why we're better off sober."

Touched, I fingered the card. "That's very kind of you."

"Like I said, we've all been there and needed a bit of encouragement to walk away from the bottle."

We watched the group drive away, then Hubert and I walked back to the church in silence. When we reached the parsonage, Hubert turned to me, but didn't speak.

"Thanks for inviting me. That's a great group of people."

Hubert jammed his hands into his pockets and stared at me. "Did they solve your murder?"

"I don't think so, although Gene offered some interesting comments."

"Do you ever stop being a cop, Doug?"

The question caught me off guard. Thoughts about my ruined first marriage and my past drinking flashed through my mind. "Not often."

"You asked questions about your murder when we're all just guys talking. Can't you just be...you?"

Dodging the question, I replied, "Local knowledge is often the key to solving a case. No one seemed reluctant to offer an opinion, and I didn't hide that I was an investigator."

Hubert considered my reply. "They knew who you were and what they were saying. I hope it was helpful."

"Did I embarrass you or cross over a line?"

Hubert considered my question for a moment, then shook his head before turning away and walking to the parsonage's basement door.

* * *

Realizing I might be out later than her curfew, Bitsy had kindly left the door unlocked. A note on the dining room table asked me to lock the front door and turn off the lights. I put the Tupperware in the sink and checked all of the doors and windows before turning off the lights.

Jill rolled over when I walked into the bedroom. "Late night. Did the alcoholics solve the murder?"

"Not entirely," I replied as I stripped down to my boxers. "They're convinced that Alistair McInnis was having an affair with the distillery manager and Tamsin knew about it."

Jill rolled over. "That's nice. Can we talk about it tomorrow?"

"I've had lots of caffeine and there's no way I'm falling asleep any time soon."

"There's a bookcase full of reading material downstairs. Try to be quiet when you come back to bed."

Chapter 20

Jill's showering woke me. I'd started a thriller and read until 2:00 AM. My eyes felt like they were filled with gravel, and my mouth tasted like a small animal had nested there. I was trying to blink the grit from my eyes when Jill came out of the bathroom. "Look who's awake."

"Sorta awake," I croaked.

"You tried to tell me something in the middle of the night."

"Charlotte and McInnis were having an affair. Tamsin knew about it."

"Bitsy probably has breakfast waiting for us. Tell me about it after we eat."

"Call Kristina while I shower."

"The sheriff gave her a day off. I don't think we can use her today."

* * *

Bitsy chatted as we ate. She thanked me for returning the Tupperware and asked about my evening with Hubert's AA group. After breakfast, I announced that we were taking a walk around the block. While walking, I explained all I'd heard from the

AA group. "I think they may be right. Charlotte and Alistair having an affair puts the case in a different light. If Tamsin threatened to return to Scotland without Alistair, he may have told Charlotte to meet him somewhere away from prying eyes to end the affair. According to the school bus driver, they'd been having their tryst somewhere in the park. McInnis probably met her there to end the affair, and Charlotte didn't take it well."

Jill frowned, then shook her head. "The murder location doesn't work. Charlotte is prim and proper. I can't see her traipsing around the trails and having a tryst in the woods."

"The tourist cabins are closed. Gene suggested that they were probably meeting there."

"I can't see Charlotte having a love fest in a deserted cabin. She looks more like a high-end hotel kind of woman."

I punched Kristina's number into my phone. "Hey, we need to go back to the murder scene. When can you pick us up?"

"Doug, the sheriff told me to take a day off."

"Do you remember when Tamsin McInnis accused her husband of having an affair?"

"Um, yeah. She thought Alistair and the chemist were getting together. That thread ended when Sophia told us she was a lesbian."

"What if Tamsin was right about the affair, but wrong about the partner? I think McInnis was having an affair with Charlotte, the distillery manager. She had the most to lose if Alistair McInnis ended their relationship."

"That's an interesting theory, but the sheriff sent me home."

"You still have a badge and pistol, right? So, you're technically just off duty."

"Doug, I'd have to pick you up in my minivan."

"Great! We'll be undercover."

Jill rolled her eyes while I waited for Kristina to reply.

"Fine. I'll be there in fifteen minutes."

"We'll be waiting out front."

Jill shook her head. "We're going to get her into trouble."

* * *

As we got into Kristina's minivan, she advised us to brush the crumbs and fries off the seats. "The kids are slobs, and cleaning the van hasn't been a priority."

"No problem," I replied. Jill inspected the two second-row captains' chairs and opted for the one behind Kristina as the door slid shut.

"Why are we going back to Lincoln's birthplace? The crime scene people have been over that spot where the body was found and the whole acre around it. If there was a clue, they would've found it."

"They were looking for pieces of evidence where he died. We're looking for something else."

"What's the missing piece?" Kristina asked.

"Was Charlotte at the park when McInnis was killed."

Kristina grimaced. "And you hope to determine that by returning to the park?"

"If there's a clue to their relationship there, we need to find it."

Kristina drove past the visitor center and parked in the lot farthest from the entrance. Jill paused next to the car, looking up the hill. "This is so impressive. A long set of stairs leading to a replica of the Lincoln Memorial."

Kristina joined her. "We came here on a school field trip when I was like ten years old. The fifty-six steps represent Lincoln's age when he died. The replica of Lincoln's homestead inside the monument seemed small even at that age. The ranger pointed out the wooden chimney. It's built to separate from the house. If it caught on fire, the chimney could be pushed away from the log cabin to keep it from burning down."

"A log chimney seems like a poor design," I observed. "It seems like you would build your chimney out of stones, at least."

Jill seemed deep in thought. "I suppose they viewed those cabins as temporary.

Folks moved every few years. I think the Lincoln family only lived here at Sunken Spring Farm for two years, then they moved to Knob Creek farther north. The family lived there for a few years before moving to Indiana."

We walked down a paved trail that led away from the birthplace monument and into a wooded area. A dirt path cut away from the main trail about a hundred feet from the parking lot. I saw the yellow crime scene tape strung between trees and bushes at the split. We followed Kristina down the well-worn dirt path where dozens of cops, the EMTs, and the coroner had passed in the previous days.

"Here it is," Kristina said, looking at the muddy spot in the creek where the body had been found.

I stood next to the yellow tape and made a 360° turn. As Kristina had pointed out, the crime scene techs had crushed every plant and overturned every stone within one hundred feet of the murder scene. Focusing farther away, I made another turn. "There!"

Jill and Kristina had been kneeling next to the creek. They stood and looked in the direction I was facing. "What? Where?"

"The guest cabins. There's a path leading here from over there."

"They're boarded up," Kristina replied. "The operator stopped renting them during the Covid outbreak, and they didn't reopen."

I walked through the bushy underbrush until I hit an older, overgrown trail that led from the nearest cabin to the creek. Although it was overgrown by weeds, there were fresh footprints in the dirt. The wooden steps looked unstable but held my weight as I climbed them. The door looked like it had been secured by a single board nailed in place. The nails into the door were intact, but the nails driven into the wood molding were gone.

I reached for the doorknob, but Kristina stopped me. "We don't have a search warrant."

"No problem. This is an abandoned building on a Park Service property. It appears to have been vandalized, and I'm inspecting the damage."

The rusty hinges creaked as the door swung open. The cabin was tiny, containing only a double bed and a bathroom. I gestured for Kristina and Jill to follow. "Why would there be crumpled sheets, two pillows, and a blanket on a bed in an abandoned cabin?"

"Do you think this is the McInnis hideaway?"

I shook my head. "It's more likely that Charlotte has known about this spot for years. Maybe she and her previous lovers snuck out here. And the spot is perfect. Everyone knows the place is boarded up, so they ignore it."

Kristina pulled on plastic gloves and approached the bed. Gently lifting the sheet, she pulled it back. Finding nothing, she got on her hands and knees to look under the bed. "There are a couple of booze bottles under here. Let's back out of here and close the door. I'll call the crime lab and ask them to collect the sheets and bottles for prints and DNA."

Jill stared into the distance while Kristina made her calls. "This setting is too woodsy for someone like Charlotte."

"Let's check the other cabins and the lodge's back door."

As I had expected, all of the other buildings were boarded up with the nails intact. The only signs of habitation were mouse droppings and bugs. Seeing the house across the open lawn from the lodge, I walked over and rang the doorbell. The matronly owner answered a minute later and introduced herself as Greta.

"We noticed that the most distant cabin has a broken back door. Have you noticed any activity down there?"

Looking past me, Greta said, "I can only see the lodge and the first cabin from the house. I wouldn't know if anyone was down there, especially if they used the back door." Thinking through the implications of my question, her eyes went wide. "You don't think McInnis was killed there, do you?"

"I doubt it. However, it does look like someone has used it for..." I searched for a more appropriate term than the one that sprang to mind, "romantic interludes."

Chuckling, Greta shook her head. "Those darned teens will mess around anywhere they find a secluded spot. There's a rumor that a ranger chased a couple out of the replica of Lincoln's homestead housed inside the monument when he was locking up."

Looking back at the parking lot, I could see the top half of Kristina's minivan from our vantage point. "Have you noticed any vehicles parked where our minivan is on the day that Mr. McInnis was killed?"

Greta looked past my shoulder again and paused. "I don't recall any cars down there that day. But now that you mention it, the same pair of cars have been parked down there off and on for the past month or more."

Aware that the license plates were out of sight, I asked, "Can you tell me their make, model, and color?"

"I'm not sure I'd know your vehicle was a minivan before you told me it was." Greta paused for a moment, deep in thought. "One of them was really strange, the color was different depending on the light. It looked gray a lot of the time, but as the sun moved, it looked blue, then purple."

"That's a great observation. What do you recall about the other vehicle?"

Responding to my praise, she dug deep. "The other was a dark green sedan. I remember its chrome hood ornament. It stuck in my mind because modern American cars don't have hood ornaments. At first, I thought it was an older car, but then I reasoned that it was probably something foreign."

"Did you see the driver?"

"I think the windows were tinted. I don't remember seeing the driver."

I thanked Greta, then Jill and I walked across the parking lot toward the visitor center. Patience was at the welcome desk, and her face lit up when she recognized us. "Hey, Fletchers! Have you solved our murder yet?"

"Not yet," I replied with a laugh. "But we're working on it. I understand there've been cars parked at the bottom of the lot, near the creek access. Have you noticed them?"

Patience tapped her long fingernails on the counter as she thought. "Yeah, sure. They drive by separately, at slightly different times. They always park side-by-side at the farthest corner of the lot."

"Have you seen the drivers?"

"Not really. I mean that's a long way away and I'm usually more focused on the people inside the visitor center."

"Did you recognize the model of car?"

Patience smiled. "That green one's a nice ride. I Googled it. It's a Jaguar XJL."

"That's great. How about the gray car that parks next to it."

"The one that changes color? It's a Mustang."

Surprised by her quick response and my lack of knowledge about color changing cars, I paused. "A Mustang?"

Patience turned away from me and called to a young male ranger. "Hey, Tad. Come over here for a second."

The young ranger looked annoyed, and then shuffled over, displaying his displeasure at being summoned. "Tell my friend about the color-changing Mustang that drives through every once in a while."

Tad, who looked nerdy as hell, drew himself up, as if preparing to recite insider information to the uninformed. "It's not a *Mustang*, it's a Terminator Cobra. There were fewer than a thousand ever made with the Mystichrome color-shifting paint. They were only produced in 2004, four-hundred-eighty-five were convertibles and five hundred were coupes."

"Wow, who around here would drive a collector vehicle like that?" I asked, hoping to stroke Tad's ego and get him to spill more.

Tad's expression turned from appearing superior to disgust. "A woman my mother's age," he replied, nearly spitting out the answer.

"Do you know her name or where she lives?"

"No. Someone should take it away from her. She drives it like a Camry. A car like the Cobra needs to run wide open once in a while. You don't drive something like that to church or the grocery store."

"Or to a national historic site."

Tad shook his head dismissively. "Whatever. Do you have any other questions, or can I get back to work?"

I could see Jill bristle. Having been a superintendent, she *knew* that most of a ranger's job was answering questions. "One other thing, Todd."

The young man stopped mid-stride, turned, and glared at Jill. "Tad. My name is Tad, short for Thaddeus."

"Did you notice where the drivers of the Cobra and Jaguar went after they parked?"

"Do you mean after they kissed and walked away holding hands?"

"Describe them," I said.

"Two cheating old people shacking up somewhere their spouses won't catch them."

"A man and a woman, right?"

Tad shrugged. "Sure. Whatever."

"Did you recognize them?"

"Nope."

Getting irritated by Tad's insolence, I said, "This is part of a murder investigation, Tad. Describe the woman in detail."

"Was the guy the body they found in the creek?" Tad's interest was suddenly piqued.

"I'm not sure," I replied. "Start with the woman's description. What color hair did she have?"

"Blonde, I guess."

"Was she tall or short, fat or thin?"

"Medium height. About the same as the guy. She wasn't fat. I don't know. I didn't see her up close."

"You described her as old as your mother. You must've seen something that hinted at her age."

Tad considered that for a moment. "I think it was her shoes and the way she walked. She had fancy shoes that no one my age wears. And she took short steps, like old people do when they're afraid of falling down."

"Tell me about the man."

"He had kinda gray hair." Tad tilted his head. "You know how most people wear a jacket in the fall and spring? Well, this guy had some sort of brown suit jacket thingy."

"A tweed sports coat?" I asked.

"I guess."

"Where did they go after leaving the parking lot?"

"I never paid much attention. They went down the trail toward the creek. It looked like they needed a motel room. The woman was hanging all over him. It was...disgusting."

Kristina joined us in the gift shop just as Tad described the man. I saw her scribble a note she handed to Jill, who nodded and said, "Thanks, Tad and Patience."

Kristina led us out of the visitor center, stopping next to the handicapped parking spot. "Alistair McInnis was wearing a herringbone tweed sports coat when his body was found."

"Do you know a woman who drives a Ford Cobra with color-shifting paint?"

"Not off hand."

"Contact your dispatcher and find the ID of a woman who owns a 2004 Ford Cobra Terminator."

"That shouldn't be hard," Kristina replied as she took out her cell phone. "I imagine half the deputies in the county have pulled her over. A car like that looks like it's going a hundred-miles-an-hour when it's sitting still."

Kristina called in her request while Jill and I lingered outside the visitor center. Jill looked into a tree where a woodpecker was squawking. "A sports car fits Charlotte's persona."

We watched Kristina explain her request to the dispatcher, then waited. A moment later, Kristina broke into a smile. After ending the call, she approached us. "Charlotte owns a 2004 Cobra and a 2018 Ford pickup. I suppose the pickup is her foul-weather vehicle."

The pickup comment triggered a memory. After a few seconds, I recalled my discussion with Bitsy's parishioner at the barbeque restaurant. "A guy told me he'd seen McInnis going into an E-town motel with a blonde driving a jacked-up Ford pickup a couple of weeks before his murder."

"I don't suppose he got the license plate number," Kristina joked.

"No, but he said it was a place that rents rooms by the hour. I assume there aren't many blondes driving that kind of pickup."

Something on the road caught Kristina's eye. She snorted and shook her head. "It's the sheriff. The dispatcher warned me he was on the warpath and drivin' in this direction."

He burst out of his car and stalked up to us. "What in hell, Kristina? I told you to take the day off." He glared at me. "I suppose you dragged her into this!"

"I think we identified Alistair McInnis' murderer," I replied. "I invited Kristina along. She deserves to be part of this."

With his hands on his hips, the sheriff tipped his head back as if imploring God's assistance. "What have you discovered?"

I spent ten minutes updating the sheriff on our interviews and observations. I reassured him that Hubert wouldn't be called to testify. We'd used his information to focus our investigation, and not as the basis for search warrants or arrests. Following that discussion, Kristina led him to the back door of the tiny cabin and talked him through what we'd found. After that, she showed him how close the cabin was to the site of the murder.

Looking less skeptical, the sheriff asked Kristina, "What's your plan?"

"I'm going to contact the district attorney, so he's not surprised if forensics finds enough evidence to justify search warrants. We'll bring Charlotte in for questioning and impound her car for forensics." She waited while the sheriff mulled her plan.

Turning to me, the sheriff asked, "Are y'all in agreement?"

"One hundred percent."

Giving a nod of approval, the sheriff gestured for Kristina to lead us back to the parking lot where we met the forensics team, who were putting on coveralls. The sheriff said, "I hope to hell you're not stepping into a hornet's nest."

"Isn't that how every investigation goes?" she replied. "We constantly ruffle feathers and kick hornets' nests."

Snorting, the sheriff replied, "The country club hornets have bigger stingers than some of the others."

Chapter 21

After picking up the warrant from the district attorney, Kristina picked us up in front of the sheriff's office. A pair of uniformed deputies followed us to the distillery. Instead of parking in the guest spots in front of the distillery, Kristina circled in back where the workers parked, leaving the deputies out of sight from the building, but with a view of the driveway. In the farthest corner of the rear parking lot was a 2004 Cobra. Kristina smiled at me and said, "Don't you love it when a plan comes together?"

Jill stepped out of Kristina's squad and commented, "Doug has an amazing ability to cause turmoil. Don't puff up his ego yet."

Kristina chuckled as we walked across the parking lot. "Ah, yes. Doug the bull buffalo."

Walking onto the loading dock, we were met with a mixture of bourbon and oak aromas. We startled a forklift operator who was unloading a semi-trailer. Seeing his look of surprise, I held up my badge and put my finger to my lips. Kristina announced our entrance to the sheriff's department team watching the front of the building as we moved quickly through the warehouse to the reception area.

Passing the stairs to the lab and the upstairs offices, Kristina signaled for Jill to check the upper level. Assuming that Charlotte was in her office, I followed a step behind Kristina. Walking quietly across the reception area, Kristina signaled for me to pause on the right side of the office door while she took the left. We could hear one side of Charlotte's discussion from outside the office.

"Who was asking questions about my car?"

Kristina turned, preparing to step into the office. I signaled for her to wait. I was curious about Charlotte's phone conversation.

"That snoopy Park Service guy? Why did he want to know about *my* car?"

The question was followed by silence as Charlotte listened to the caller's reply.

"Shit, I've got to get out of here."

Kristina stepped into the office. "We'd like to ask you a few questions, Charlotte."

I stepped in a fraction of a second later, as Charlotte ended her call. "There must be some mistake," Charlotte said.

"We'd like to ask you about Alistair McInnis' murder."

"I didn't kill Mac."

"We found your love nest in Lincoln's Birthplace," I said, "that last guest cabin with the unsecured back door overlooks the murder scene."

First, Charlotte glared at me, then at Kristina. I sensed that she was in panic mode, trying to explain away the love nest comment. As many liars do, she broke eye contact with us and looked at the corner of the office. "I've never been there."

"Your car has been seen there frequently, including the day of the McInnis murder," Kristina explained. "We have crime scene techs checking for fingerprints on booze bottles and for DNA on the sheets."

Charlotte's confidence faded. "Fine. Sure. Mac and I were having an affair, but it was just meaningless sex."

"Your car was at the crime scene at the time of Mac's death," I said.

Charlotte couldn't let go, adding to her string of lies by responding to each of our comments. "Fine. Yes. Mac and I snuck over to that cabin the afternoon he died. We drank some and romped in the sheets. It was just fun. That's all. He was sleeping in the bed when I left."

"He was sleeping in the middle of the afternoon?" I asked.

"Yeah. He works...worked crazy hours and was always tired. He'd often fall asleep after sex. His libido was like a microwave; heat up, boil, then immediately cool down. I was okay with that. I didn't need post-coital reassurances and lies. We were just having sex that we both enjoyed." Reading our skepticism, she added, "We were consenting adults committing adultery. That's not illegal, even in Kentucky."

Playing along with her fiction, I asked, "What time did you leave the cabin?"

Charlotte froze, trying to frame her answer to fit the timeline of Mac's death and whatever alibi she was concocting. "I don't wear a watch, and I didn't look at the time on my cell phone."

"Where did you go after you left?"

"I probably went home and fed my cat."

"Did anyone see you there?"

Charlotte smiled nervously and snorted. "Only the cat and he's a poor witness."

"You didn't stop to buy gas or groceries on the way home? The security tape at a business would help establish your timeline."

"No. I don't know. I don't think so," Charlotte backpedaled as she tried to construct a story for us.

I glanced at Kristina and suggested, "Let's take another look at the visitor center's security footage."

"I wasn't there when Mac was killed, and I didn't do it." Seeing that we weren't buying the story, she continued constructing lies. "It was probably Robert Carlisle. He wanted control of the distillery before the bourbon release."

"Doesn't Carlisle own most of the distillery?" I asked. "He supplied the start-up funds."

"Um, no. Um, Robert has been selling off some of his shares, hedging his bets ahead of the release. Now that we know how good this bourbon is, he wanted to buy part of Alistair's shares to maintain control."

I cocked my head, "I'm confused. Robert Carlisle has been selling his shares in case the bourbon wasn't good. Now that he knows the bourbon is good, he wanted to buy shares from McInnis? Was Alistair interested in selling to him?"

Charlotte shook her head. "Not at all! That was Carlisle's problem. Mac didn't want to sell. However, Tamsin is sick of living here. Robert probably thought she might pressure Mac to sell their shares just to move on."

Kristina shook her head. "That's disgusting. There's nothing worse than taking advantage of a grieving widow."

Charlotte reached for her phone on the desktop. "I've got pictures of them arguing about the ownership."

"Do not touch your phone!" Kristina ordered.

"No, you have to see the pictures." Charlotte paused with her fingers a few inches away from the phone.

"Actually, we'll be taking your phone, computer, and impounding your car."

"Why are you searching *my* stuff?" Charlotte shrieked. "I'm a victim, too."

After pulling on purple gloves, Kristina picked up Charlotte's phone. "You were the last person to see McInnis alive."

"I was…"

I cut off Charlotte's retort with, "You were seen at Lincoln's Birthplace the afternoon McInnis was killed. We have crime scene techs processing evidence at the cabin you and McInnis had been using as a love nest."

Charlotte stared at me, then watched Kristina place her phone into an evidence bag. Her eyes fluttered, then teared up. "Mac was alive when I left."

"Do you admit being at the cabin with McInnis the day he died?" I asked.

Charlotte nodded her head. "It's not what you think."

Kristina sealed and signed the evidence bag. "What's not what we think?"

Charlotte sighed. "Mac and I weren't having a sleazy hook-up. We were in love. I wouldn't kill him."

* * *

Kristina guided Charlotte into a sheriff's department interview room as I held the door. Charlotte rubbed her wrists as if the cuffs had chafed. Once they were seated on opposite sides of the small table, I closed the interview room door and joined Jill in the adjoining room where we watched the interview through a two-way mirror.

Kristina opened the interview by repeating their names, the date, and that Charlotte had waived her right to have an attorney present. With the formalities complete, Kristina jotted notes and asked, "What was the nature of your relationship with Alistair McInnis?"

"Mac...Mr. McInnis was my employer."

"You also had a personal, non-work relationship with Mr. McInnis, correct?"

Charlotte hung her head. After drawing a breath, she straightened up and looked at Kristina. "Yes. Mac and I were in love."

"How long had you and Mr. McInnis been in a relationship?"

Charlotte stared at the mirror as if visualizing Jill and me sitting on the other side. "It's been several months now." Kristina let the answer hang, and after a few moments, Charlotte added, "We'd spent a lot of evenings with suppliers, potential customers, and distributors. The meetings always involved alcohol and late evenings. One night, after the others left, Mac and I were cleaning up. We were both emotionally spent, having used all of our energy convincing a Midwestern distributor that we were real and worthy of him stocking our bourbon. Mac poured each of us 'a wee dram more' and we collapsed, laughing about what business whores we'd become, selling ourselves and our souls to get some rich businessman with an overinflated ego to sell

325

a product that we knew would be better than ninety-nine percent of the booze he carried."

Charlotte closed her eyes and bit her lower lip as memories flooded back to her. Kristina waited for a bit, then asked, "And that was the first time?"

Charlotte nodded. "Yeah. We didn't intend for it to happen. I mean…" Charlotte sniffled and Kristina handed her a tissue. "It wasn't just the alcohol. Mac's marriage had become soulless since they'd moved to the US. His wife hated it here and was lobbying for them to return *home* after the bourbon release. She didn't get that Mac had put his heart into the distillery and it was his baby, not just a job."

"Did you make plans together?"

"We planned the future of the distillery and what our roles would be. I was going to be the vice president of operations and in charge of the distillery. Mac was going to expand his marketing role. Our future together was undefined but understood."

"Where did the Carlisles fit into the future?"

"Robert didn't want to be involved in anything operational. He wanted to have his horse on the label so he could brag about being a distillery owner. Glinda didn't give a shit about the distillery, or anything associated with it."

Kristina made notes and asked, "You said Tamsin McInnis was moving back to Scotland?"

"That's what Mac told me. She's been frustrated because her visa doesn't allow her to work in the US. She wants to teach. And..." Charlotte stopped talking and stared at her hands.

"And..." Kristina prompted.

Charlotte shrugged. "She thought they could slip back into their Scottish life."

"Their Scottish life being, what?"

Shrugging again, Charlotte bit her lip. "I suppose her Scottish life where her husband was the lord of the manor, and she had tea with the other ladies."

"Did his wife know you were having an affair with him?"

"Mac told me Tamsin suspected he was cheating on her. I don't think she realized I was the other woman."

"Tell me what happened at the cabin the day Alistair died."

"We always drove separately, you know, to keep up appearances. Mac was doing something on his phone when I got there." Charlotte looked at Kristina with apprehension. "You don't want me to talk about the sordid details, do you?"

"After you had sex, what happened?"

"We snuggled a bit. We talked about the future."

"What about the future?"

Charlotte stared at the tabletop. "Tamsin gave Mac an ultimatum: Either he returned to Scotland with her, or she was going to return alone and divorce him."

"That's a big ultimatum. What was he planning to do?"

Charlotte wrung her hands. "He'd been talking about leaving her and marrying me. I think that having the divorce thrown at him had put him off balance. I mean, it's one thing to talk about something way off in the future. It's another thing to be standing at the brink, being pushed to jump."

Jill whispered, "Do you think she's telling the truth?"

"She's expanding on what we've heard from Glinda and Tamsin."

Kristina waited to see if Charlotte would add to her comments. When no more was forthcoming, she asked, "Did you give him an ultimatum too?"

Tears formed in Charlotte's eyes as she nodded. "I needed him to commit or walk away. I was tired of sneaking off to that musty cabin. Of being the other woman. Of being in limbo."

"Did you kill him?"

Charlotte stiffened. "God no! I LOVED him!"

I took out my phone and typed Kristina a text. *Take a break.*

Kristina's phone must've vibrated because she pulled it from her pocket and read my message. "I need to follow up on this. Would you like a cup of coffee or a bathroom break?"

Charlotte shook her head. Jill and I met Kristina outside the interview room. She looked tired. "What do you two think?"

Jill looked at me, expecting an answer. "She's not prevaricating or looking into the distance. I don't think she's lying."

Kristina looked through her notes. "She's either the best liar I've ever interviewed, or she's innocent." Kristina picked up her phone and dialed the crime lab number. "Have you processed the fingerprints from the park cabin?"

We watched Kristina nod and make notes. "Okay, the only prints belonged to the decedent and Charlotte. Okay. How about the murder scene? You found a woman's footprints at the scene. Do they match Charlotte too?"

"Well?" I asked as she replaced the phone.

"Charlotte's fingerprints are all over the cabin, as are Alistair McInnis' prints. However, the women's footprints in the mud alongside the creek are size five with a deep cleated sole, like barn boots. Charlotte wears size seven and a half. Charlotte is a city girl who wears shoes, not boots."

"We need a search warrant for the McInnis house, phones, computers, and Tamsin's boots," I said.

Chapter 22

By rural Kentucky standards, the brick two-story house on a five-acre lot was darn nice. I imagined it was more modest than whatever the McInnis family lived in when in Scotland. Tamsin McInnis answered the door wearing a cotton shirt and jeans. If she was surprised to see us, it didn't register on her face. "Yes?"

"We have a search warrant," Kristina said as she pushed into the house. "We are here to collect your phone, computer, laptop, tablet, smartwatch, and whatever other electronic communication devices we find."

Tamsin tried to stand her ground. "You'll have to wait until I contact the consulate. They may not be able to get here for a few days."

Kristina pushed past as Jill guided Tamsin into a living room off the entryway. "I believe the protocol is to notify them when we arrest you. Until then, they're not officially involved."

"I have to protest!" Tamsin argued, pulling her elbow free from Jill's guiding hand as two uniformed deputies and a crime scene tech followed us into the house.

I gestured to a chair, noting the dozen or more beautiful hand-blown vases and art pieces arranged around the room. "Please take a seat and give me your phone."

"I will NOT *give* you my phone! I plan to call my solicitor."

I watched her remove the cell phone from her pocket and type in the code to unlock it. I snatched it from her hand. "Thanks for unlocking it. Figuring out those codes sometimes takes hours or days."

"Damn you!" Tamsin swore. "I'll have you all reprimanded for this!"

"I don't think so," I replied, handing the phone to the crime scene tech who pulled up Tamsin's call and text message history as he walked away.

"There's a pair of muddy size five rubber boots next to the back door," Kristina called from deeper inside the house.

Tamsin glared at me. "Of course, there are muddy boots near the back door. I wouldn't traipse through the house in them!" Seeing my smug grin, she added, "As I said before, I would like to call my solicitor now."

"That call will have to wait until after the search, although you don't need to answer any of our questions without your *solicitor* present."

Kristina appeared wearing purple gloves and carrying the muddy boots in a clear evidence bag. She held them up and said, "The size and tread match the casts made at the murder scene."

Tamsin glanced at the boots absently. "I have no idea who those belong to."

"So, they won't have your fingerprints on them?" Kristina asked.

"No comment."

I noticed Tamsin glance at a door off the living room. "Is there someone hiding in the closet?"

Looking annoyed, Tamsin glared at me. "I'm annealing pieces in the workshop kiln. The cycle is time and temperature sensitive. If they're in too long or cool too quickly, they turn from thousand-dollar art pieces into slivers of glass."

"Is there someone you can call to take care of them?"

Tamsin consulted her watch. "Not anyone who can get here in time to turn down the kiln to start the next step of the annealing."

Having watched the class at the museum handling globs of molten glass attached to the ends of long tubes and rods, I had no interest in letting Tamsin pull glowing glass out of the kiln. "Can you talk one of us through it?"

"I can hardly turn a...baboon into a glass blower in five minutes." Tamsin's eyes sparkled. "Did that sound insulting?"

"I've been called worse," I replied. "I'm not going to allow you to handle molten glass while we stand back watching. If there's a way to remove your art from the kiln to protect it, I will. Otherwise, show me the switch and I'll turn off the kiln. But first, turn your pockets inside out. Do you have any weapons, drugs, razor blades, or needles?"

Tamsin glared at me, then Jill and Kristina. "If you lay a hand on me, I'll sue you for every penny you're worth."

Undaunted, Kristina set the evidence bag down and stepped in front of Tamsin. "Fine. Put your hands behind your head."

Kristina patted Tamsin down, removing a used tissue from her front pocket and an engraved flat metal cigarette case from a back pocket. "What's in this?"

Tamsin glared daggers at her but didn't answer.

Carefully opening the metal case, Kristina held it so Tamsin, Jill, and I could see the contents. "There appear to be three joints here. We'll have them tested."

"It's medicinal cannabis," Tamsin said. "For my glaucoma."

"Great! We'll talk to your doctor," Kristina said as she patted down Tamsin's legs.

"I hope you enjoyed that," Tamsin said as she straightened her jeans and shirt. "May I deal with the kiln now?"

Ignoring the question, Kristina looked at me. "Will you and Jill watch her while I finish the search and log evidence?"

"Sure," I replied, gesturing for Tamsin to sit in a chair.

She glared at me. "The kiln. Are you going to do something about it?"

"What needs to be done to the kiln?"

"I need to lower the temperature another hundred degrees."

"I assume there's some kind of thermostat I can adjust."

Tamsin rolled her eyes. "It's digital. I could train a monkey to adjust it. Do you think you can handle it?"

Ignoring the insult, I pointed to a door marked *studio*. "The kiln is in here?"

"Of course, it's in there. Where did you think it was, in the library?"

The digital controller was mounted on the front of the kiln, and I entered the new temperature as requested. I looked at the workspace, which was haphazardly strewn with pipes, tongs, and other glass-handling tools. A shelf along one wall supported a dozen glass sculptures. Some were abstract. Others were identifiable as horses, dolphins, flowers, and turtles. *Tamsin is very talented*.

Jill sat on the arm of the sofa, watching Tamsin, whose head was down, her arms crossed. She appeared to be asleep except for her foot which seemed to be tapping in rhythm to some song playing in her head. Her foot stopped abruptly, and she looked at a bar built into the wall. "I don't suppose you would whip up a dry martini?"

"No," I replied. "I can get you a glass of water."

"Water isn't what I need."

I stood next to Jill, and we watched Tamsin, who was fidgeting and squirming, making me wonder if she'd missed a dose of ADHD medicine. "We heard you were considering a move back to Scotland."

"God, yes. I have to get away from these...people."

"Which people would that be?" Jill asked.

"Everyone in this damn state! They're all so...backward. What was the word Glinda used? The local police are unprofessional." She paused to think. "Glinda calls the local police 'Bubbas who can't find their own butts with two hands.'"

"I take it that you agree with her?"

"Scottish police are professional and polished. You people are...incompetent Yankees. If you had a clue, my husband's killer would be in jail, and I'd be on a plane to the civilized world."

"I'd be delighted to arrest your husband's killer. If you know who it is, please tell me."

Tamsin frowned. "Are you joking? You don't think the whore he's been screwing killed him?"

"Which whore is that?" I asked.

Looking exasperated, Tamsin sighed. "I told you. The chemist. The one who spends day and night with him."

"She has an alibi."

Flipping her wrist, Tamsin replied, "Fine, the other one. The blonde secretary who answers the phone."

"What's the office manager's motive?"

Blowing out a breath, Tamsin threw her head back dramatically. "Motive? I'll tell you the motive. Alistair told her their fling was over. He was going to fire her and kick her blonde butt into the street."

"Huh. I hadn't heard that story."

"Incompetent Yankee," Tamsin uttered.

When Kristina appeared in the doorway and I directed her outside, "Are you through?"

She grinned. "What's the matter? Are you tired of babysitting?"

"I'm missing something, and Tamsin's annoying chatter is distracting."

"What are you missing?"

"If I knew what *it* was, it wouldn't be missing."

"What's the context of the missing *it*?"

"Tamsin is talking about her husband breaking off the affair. First, she accused Sophia, the chemist. When I said she had an alibi, Tamsin accused Charlotte, describing her as the blonde secretary."

"She suspected Alistair of having an affair, but didn't know who his partner was? Your AA buddies said the affair with Charlotte was common knowledge. If everyone in town knew who his partner was, how would Tamsin think it was Sophia?"

"Different social circle, I suppose? Maybe the country club rumor mill isn't as accurate as the AA group."

Chapter 23

As we drove away from the McInnis house, the missing tidbit bubbled to the surface of my thoughts. "I didn't see the green Jaguar in the crime scene pictures."

Kristina glanced at me, then drove silently, trying to envision the pictures. "It wasn't in the park."

"Where did you find it?"

"There's a picnic area across the highway from the park. It was parked there."

"Greta saw the Jaguar parked at the bottom of the parking lot the day of the murder. Someone other than Alistair moved it across the highway after the murder."

"Charlotte must've had an accomplice who drove the Jag out after the murder," Kristina suggested.

Jill leaned forward. "Or Charlotte parked her car in the picnic area, then drove the Jag across the road after killing Alistair."

"Killers don't hang around, particularly amateurs who've never killed before. They panic and try to get as far away as they can as quickly as they can."

Kristina nodded. "Crimes of passion are messy, and the killers are unprepared. Can you see Charlotte, who never has a hair out of place, whacking Alistair in the head with a weapon we've never found, then drowning him in the creek? I don't buy it. She would've ruined her manicure."

"And been muddy," Jill added.

Kristina pulled into a gas station and parked next to the pumps. "I'm going to make a call. Would you grab me a Pepsi and a bag of Fritos? I need carbs and caffeine to think."

She was sitting in the idling car when I carried out our drinks and a large bag of Fritos. "What did you find out?" I asked as I handed her the Pepsi and Jill climbed in the back seat.

"The Jag had been wiped clean. There were no prints in it."

"I doubt Alistair would bother to wipe his own prints out of his own car," I summarized.

"The only prints inside the cabin belonged to Alistair and Charlotte." Kristina pulled out of the gas station. "The park security camera video is on my computer."

* * *

At Kristina's desk, Jill and I looked over her shoulders as she logged onto her computer and pulled up the video. "I looked at it before and saw the Jag arriving and leaving. I didn't notice who was driving it. I'll go to the afternoon of the murder and fast forward until a vehicle shows up."

I thought back to Gene's comments at the AA meeting. "Go to 3:30."

Kristina glanced at me. "That's very precise."

"Trust me."

The video showed the empty driveway until 3:34 when the Jaguar passed the visitor center. "Fletcher, you amaze me."

At 3:39, Charlotte's Cobra passed. "The camera is mounted on the building, so it shows the passenger side of the incoming vehicles. We can't identify the driver."

"I think we can assume that Alistair and Charlotte are the drivers," I suggested. "I'm more curious about who's driving when the cars leave."

The remaining afternoon video was of the few visitors' cars who arrived later. Virtually all of them parked at the visitor center, most likely delivering tourists who spoke with the rangers, then walked to the memorial. They were parked for less than fifteen minutes. As Kristina fast-forwarded through the video, we saw a couple flashes of the superintendent and Patience as they walked in and out of the visitor center.

At 4:21 the departing Cobra flashed on the screen. Kristina stopped the video and backed it up. In slow motion, she ran it again. "That looks like Charlotte," she observed.

A moment later a hooded figure wearing sunglasses walked past the visitor center.

Kristina stopped the video. "If I were a suspicious person, I'd say that person had been waiting for Charlotte to leave. He or she knew the camera was there and turned their head so we couldn't see their face."

With the video moving again, we watched the last car leave the visitor center at 4:39. Patience walked past, emptying the waste bins. At 4:48, the Jaguar appeared. Kristina stopped the video with the driver's window centered on the screen.

"It's our hooded person, still in sunglasses."

Jill reached over Kristina's shoulder and pointed at the screen. "Look there. The ring. The driver used her left hand to obscure the side of her face. That's Tamsin McInnis. She wears a two-carat diamond ring. Didn't you notice it when we were at her house?"

I shook my head. "It didn't register."

Kristina chuckled. "It took my husband six months to pay off my quarter-carat engagement ring. That's one honking diamond, and yes, I noticed it too. I'll wager that there are fewer than five people living outside of Louisville who wear a stone that size."

Kristina ran through the rest of the security video. The day ended when the superintendent drove past shortly after 5:00, probably closing the gate behind himself. She shut down the computer and turned to face us.

I straightened up and stretched. "Now we know how the Jag got parked across the highway. And we know that Tamsin didn't want to be identified as the person who drove it there."

"And her boots match the crime scene footprints," Kristina added.

Jill pinched the bridge of her nose. "I don't get it. She talked to us for half an hour during the search. I didn't sense anything in her demeanor that hinted at her being the killer."

"Glinda told us she has a Bachelor of Fine Arts degree. I wonder if that includes acting?" I suggested.

"I think actors get theater arts degrees," Kristina said as she shut down the computer. "Tamsin certainly has motives. She now owns more than half of a distillery and she's rid of a cheating husband."

"And opportunity," Jill said.

"I think it's bigger than that," I added. "She framed her husband's lover for the murder. For her, it's win, win, win."

Continuing to pinch the bridge of her nose, Jill asked, "How do we prove it? We don't have a murder weapon. We don't have any DNA evidence. We don't have a witness. The only fingerprints at the scene belong to the victim and his lover. All we have is a video of someone with a big diamond ring wearing a hoodie and a pair of boots whose tread might match those left at the murder scene."

After a moment of consideration, Kristina lit up as a thought came to mind. "We've been focused on what was left at the scene. Every criminal takes something from the murder scene with them. We need to impound the Jaguar, and swab every boot, shoe, and pair of pants Tamsin owns for blood, hair, and DNA."

"Do you think she threw the hoodie away?" Jill asked.

"The ring!" I blurted out, "There are nooks, crannies, and crevices all over an engagement ring."

"Let's find the district attorney!"

* * *

"We've got her!" Kristina said as we raced from the courthouse to her squad.

"Let's hope she hasn't cleaned her ring in bleach," I said, hoping to contain the enthusiasm.

Kristina glanced at Jill in the rearview mirror after pulling onto the street. "Is he always a Debbie Downer?"

"Doug's the fun sponge—he can suck the fun out of any situation."

"I'm not the fun sponge. I'm the voice of reality. I've been burned too many times by hoping for an outcome. Criminals have a way of dashing your hopes."

We drove in silence the rest of the trip. I noticed the doors were open on the three empty garage stalls as we pulled into the McInnis' driveway. "Tamsin is in the wind."

"Damn, damn, damn," Kristina swore. She picked up the radio mic and asked the dispatcher to get descriptions and license numbers of all vehicles registered to Tamsin or Alistair McInnis.

"Maybe she's just at the grocery store," Jill suggested.

Kristina and Jill approached the front door while I circled to the back. There was no sign of activity in any room I passed. The back door was ajar, so I stepped inside. "Tamsin McInnis, are you here? This is Doug Fletcher from the US Park Service. We have a warrant for your arrest."

The front doorbell rang, and I heard Kristina knocking and identifying herself. With no one home, I pulled on a pair of gloves, walked down the hallway, and opened the front door. "She's not responding. I'll check upstairs."

The only room that wasn't immaculate was the master bedroom. Clothes were strewn haphazardly around the floor. The closet was open, and it appeared half of the clothes were gone. An impression on the bedspread showed where a suitcase had probably been placed while being packed.

I met Jill and Kristina at the bottom of the stairs. "It appears she packed a suitcase and left. Do you have the phone number of that guy from the consulate?" I asked.

Returning to the squad, Kristina dug into the car's console and pulled out a business card. She punched in a phone number and waited. "I'd like to speak with Mr. Derek Sandborn, please. This is Detective Blake from the LaRue County Sheriff's Department." Kristina's head bobbed as she listened to the receptionist. "Please interrupt him. This is an urgent police matter regarding Tamsin McInnis."

With Kristina on hold, I asked, "He's in the office, not here, right?"

"He's dealing with a tourist who was mugged and needs a new passport."

"You have Tamsin's passport, right?"

Kristina nodded. "It's locked up at the office." A moment later, her eyes locked with mine. "That means she can't fly commercially. If she found a less than ethical charter pilot, she could take off and deal with immigration and customs wherever she landed."

"Not wherever she landed," I replied. "Wherever she got off the plane. The plane could land in Gander, Newfoundland to refuel. If no one officially left the plane, there'd be no immigration involved. The pilot would hand his credit card to the fuel truck and never set foot on the ground."

"She might be driving to Canada," Jill suggested. "I wonder what reception a

British citizen without a passport would get at the border?"

The dispatcher responded with the license number and description of the two McInnis vehicles, the Jaguar and a Land Rover SUV. "Broadcast a BOLO on those two vehicles with a description of Tamsin McInnis and orders to arrest her if she's stopped."

A man's voice came from Kristina's phone, and she put it to her ear. "Mr. Sandborn, this is Detective Blake. I have an arrest warrant for Tamsin McInnis and she's not home. Do you have any idea where she is?"

Kristina's look of disgust preceded her eye roll. "I understand that Mrs. McInnis isn't the only British citizen in need of your assistance. I need to know if she was planning to leave the country, or if I should be looking for her at the grocery store."

Kristina nodded and listened. Unable to put up with anymore, she interrupted the monologue. "Mr. Sandborn, we have evidence that Mrs. McInnis murdered her husband. We want to locate and arrest her. Do you know where she is or where she's going? Yes, or no?"

Kristina's eyes went wide. "Canada or the British Virgin Islands? She told you that?"

"Hit the speaker," I ordered.

"Sandborn, this is Doug Fletcher. If you recall, I'm a US Federal law enforcement officer."

"You're a park ranger."

"No, my partner and I are federal law enforcement officers, with the same powers as an FBI or DEA agent. Are we clear about that?"

"That's irrelevant, Fletcher. I'm an official in the British Foreign Office. My job is assisting British citizens in the United States."

"I understand, Mr. Sandborn. However, you work in cooperation with the US State Department, and you understand that British citizens in the US are subject to our laws. Detective Blake has an arrest warrant from LaRue County, Kentucky. I'm formally requesting your assistance in locating Mrs. McInnis and taking her into custody. If you have any knowledge of her location or plans, please tell us now."

"As I told Detective Blake, Mrs. McInnis informed the consulate of her intention to take her husband's ashes to Scotland for burial. I advised her that she needed her passport to travel. She said she'd misplaced it and asked me to issue a replacement. I was aware that she'd surrendered it to the Kentucky authorities, so I advised her I wouldn't issue a replacement, and that she wouldn't be allowed to board a commercial flight without her passport. At that point, she asked what would happen if she arrived in a

British Commonwealth, like Canada, without her passport. I told her she'd most likely be held until her immigration status could be resolved."

"You mentioned Canada and the Caribbean. Did Mrs. McInnis discuss those destinations with you?"

"She did, although I made it clear that regardless of where she arrived, without a passport she'd probably be held until the local authorities could resolve her status with the local British consulate."

"How long ago did you have that discussion with her?"

"I responded to her message this morning, about nine o'clock Central time."

I looked at my watch and realized Tamsin had several hours' head start on us. "Thank you, Mr. Sandborn. If Mrs. McInnis contacts you, please advise her to turn herself in to the local authorities and then call Detective Blake at this number."

"Your request has been noted and I will comply."

Kristina ended the call and grimaced. "Do you think she'll try to talk her way onto a flight at Louisville?"

"Tamsin is smart, and she has money. My bet is on a private charter."

Jill was busy on her phone as we spoke. "Okay, there are five charter air services in northern Kentucky. If I expand the search to southern Ohio, there are three more." She paused. "We can rule out two who only fly small propeller planes with limited range. The others all offer jet charters."

"I wonder what the cruising range of a business jet is?" I asked rhetorically.

Jill went back to her phone. "Hang on. A Gulfstream G550 has a cruising range of 6,750 miles."

Kristina stared out of the windshield. "I wish I'd paid attention in my geography class. How far away is Scotland?"

After a minute of research, Jill replied, "Glasgow, Scotland is 3,773 miles from Lexington, Kentucky. The British Virgin Islands are 1,800 miles away."

A plan came to mind. "Jill, call all of those charter airlines and ask if they've booked a flight anywhere out of the US today or tomorrow."

Kristina nodded. "I'll alert the TSA at Louisville, Nashville, and Cincinnati."

Taking out my own phone, I dialed our boss, "Jack, we've got an arrest warrant in the Lincoln's Birthplace murder."

"Great! Are you and Jill going with the sheriff's office to make the arrest?"

"There's a slight glitch in that plan. The suspect is the victim's wife, a British citizen, and she's in the wind. We think she's going to charter a plane to fly out of the United States. The sheriff's department has her passport, so no commercial airline will let her on an international flight. We think she's going to book a charter."

"What's the driving distance to Canada?"

"Jill asked about that too. I'm trying to envision the geography. We're only a few miles from Ohio and it borders Canada. I think the entire Ohio/Canadian border is Lake Erie. I suppose there may be a ferry across somewhere." An idea struck me. "The sheriff's office seized the suspect's computer. I'll have the techs look at her search history. That may provide us with a clue."

"Keep me posted. I'd like to alert our bosses about arrests we've precipitated. They hate hearing about them on the news."

Having overheard the last of my conversation with our boss, Kristina was on the phone to her crime scene people. "Have you accessed the suspect's computer?" She nodded to me as she spoke. "Look at her search history. Tell me about anything related to airplane charters, airports, and travel destinations."

"They're already into Tamsin's computer?" I asked.

"They're rebooting it now."

I heard Jill talking to an air charter company in the backseat. "None of the Louisville airport charter companies have a reservation from an unknown woman today. It sounds like they mostly handle repeat corporate customers. I'm calling Lexington now."

"Give them to me," Kristina said to the computer techs as she pulled out a small notebook. "She opened websites for Commodore Air out of Lexington and Ohio Express Service out of Cincinnati. How about her location searches?"

"Ask if she checked for countries without extradition treaties and countries with lax entry requirements," I suggested.

Kristina nodded but was multi-tasking with my conversation and the phone call with the computer techs. "Okay, she checked Canada entry requirements for British Citizens, then a bunch of Caribbean and Central American countries. Trinidad-Tobago, Anguilla, the Bahamas, Belize, Guatemala, the US and British Virgin Islands, Bonaire, and Costa Rica." She paused her notes and stared at me. "That's interesting, she checked on cruise lines too. Some don't require passports, depending on their itinerary."

I looked at the list Kristina had written and thought about the range of a corporate jet. "Let's face it, she could be going anywhere."

Jill was on her phone the entire time Kristina and I had been discussing Tamsin's search history. Her voice changed, expressing excitement. "Okay, you've booked a charter this afternoon for Rona Bradbury. Where is she going?" Jill waited. "Taddy Bay airport? Where is that located?"

Unfamiliar with that airport, I turned to Kristina and mouthed *Taddy Bay?* She shook her head.

"Thank you so much," Jill said before ending the call.

"Where is Taddy Bay airport?" I asked.

"It's a small airport on Virgin Gorda, one of the British Virgin Islands."

Kristina started the engine and shifted into gear. "Which airport does the charter company fly from?"

Jill glanced at her notes. "Scott County Regional Airport."

Kristina nodded. "That's northeast of Lexington."

We were driving down the driveway when the dispatcher radioed Kristina. "KHP has stopped one of your vehicles, the silver Land Rover."

"Where?" Kristina asked as she stopped at the end of the driveway.

"About a mile east of your location," the dispatcher replied.

"Who is driving? Tamsin McInnis?"

"Holden Young."

"Do you know who that is?" I asked.

Kristina shook her head. "I don't have a clue."

We sped to the location, spotting the flashing lights on the Kentucky Highway Patrol SUV. The trooper and driver were standing in the ditch to the right of the vehicles, and we walked over to them.

Holden was young, his brown hair sticking out from under a University of Kentucky cap. His jeans were tattered and his t-shirt smudged, in stark contrast to the trooper who looked like his uniform had just come back from dry-cleaning.

The trooper nodded his acknowledgement to us and handed the boy's driver's license to Kristina. "Holden runs a car detailing business out of his barn, in Hodgenville. He's returning the vehicle he just finished cleaning and waxing."

Holden fidgeted and shifted on his feet. He stared at Kristina expectantly as she read his driver's license. "Who hired you?" Kristina asked.

"Mrs. McInnis asked me to wash and clean out her Rover. I've been working on it for a couple of days. It was kind of a mess."

"A mess, how?" I asked.

"It had been on some dirt roads, so it was kind of muddy and dusty."

"The inside, too?"

"Yeah, there was a bunch of trash in the back, and someone had been stomping around in the mud before they drove it."

"Did you notice any blood inside of it?"

Holden frowned and shook his head. "It's not hunting season. I only find blood in trucks when people have been hunting."

"Do you still have all of the trash you removed?" Kristina asked.

"It's still bagged up in the barn. I haven't been to the dump for a couple of days."

Kristina looked at me. "What do you think about checking the trash?"

"The vehicle driven from the scene was the green Jag. I doubt anything in the Rover is going to provide evidence." As soon as the words were out of my mouth, I was struck by a thought. "Holden, were there any of the owner's personal items in the Rover?"

"That's funny you'd ask," he replied. "Mrs. McInnis asked me to look for her tennis racket. I guess she'd lost it."

"Did you find it?"

"She must've had it laying on the back seats when she had them folded down. It slid down behind the seats when she folded them up. I think she'll be really happy about me finding it. It's one of them expensive carbon fiber ones. I even cleaned it up for her."

"She had a dirty tennis racquet?" I asked.

"Yeah, it looked like she'd dropped it in the mud or something."

"Is it in the Rover now?" I asked.

Holden nodded. "It's laying on the backseat."

I took out a pair of rubber gloves as I walked to the Rover. As promised, the tennis racquet was on the seat. It looked like it had just been polished. I picked it up and inspected the outer edges until I got about a third of the way around where I noticed dirt deep in the groove where it was strung. I carried the racquet to Kristina and nodded for her to step away from Holden and the trooper.

"We need to get this to the forensics people." I held the racquet so she could see the groove. "I can't tell, but it looks like there might be a hair or two in the mud. I bet a good crime scene tech might be able to tell you if there's blood in the mud, too."

Kristina smiled, then sighed. "He wiped off all of the prints."

"That's okay. If there are traces of Alistair's blood and hair, we've got a murder weapon. And we've got Holden who was asked to find a lost tennis racquet for Mrs. McInnis. I'm sure a good defense attorney would dispute the chain of evidence, but a jury might connect the dots."

Kristina put the racquet into an evidence bag, then locked it in the trunk of her squad. She locked the Rover and told Holden not to touch the bags of cleaning supplies he'd used while detailing the SUV. After calling to have the Rover towed to the secure impound lot, she asked the trooper to drive Holden home.

Her phone rang as we got back to the squad. We only heard her side of the conversation. "Okay, thanks!"

"That was Scott County. They've got a deputy at the airport. There's no sign of Tamsin, but it's still more than an hour until the charter is scheduled to fly." She checked her watch. "If we hurry, we should get to the airport a few minutes before she's scheduled to leave."

Chapter 24

With lights and siren, we made it to Scott County's Georgetown airport in twenty-three minutes, arriving a full half an hour before the charter's scheduled departure. A marked squad was parked outside of the small cement block terminal building.

"Shit," Kristina said as she turned off the lights and siren. "If Tamsin sees the cops here, she'll just keep driving."

"Yeah," I agreed. "We need to have the deputy move his car. You need to get this squad out of sight too. It's not marked, but it looks like a cop car."

We rushed inside and spoke with the middle-aged man behind the counter wearing a uniform shirt and epaulets with four bars, indicating he was the pilot. He explained that he was a one-man show, checking in passengers, loading luggage, and piloting the plane.

"Is there somewhere where we can put the squads out of sight?" I asked.

"Um, sure. Park them in the hangar. The plane is on the tarmac outside of the terminal, so the hangar is empty."

Kristina and the Scott County deputy moved the cars while Jill and I waited inside of the terminal. "I suppose this messes up your lucrative charter."

The pilot smiled and shook his head. "I have her credit card number. The cancellation penalty is about the same as the profit I'd make on the flight. And there would be fewer hours on the plane plus a free day to catch up on paperwork."

"How were you planning to get Mrs. Bradbury past the Customs and Immigration people in Virgin Gorda?"

The man smiled. "My responsibility ends with her delivery to the destination. It's up to her to deal with the local authorities."

"Are the Customs people in Virgin Gorda diligent?" I asked.

The pilot shrugged. "It depends. If Taddy Bay is like most Caribbean airports, if the customs agents aren't off to lunch, they're sometimes thorough. If they're late for lunch, at the end of their shift, distracted, or busy, they're less concerned about contraband, cash, or passports."

"I've been to some places in Mexico and Central America where $20 will suffice for a missing passport," I suggested.

The pilot chuckled. "Most of the Caribbean is good. There are a few islands where you need that $20 even if you have a passport. Otherwise, there will be an intense search of your bag, involving a long delay. Twenty dollars greases the process. On the other hand, too large of a tip makes them suspicious.”

“Is there any chance Mrs. Bradbury might ask you to deviate from the flight plan?”

“You’ve been watching too many spy movies. We generally file the flight plan, then stick to it.”

“Always?”

The pilot considered my question for a minute before answering. “If there are weather considerations, we sometimes need to make an intermediate stop or divert from our planned destination. That doesn’t happen often.”

“If you’re paid enough extra...”

The pilot shook his head. “I won’t risk losing my license or going to prison for a couple of hundred dollars. Like I said, you’ve been watching too many spy movies.”

Jill chuckled. “My partner sees the negative side of everything.”

Looking out of the windows facing the small parking lot, the pilot nodded. “I think my passenger has arrived. Did you expect her to be driving a green Jaguar?”

I nodded. “Can we slip into your office for a minute?” I asked.

He gestured toward the door behind the desk, then paused, noting our bulletproof vests. “This woman isn’t likely to shoot me or something?”

“Nah, she’s a pussycat,” Jill replied.

"Pussycats sometimes have sharp claws," he said as we slipped into the office.

From the doorway, I looked past the pilot at the woman who was unloading luggage from the Jag's trunk. Seeing only flashes of her as she walked behind the open trunk, I questioned whether I was seeing Tamsin McInnis, or another person. The woman's gray hair threw me, as did her less than fashionable clothes and face without makeup.

I gestured for Jill to join me. "Is that Tamsin?"

"It looks like Tamsin's mother, maybe."

We backed away from the door to be out of sight when the woman walked in. I heard the pilot ask, "Mrs. Bradbury?"

"Are you prepped and ready to take off?" the passenger asked in a heavy Scottish accent.

The door behind us opened and Kristina walked in with the Scott County deputy. "Why are you in the office?" she asked.

I put my finger to my lips and nodded to the door.

"Get out here!" Tamsin commanded, holding a small pistol in her hand.

Our subterfuge was over. Jill, who was nearer the door, stepped forward with me a step behind. I bumped into her when she stopped abruptly and raised her hands. "Take it easy," she said.

"Get everyone out here." Tamsin commanded. "Your Yankee partner and that female deputy too."

"I'm coming out with my hands up," Kristina said, using her outdoor voice while gesturing for the uniformed deputy to move into the office's most remote corner.

"I'm right behind her," I said, easing past Jill who was just past the doorway.

Tamsin was behind the counter with a compact pistol pointed at the pilot. "All of you take your guns out slowly and drop them on the floor."

"That only works on television," I said. "We're trained to never surrender our weapons."

"I'm not taking your guns. I'm just asking you to put them down until the pilot and I are safely on the plane."

"Shooting the pilot would put a dent in your plan to fly out of here," I said. "Why don't you set down *your* weapon. We can discuss how to best end this."

Tamsin smiled. "Good point." She pointed her pistol at Jill. "You, Yankee cop, drop your gun and step over here. You're going on a trip with me."

Jill drew a shaky breath to stiffen her resolve. "No."

Tamsin's smile was scary, like something out of an eerie movie right before the vampire lunges at the hero. "You might think this little gun isn't too lethal. I'll bet you were trained to respect all guns. Even little ones cause damage that takes years to heal. Experienced cops like you know that. I see that you're wearing a bulletproof vest, so I'd have to shoot you in the hips or legs, right?" Tamsin lowered her aim from Jill's torso to her waist. "Drop your gun. Three... Two..." I saw Tamsin's grip tightening on the pistol as if she was squeezing the trigger.

"Fine!" Jill replied. "I'm using my fingers to remove the pistol. I'll lower it, then drop it on the floor."

"That's better," Tamsin chuckled. "It's easier now that you understand how serious I am. Before you knew I'd killed my husband, I wasn't nearly as scary. But now, you know that I'm capable of killing not only strangers, but people I used to love."

"Used to love?" I asked as Jill lowered her pistol.

"It's hard to love someone who's never there, even when he's physically there." Tamsin gestured with the pistol for Jill to step away from the counter and me. Leading the pilot to the front door, Tamsin asked, "When did you figure out I'd framed the blonde slapag?" Seeing our confusion with her Scottish slang, she asked, "Whore?"

"Does it matter?" I asked as Tamsin opened the door and backed out.

"Not really. We found the missing tennis racquet. Alistair's blood and your fingerprints. The jury shouldn't need anything more."

Gesturing for Jill to back out of the door, Tamsin had one last comment before the door closed. "There's never going to be a jury."

At some point in the standoff, I'd heard the back door open behind us when the deputy slipped out. I picked up Jill's pistol and slid it into the back of my waistband.

Kristina watched and said, "I assume you've got some sort of plan that involves us setting our pistols down and you drawing that hidden gun to shoot Tamsin."

I led Kristina out of the back door. "I'm still working on the plan."

"Great. Let me know when it gels. I hate surprises."

We stood with our hands in the air and watched as Tamsin led Jill and the pilot to the small business jet that was parked thirty yards away. "I'm more concerned about what our missing deputy has up his sleeve," I whispered. "Young guys are sometimes overly eager and assume they're bulletproof."

"I think everybody in law enforcement respects the gravity of an armed hostage situation."

"Where in hell is he?" I asked, casting my eyes around the plane and surrounding area without turning my head to tip off Tamsin.

"I don't see him. Maybe he's calling for backup."

"There's not much hope anyone else will be here before that plane takes off," I whispered.

At the bottom of the steps, Tamsin told the pilot to climb into the plane and prepare for takeoff. I started walking toward the plane with my hands still in the air. "We can still sort this out, Tamsin. Flying away only delays the inevitable. Your life would be like a prison, even if you escape. You'll be looking over your shoulder all of the time, wondering if someone behind you isn't from Interpol or the FBI there to arrest you."

Tamsin pressed the pistol against Jill's neck as I walked toward them. "Stop walking. Now!"

"Yes. You're in control. I'm just trying to get close enough to talk."

Tamsin called over her shoulder, "Are you about ready, Mr. Pilot?"

"Just completing my pre-flight checklist."

"Don't worry about your partner, Mr. Ranger. You'll get a call from her in a couple of days to let you know she's safe and ready to be retrieved."

"Where will she call from?" I asked.

Tamsin stepped backward onto the plane's first step. "It'll be a surprise," she said as she grabbed Jill's collar and pulled her up the steps with the pistol pointed at the back of Jill's head.

The right engine whined, then fired and started to roar. Tamsin reached the top step with Jill still two stair steps behind her. With limited space for two people to maneuver inside the plane, Tamsin struggled to find space to stand as she pulled Jill up the last steps.

"What's your plan, Fletcher?" Kristina asked.

"I'm out of plans. There's nothing I can do while she's got a gun pointed at Jill's head."

Trying to step backward from the top of the ladder into the plane, Tamsin's foot slipped, and she fell hard on her butt. Jill was pulled back until she completely lost her footing, causing her to slide down the six narrow steps.

Tamsin struggled to maintain her grip on Jill's collar, then yelled something that was lost in the sound of the second jet engine firing up. I heard a POP as Tamsin released Jill. Tamsin aimed at us. I lowered my hands, moved to the side while reaching for my pistol. Kristina stepped in the opposite direction as she pulled her pistol. A fraction of a second later, Tamsin's face disappeared into a cloud of pink mist as her body pitched forward. She slid headfirst down the stairs onto Jill.

"What the hell just happened?" Kristina yelled as we sprinted toward the plane.

The jet engines started slowing as the Scott County deputy stepped into the plane's doorway. He aimed his pistol at Tamsin's crumpled body as Jill tried to push herself free from the weight that had fallen on her.

I grabbed Jill's arm and tried to have her lie down next to the plane. She was having none of that and instead pulled herself up. One side of her head and shoulder was covered with blood.

"Where are you hit?" I asked.

"What in hell are you talking about?" Jill asked as Kristina kicked Tamsin's pistol aside. The Scott County deputy leapt down the stairs and landed next to Tamsin's inert body.

"Tamsin shot you when you slipped. You're in shock. It'll hurt like hell when the adrenaline wears off."

"Geez, Fletcher," Jill said, pulling her arm free from my grip. "I wasn't shot. I don't know what you're talking about."

I touched the left side of her face and held out my fingers so she could see the blood. "You're hit."

The sight of the blood caused Jill to pause. She touched the side of her head, then her neck, shoulder, and arm. "I think I'm okay. I don't feel anything."

I turned her so I could inspect her head. I pushed her hair aside and searched for a tiny bullet hole. "I don't see anything."

A siren whined in the distance, and the Scott County deputy jogged over. "That's the ambulance. Are you hurt badly, ma'am?"

"I think the bullet missed."

"There's an awful lot of blood on your head, ma'am."

"I think it's from the victim."

"Let's go inside and let the EMTs have a look at you, okay?"

Jill let the deputy take her arm and lead her inside. I followed behind, while Kristina stood next to Tamsin's crumpled body, talking to someone on her cell phone. The pilot appeared at the plane's door and just stood there, taking in the scene.

Kristina stepped next to me while the EMTs were checking Jill for injuries. She took off her vest and let them check it for a bullet hole, but refused when they suggested she remove her shirt so they could check her shoulder and torso.

I chuckled and whispered, "That's not happening."

"Jill's a bit shy?" Kristina asked.

I was going to give a more detailed answer and then rethought that. "Yeah."

"She might've caught some bullet fragments when Tamsin's shot hit the stairs."

"Ah, you know where that shot went?"

"I don't know exactly where Jill was when Tamsin fired, but I assume the bullet hit behind her as she slid down the steps."

"Tell me about the Scott County deputy."

"He was hiding inside the plane's toilet. He'd planned to jump out after they'd settled into their seats. He peeked out and saw the hostage situation and decided he needed to intervene. He'd planned to order Tamsin to drop her gun until he heard the shot. He didn't aim. He fired a shot as Tamsin bent forward."

"Remind me to buy him a bottle of expensive bourbon."

Kristina turned so she was facing me. "He's the only one who gets a bottle?"

"I thought you were Baptist."

She snorted. "Yeah, right. Nice try, Fletcher."

* * *

Bitsy met us in the B&B living room when we returned from the sheriff's office. "Is that blood yours?" she asked, touching Jill's shoulder.

"No. I'm fine. Really."

Still looking concerned, but smiling, Bitsy gestured for us to follow her into the dining room, where Hubert was seated. There was a coffee mug and a crumb-covered plate in front of him. He looked at us and seemed to blush, although it was hard to tell under the grime.

"Miss Bitsy gave me cookies and coffee to celebrate us solving that Scottish guy's murder." His smile faded when he saw the blood on Jill's shirt. "Are you okay?"

"I'm fine, Hubert."

I took a seat next to Hubert while Jill and Bitsy went into the kitchen. "I was meaning

366

to thank you. I'm glad Miss Bitsy rewarded you for your contributions."

Hubert's attention was diverted when Bitsy arrived with a plate covered with homemade cookies. She stopped just out of his reach. "They aren't all for you. They're meant to be shared with Doug and Jill."

Hubert's disappointment wasn't masked. "Can I take some when I go, if there are any leftovers?"

Bitsy put the plate between Hubert and me, then patted him on the shoulder. "I've got a whole container of them for you to take home. Don't eat them all at once or you'll get sick."

Although Hubert nodded, I was sure they'd be gone before he reached the parsonage. Jill sat across from me and took one cookie off the plate as Bitsy poured coffee. "Hubert, did you know Charlotte was having an affair with Mr. McInnis?"

Hubert thought for a moment, then asked, "Is having an affair the same as screwing like bunnies? I overheard the people at AA saying they were screwing like bunnies."

I snorted a half swallow of coffee, laughing at Hubert's simplification of the relationship. "How long have they been screwing like bunnies, Hubert?"

"I don't exactly know when they started. I think it's been a while. Probably more than a month of Sundays."

Bitsy nodded. "Hubert's job is to make sure the church is ready for Sunday worship. His life is measured in Sundays."

"Have they been together more than eight Sundays?" Jill asked.

"Oh, yeah. I think it's closer to sixteen."

"It doesn't seem like Mrs. McInnis knew about it," I said, hoping Hubert might have some thoughts about her knowledge.

"I don't think so. Most people say she's as dumb as a sack of rocks. I don't think that's true. She's been nice to me, although it's hard to understand what she's saying. I have to listen hard."

"You've spoken with Tamsin McInnis, Hubert?"

"Sure. She bought a big bunch of gardening stuff in town and needed help loading it into her car."

After a few more minutes of discussion, I suggested that Jill needed to shower.

Chapter 25

Kristina was seated at the table when we came down for breakfast. After serving coffee and confirming our breakfast selections, Bitsy left us alone. I was struck by a sudden thought. "Where did Tamsin get a pistol? She's a non-resident."

Kristina shook her head. "She couldn't legally buy a pistol..."

I nodded. "Not legally. I assume there are places where someone could buy a gun without involving paperwork."

Jill frowned, then added, "There was a bulletin board in the country club pro shop. Most of the items were golf clubs or tennis racquets. There were a shotgun and rifle for sale, too."

"Yeah, this is rural Kentucky. We have a long history of not complying with federal laws. Think of our history with moonshine and federal 'revenuers.' We'll check the pistol's serial number. We'll be able to identify the original buyer. It might've been stolen, or it may have just been a private sale."

"What happened to the investment counselor/bookie and the tennis pro?" Jill asked.

Kristina smiled. "I'm sure they're no longer together. She couldn't wait to throw him and Glinda Carlisle under the bus. According to her, Glinda was unable to pay off her gambling debt, so she offered them a way to steal a few cases of very valuable bourbon in exchange for suspending the interest on her debt. She gave them copies of Robert's keys, information about where the bourbon was locked up, and a tip about what hours the building was empty. The idea for smashing the cases was all Reggie. He reasoned through increasing the value of the booze by destroying ninety percent of the batch. The tennis coach was the lookout and getaway driver. In her words, 'she was involved under extreme duress.'"

"What deal did she cut with the district attorney?"

"She wasn't smart enough to lock that down before she gave her statement. I suggested the judge might be more lenient if she volunteered to testify against the others, and she started baring her soul." Kristina paused. "I imagine her court-appointed attorney will work something out with the district attorney in return for her testimony. I've got her signed statement and recordings of the interviews in case she gets cold feet."

Bitsy delivered bowls of fruit, followed by grits for Jill and Kristina. "When are you two leaving?" Kristina asked as she poured gravy on her grits.

"Why?" I asked. "Are you getting used to having Bitsy's breakfast every morning?"

"There is that," she replied as Bitsy delivered my biscuits covered in sausage gravy.

Bitsy patted her shoulder. "Miss Kristina, you're welcome at my table anytime."

"When is the sheriff's news conference?" Jill joked.

"Do you remember when the sheriff commented on the country club having a lot of clout? What did he say? 'Those bees have bigger stingers.' There's no news conference. There will probably be an article about the bourbon thefts and resolution of the murder case on page three of the weekly newspaper."

"What's Glinda's situation?" I asked.

"She's out on bail. Robert hired a big-name Louisville defense attorney for her. I imagine she'll get probation."

"How are you and the sheriff getting along?" Jill asked.

"He's a politician. Breaking a big case looks good to the majority of the voters, so that's good. On the other hand, arresting country club members is probably going to hurt his campaign contributions. As for me, it was another day at the office. Solve a murder. Solve a couple of burglaries. Arrest the biggest illegal bookie in the county. All in a day's work." She paused and smiled.

"Personally, it was good because the notoriety has embarrassed my son."

Bitsy had been listening politely. Taking advantage of the break in conversation, she commented, "If you two aren't rushing back to Texas, there's an auction at the Lincoln Museum tonight."

I grimaced, but Jill perked up. "In South Dakota, auctions are big community events. They generally serve food, and people show up to talk to their friends."

"That's what happens here, too," Bitsy offered. "I heard there's going to be a couple of food trucks there."

"What's being auctioned off?" I asked.

"Hubert told me Robert Carlisle donated two bottles of Running Acres bourbon as the final lot. There are also a couple of homemade quilts and some antiques."

Jill grabbed my arm. "We could buy bourbon for Dad and Chet."

Sighing, I replied, "We're not bidding on insanely expensive bourbon for your dad and Chet. We can buy something at a Rapid City store and not have to lug it across the country."

"Come on," she chided. "Let's go just to see how high the bidding goes."

"When is our return flight?"

"Tomorrow at noon."

I looked at Bitsy and Kristina, then asked, "I don't suppose there's anything else we need to do tonight."

Jill's sly smile made me cringe. "I suppose you could attend another AA meeting with Hubert. Didn't he say there's a meeting every night of the week?"

Kristina glanced at the clock as she folded her napkin. "I hate to eat and run, but the assistant district attorney expects you two to make formal statements this morning."

Bitsy put her hand on my shoulder. "I do believe I'll come with you to the auction. One of those handmade quilts would look nice upstairs."

"Don't you think they'll go high?" Kristina asked.

Bitsy smiled politely. "It's a charity. The money helps keep the museum open." She patted Jill's shoulder. "Wouldn't your mother enjoy a nice quilt?"

"I'm sure she would, but there's no room in my suitcase."

"If you bid high enough, I bet they'd ship it to you."

"You don't need to be quite so helpful, Miss Bitsy," I whispered as I walked past her.

* * *

Because of the auction, Bitsy had to park three blocks from downtown Hodgenville. The city set up barriers, blocking off the street in front of the museum. A platform was set up with tables displaying the antiques and quilts. The food trucks had eight or ten people in line for tacos or barbecue. The ice cream shop around the corner had a longer line than the food trucks. We joined the crowd milling around in front of the auction table. Several people we'd met at the church dinner spoke to us, and Hubert made his way through the crowd to greet me. He smiled, but didn't say anything.

"Hubert, are you skipping tonight's meeting?"

He shook his head. "They cancelled. Because of the auction." He gestured toward the side of the auction platform. "Jerry and Ske are on the museum board."

"How do they feel about auctioning off liquor?"

"I s'pose they don't care. It's going to raise money, right?" He paused, then added. "I don't s'pose they'll bid on the booze."

A gentleman, who could've been Colonel Sanders' brother, stepped onto the platform and rapped a gavel to get everyone's attention. "Let's get this started."

Conversations ended, and the crowd drifted toward the main table. Someone bumped into me, and I turned to see who would be so pushy. I was surprised to see Robert Carlisle smiling at me. "You made it!"

"Auctions aren't my thing, but my wife was excited about attending."

"I gave a bottle of my bourbon to E.W. Graves." When I didn't react to the name, he added, "E.W. writes bourbon reviews for *Whiskey Monthly* magazine."

"What did he say?"

Robert nodded toward the auction platform. "Cordell is going to read the review before bidding on the bottles I donated."

The first auction item was a rusty kerosene lamp that looked to me like it had been picked out of a dump. The bidding crept up to twenty-five dollars, then stalled. "Sold to the man in the John Deere cap!"

The next item was a cavalry sword from the collection of a local doctor. The bidding started at one hundred dollars and quickly reached five hundred. A quilt sold for four hundred dollars.

The auctioneer paused to let the buyer collect her quilt, then he had his assistants hold up a quilt with a more intricate pattern. "This quilt was donated by Mary Martinson. It won the blue ribbon at the 2023 county fair."

A murmur passed through the crowd. Bitsy opened the bidding at one thousand dollars, which brought a collective gasp from the crowd. A woman, whom I assumed was Mary, nodded to Bitsy. Bitsy's final bid was two thousand five hundred, which ended the bidding process.

The auctioneer removed a sheet of paper from the pocket of his white suit coat and put on a pair of readers. "Ladies and gentlemen, I have two bottles of bourbon donated by Robert Carlisle and the Running Acres Distillery." He went on to read the E.W. Graves review, which mentioned vanilla, smoke, dark chocolate, and leathery flavor notes. "Mr. Graves rated this liquor ninety-seven, on par, or better than, the best bourbons from the big distilleries."

Robert Carlisle tapped me with his elbow. "I was hoping for at least a ninety-five!"

The auctioneer removed his glasses and looked around the crowd. "This sounds like a fine bourbon, folks. Will someone open the bidding with one hundred dollars?"

"One thousand!"

I turned to Jill, who had her hand up after offering that opening bid. "What the hell?"

"It's for charity," she hissed.

The price jumped by hundreds and quickly passed two thousand. I could see Jill thinking about upping the bid, and I grabbed her wrist. "Really? Are you crazy?"

"It's Dad's eightieth birthday. How many more do you think he'll have?" She waited a moment until I nodded. "Two thousand five hundred!"

That bid stalled the other bidders. The auctioneer tried to cajole the crowd into one more bid, but he rapped the gavel. "Sold!"

"How are you paying for it?" I whispered.

"Cash. Kristina took me to the bank while you were with the district attorney."

"How high were you willing to go?"

She removed a roll of $100 bills from her pocket. "You don't really want to know, do you?"

"Probably not," I replied as the crowd split to let her approach the auction table.

Robert Carlisle tapped my elbow. "I thought you weren't a drinker."

"It's for my father-in-law's eightieth birthday."

He slapped my shoulder. "Thanks for your generosity."

Jill returned with the bottle wrapped in a fancy bag as the bidding on the second bottle surpassed fifteen hundred dollars.

"Please tell me you're not bidding on the second bottle for Chet."

"He and Dad can share."

The bidding stalled at two thousand dollars despite the encouragement of the auctioneer. He was about to rap the gavel when Robert Carlilse stepped onto the platform and whispered something to the auctioneer.

He nodded and turned to the crowd. "Because this is a charity auction, Mr. Carlisle has offered a matching donation equal to the highest bid." He turned to Carlisle, who was grinning broadly. "You're not going to let Bobby off for only two thousand, are you?"

A male voice yelled, "Twenty-one!"

"The sheriff just bid two thousand one hundred! What other civic-minded people are out there!"

The bidding swept past three thousand and ended at thirty-five hundred. The gavel fell and Robert Carlisle was grinning like a proud father.

It took us a few minutes to find Bitsy, who was carrying her new quilt. She smiled at Jill and nodded to the bag. "Your father is going to enjoy that."

"You knew Jill was going to bid?"

Bitsy winked at Jill. "We girls sometimes have secrets we keep from our menfolk."

"You don't condone drinking!" I protested.

"I'm sure Jill's father will quit as soon as this bottle is gone."

"Yeah," Jill said. "He'll probably say, 'I'll never have another drop as good as this. I'm going to quit now.'"

I sighed, "Right. I can almost see that happening."

Epilogue

A month later, we flew to Rapid City for Al Rickowski's 80th birthday. Jill's cousin Susie arrived unexpectedly the day before the party, explaining that her job at the Bureau of Land Management had been eliminated. Rickowskis invited her to stay at the ranch while she searched for a new job. Preferring privacy, Susie offered to clean up the bunkhouse rather than staying in Junior's vacant bedroom.

Molly, Jill, Susie, and my mother prepared a smorgasbord for their relatives, neighbors, and friends. There were nearly enough candles on Al's birthday cake to burn the house down.

Despite Al's request for no gifts, a few people brought presents. Al protested, but thanked them as he unwrapped salami, cheese, and candy. After everyone left, we dove into the after-party cleanup with Jill's cousin, my mother, and Jill's Uncle Chet. With everything picked up, the garbage taken out, and the dishes washed, we collapsed around the kitchen table.

Uncle Chet excused himself and went outside. "Is he okay?" I whispered to Jill. She nodded, then went into our bedroom. A moment later, Chet returned with a paper sack containing a bottle.

Al accepted the bag, smiling. "I think I know what this is." He peeled back the brown paper, exposing a liter of Tennessee whiskey. Chet's smile was partially in recognition of Al's appreciation and partly in the knowledge that Al would share it with him.

Jill emerged with the padded container we'd carried from Kentucky. "Here's something from Doug and me."

Because the package was so overpacked, the contents weren't obvious. Al set Chet's bottle aside and peeled open the bag, then the padding. He held up the bottle, studying the unusual horse logo. "I don't think I've ever heard of this brand."

Susie brought lowball glasses from the sideboard and set them in front of Al. "I guess we'll have to do a taste test. Compare Jill's bourbon to Chet's fine Tennessee whiskey."

Al opened the two bottles and poured a half-inch of Chet's gift into the glasses. He passed them to Chet, Jill, and Susie. Chet held his up, and said, "The Tennessee whiskey is a little lighter colored."

After sampling a taste, they all nodded their approval. Susie smiled and proclaimed the Tennessee whiskey better than the rotgut her ex-husband drank, which brought chuckles from the group. "Bottom's up!" she said before emptying her glass. Al and Chet happily drained their glasses. Jill took a second sip of her whiskey, then pushed the glass to Chet, who happily drank the rest of Jill's portion.

Al poured two fingers of bourbon from the second bottle and passed them around. As we watched in anticipation, he swirled the bourbon, sniffed it, then took a sip. Chet sampled the bourbon and wore a silly grin. Susie and Jill sniffed their samples but waited for Al's reaction before tasting the liquor.

After savoring a sip, Al set his glass down and lifted the bottle as if he was displaying the winner. "Wow." He nodded his approval.

Susie took a sip and coughed. "It's good, but that barrel-strength is potent."

Jill slid Al's chair away from the table to make room on his lap. She wrapped her arms around him and kissed his forehead. "Happy birthday, Dad."

The End

Dean Hovey is the award-winning and best-selling author of three mystery series. He uses his educational background, travel, and extensive research to craft engaging plots with relatable characters. He and his wife split their year between Minnesota and Arizona.

Other Dean L. Hovey mysteries from BWL Publishing Inc.

Whistling Pines cozies

Whistling up a Ghost
Whistling Pirates
Whistling Bake Off
Whistling Artist
Whistling Fireman
Whistling Wedding
Whistling Librarian with Anne Flagge (Late 2025)

Doug Fletcher mysteries

Stolen Past
Washed Away
Dead in the Water
Death in Shifting Sands
Devils Fall
Prairie Menace
Down River
Burnt Evidence
Gator Bait
Grave Survey
Dead End Trail
The Last Rodeo
Peril in Paradise
Western Justice
Strung Out to Die
Medora Murder

Pine County Mysteries

Killer Secrets
Deadly Mixture
Fatal Business
Taxed to Death
Conflict of Interest
Skidded and Skunked with D.L. Dixen